THE
STORY
OF
STONE

Also by N. M. Browne

Warriors of Alavna
Warriors of Camlann
Hunted
Basilisk

For my grandmother

BEFORE

THE STORY OF STONE

N.M. BROWNE

BLOOMSBURY

Fic
Browne

Published by Bloomsbury Publishing, New York, London, and Berlin
Distributed to the trade by Holtzbrinck Publishers

Library of Congress Cataloging-in-Publication Data
Browne, N. M.
The story of stone / N. M. Browne.
p. cm.
Summary: While researching her society's origins, Nela—an apprentice
archaeologist—discovers a mysterious stone that reveals to her the true story
of how her Bear-man and Night Hunter ancestors were united by a terrible magic.
ISBN-10: 1-58234-655-0 • ISBN-13: 978-1-58234-655-7
[1. Magic—Fiction. 2. Wishes—Fiction. 3. Fantasy.] I. Title.
PZ7.B82215Sto 2005   [Fic]—dc22   2005040981

First U.S. Edition 2005
Typeset by Dorchester Typesetting Group Ltd.
Printed in the U.S.A.
10 9 8 7 6 5 4 3 2 1

Bloomsbury Publishing, Children's Books, U.S.A.
175 Fifth Avenue, New York, NY 10010

ONE

The Chief Findsman was angry. A pearl of sweat, stained blue with the dye of his hair, trickled down his forehead to mingle with the deeper blue of his plaited beard.

'I don't know what in the name of scholarship and the Spirit of Enquiry you are doing, but it isn't enough.'

He glowered at his small, cowed audience of Findsman Millard, Findsman Flear and Nela, his apprentice and daughter. The two Findsmen toyed nervously with the braids of their scarlet beards and nodded their agreement: Nela's father was fond of humiliating them. Nela wiped sweat from her face with dirty hands and slapped at one of the oversized stinging insects that droned near her ear. By all the scholars and trollops of Scraal, this was a blighted place. The pervasive smell of decay, sweet as a festival pudding and rank as the Scraal City midden, made her feel nauseous. It was hard to concentrate and she found herself idly watching the camp bondsman as he manoeuvred round their fire, his economical movements barely straining his ridiculous slave-tether as he prepared food for their meal. She did not know why her father had insisted on the tether, attached by an oiled ring to the oiled rope of the perimeter cordon at one end and to the bondsman's belt at the other: no one used such things in the city any more and it hardly seemed necessary where there was nowhere to go but the wilderness, and nothing of any value to steal. Nela sensed her father's icy gaze upon her and quickly averted her eyes from the bondsman. Even away from Scraal it was not seemly to acknowledge the existence of a servant.

Her father was still ranting. 'We have to find some kind of proof soon or all our reputations will lie in tatters! We are running out of time, money and patience.'

He had a point. The Worshipful Company of Historical Archivists of Scraal had been reluctant to support this expedition, which was a pet project of her father's. Their small team had been camped by the stagnant Mordant Lake for ten days already, seeking evidence for her father's theory that this was the cradle of their people, in the stinking mud and sterile soil of the decaying forest, but they had unearthed nothing more than a few ancient shards of early dye-pots and a leather-wrapped black stone. The Chief Findsman held that stone in the palm of his hand now.

'Nela!'

She tried to look intelligent and stood a little

straighter, though she felt as if she were a child's wax doll melting and slipping away from herself in the humid heat.

'There is an ancient song, is there not, about a black stone?'

'In the ancient song cycle of exile there is a fragment of a song called "Black Stone of the Unmaking", Father,' Nela said, and clearing her throat she sang:

Weep if you will for the life that is gone,
For hunt, for caves and evening song,
Weep if you will for the life that is gone
For loss and lies and hope undone
She's grieving still and it's scarce begun
And the stain of their blood
Has seeped through her bone
Has defiled now dark lands
Unmade by Black Stone

She paused and Findsman Flear smiled at her. She had a sweet, musical voice at odds with her appearance and it always surprised people the first time they heard it.

'And . . . ?' said her father.

'I doubt that stone has anything to do with the song.'

She spoke dismissively and wished she hadn't the moment the words escaped her suddenly constricting throat. She should remember that she was not at home, that no one here cared for her opinion.

'Ah, and I had forgotten that you were such an expert Findsman,' her father said in his precise, barbed voice. 'I should perhaps leave this Seeking to you! No, go on, please, I must insist. We await your judgement. Take the stone and tell us your opinion – we are all waiting.'

The other men, Millard and Flear, smiled uncomfortably. She knew it was worry that made her father cruel. His reputation hung in the balance, but she could still have wished him kinder.

She was not as reluctant as she pretended to take the stone he offered her, nor was she sorry to hold it in her own hand. She could not see how an old song about a faerie woman called 'Black Stone' could have any connection with a real black stone: her father was clutching at straws. When she touched it, though, she understood. It was the size of her palm – smooth and black, shiny as though wet, polished by much handling. She had expected it to be cool, and its living warmth shocked her. She measured the weight of it gravely in her hand, as she had seen her father do. If his expression softened as he watched her, she did not know it. She was totally immersed in her investigation. She touched the stone delicately with the tip of her forefinger; it seemed to pulse under her finger like the fragile heartbeat of a small animal. She stroked it as one might a midget kitten and felt it vibrate like a blown bone-comb in paper. She heard a sound within her head, buzzing in the browbone of her skull. It was a long note, like the resounding echo of the prayer bell pealing high and clear. She blinked as her vision dimmed and thought she heard a sweet voice singing words she couldn't quite hear. Then there were no words, only the overwhelming flood of impressions, filling her senses with the thoughts of someone else – somewhere else.

I am shaking. I know what he wants. I thought the old tales were forgotten at last, but I was wrong. For every story of the poverty and powerlessness of the Night Hunters there are ten tales of our power and evil magics. The greed was in his eyes: I saw it in his face when he caught me – greed and longing and a strange, unexpected beauty.

I know I should not have gone the way I chose. I should have trusted my own foreboding, but I was tempted by the berry-red of his cloak, and he hid his tracks well – not so stupid, this giant Bear-man, not so greedy that he forgot his wits. He has watching eyes – eyes that notice almost as much as one of us.

He has at least put me in the cool blessed dark – in the dove cote and the carrier coop at the top of the Chief's house. There are no birds here now, though they have left their smell behind and feathers enough to make a soft bed for one with the ease to sleep. He has sworn me to silence and I gave him my promise for the sake of those eyes, not for the greed but for the beauty and the longing and the noticing – almost like one of us. I gave him my promise, but I cannot stop the shaking and the fear that sours in my empty stomach as the timber walls close in. Oh, Lady, Womanface-hidden-from-view! It is hard to be silent.

Beneath me I can hear the movement of the wives and the youngest ones. I dare not cry out nor murmur in fear, for my captor is one thing, but the others might be worse. I dare not try to escape for fear of them. The smell of roast chicken is driving me mad and my stomach is hollow as an empty cooking pot. Hunger overrides even my fear. I have had only a small handful of the end of season breadberries all day – and the stale heel of wanderer's loaf I had in my gather bag. I lost my gather bag, left it behind in my panicked flight, but it was empty anyway and, as one blessing among so many curses, my name stone, blessed by the gift of the Wandering Man, was in my waist band with my small knife, and that I have still.

I am a fool and a hungry fool, and there is nothing for it but to wait until he comes and I suppose that will not be until tonight. I can smell the morning seeping through the holes in the thatch along with the first sharp shards of sunlight. I will have to sleep, and if a natural sleep will not come (and it will not with my heart beating like a calling drum) I will wait until there is enough noise down below to mask the sleep-song-for-the-too-cold-night. I will be safer if I can sleep, still as a hibernating bear, and don't fidget for the lack of space to stretch. I have heard it said that the Bear-men have poor hearing, but the one who caught me had sharp enough ears and more patience than he is supposed to have – so that story is the wild

14

boar's ordure I always suspected it was.

One of the babies wakes, below me. I hear someone pad on heavy feet to lift it from its hammock. She murmurs softly and the wailing stops. I think I have missed my chance, and then she sings a lullaby of her own. It is a simple tune, but it is not badly sung. The woman has a strong voice, low and breathy, which suits the melody – I do not hear the words, though there seem to be a great many. So those that say the Bear-men are song-deaf too are wrong. There is little art to the song, but still it unknots some of the tension in my neck and eases my fear just a little, so it is not without efficacy. I ready myself for my own lullaby. I will sleep until dusk and hope he feeds me then.

'Nela! Nela!'

Cold water on her face and her father's insistent voice drew her back from the darkness, from the cloying stench of the coop, the smell of roasting chicken, the feel of feathers and the cool air, damp under the thatch.

'Are you all right?' The Chief Findsman's bright eyes that were bluer than his beard looked stricken. 'Nel, what happened?' He never used the affectionate diminutive of Nela's name in front of outsiders: she must have frightened him a great deal.

He helped her to sit up and Findsman Flear offered her water to drink. She was quite wet with the water that had been thrown over her and she started to shiver.

'Maybe she could use something stronger.' Findsman

Millard reached under his coat and produced a polished tortoiseshell hip flask, decorated with silver filigree, which he offered her. The dark wine it contained was strong and fine and Nela remembered that Millard was of good family and probably wealthier than her father. She smiled her thanks.

'What language were you speaking?' Flear asked, with a kind of awed reverence. He was trembling slightly, as though in shock, which was surely an overreaction. Nela's father glared at him.

'What did you experience when you touched the stone?' the Chief Findsman demanded.

'I don't know . . . it was as if I were somewhere else, suddenly. It's difficult to explain . . .' Nela did not know how to begin.

'What? Like a dream?' Her father's voice was professional now, without sympathy, as if he had never been afraid for her, as if she was just another subject for the Findsman's seeking and systematic questioning. She tried to round up her thoughts.

'No. It was real – like I was someone else.'

'Who?'

'I don't know. A girl I think, young – maybe my age, maybe older. And she was frightened – she was hiding somewhere – at the top of some circular building.'

'A Tier House? Like the ancients built?'

'Maybe. I don't know.'

Her father sketched a three-tiered circular building. Each tier had a steeply pitched thatched roof and each diminished in size so that the top floor was small – small enough and high enough to house carrier birds.

'Nela, this was the traditional layout of the family Tier House of a Chief of a Dependency in the earliest settlement times.' He spoke as if he thought her ignorant and she felt herself flush with humiliation. She knew all about that! She was an apprentice Findsman – by the Lord of the Earth! But the Chief Findsman carried on in his lecturing tone, oblivious to her discomfort, 'Some Findsmen think that this top part was for the message birds of the Chief – could you have been here?'

'Maybe – yes. Probably – it could well have been.' She tried not to sound sullen and uncooperative – it would do her no good. Then her eye was caught by the notes above the sketch, written in her father's neat notecode.

'What's this?'

'This is a sound-by-sound representation of what you said.' He spoke as if it were obvious and she were foolish not to recognise them. 'I am surprised that you used the most ancient language traditionally associated with the nomadic hunter-gatherers, but I have long suspected that the settled people spoke the same tongue.'

'You took notes?'

'Of course. Have you no idea how significant it is to find evidence of ancient power so many scholars have dismissed as old stories? It is the strongest evidence we could find that this place really is the cradle of our most ancient civilisation. We *must* know what you said. It seems you spoke in some dialect of that old tongue – I recognised many of the words, though I'm not familiar with the precise idiom so we must set to work on our return to the city to unscramble the whole.'

'The stone spoke to *me*,' Nela said with emphasis, suddenly stubborn and cold. Her father took notes while she was in the grip of who knew what. He took notes!

'Did I have a fit?'

Her father looked uncomfortable. 'Yes.' He looked slightly embarrassed. 'But I was sure you were not in any danger. This stone and its ancient power to speak to us changes everything.'

Since her earliest childhood she had been prone to fits, periods of black unconsciousness and wild exhausting thrashing; it was why no aunts would take her in after her mother's death. It was why she was permitted to accompany her father. It was why she was allowed to be a non-woman and shave her head as a sign that she was not available for courtship. It was why she was free. Even so, she could have wished that her father took her condition more seriously and put her health and welfare before his work.

She shut her eyes to block out his face, his cold and searching eyes. He was Seeking her, searching her demeanour for clues as to the nature of her experience, trying to squeeze every last drop of information out of her, like every good Findsman did, and she hated it. She felt his smooth and heavy hand pat her gently on the exposed skin of her head, like a blessing for a child, like a request for understanding, but she did not lift her leaden lids. Her father had let her down again and she wasn't even sure if he knew it. She was exhausted, and sleep came to her at once, like a heavy blanket burying her under its rough, enveloping weight.

Two

It was not so very unusual for the Chief of the Tier House to come downstairs: he regularly checked his stock, including his children, and often trained with the Hearth Guard, even though he was getting old. It *was* unusual, however, for the wives of the four quarters to come downstairs – they lived unseen and largely unheard in the Heart of the Home, the circular room above the Hall, and rarely left it.

The children, the youngest of the Chief's extensive Brood Trove who lived below in the Hall with the beasts and the Hearth Guard, the core of the Chief's Battle Horde, were not told of this moderately momentous event in advance. This was because, as a general rule, no one told the children much at all. Instead, they were set new tasks: all of them had to sweep and muck out the central section of the Hall with unaccustomed vigour, scrubbing it with 'old men's tears', a cleansing mixture of the Teller Priest's devising. Drannott of the third quarter had been sent to collect the sweet grass to burn in the pot stove to mask the pungency of the animal smells that filled the Hall. This was enough for Mirit of the first quarter to remark to Jerat of the second that something was going on.

'The wives'll be down, sure as Keran farts. They can't bear the stench of horse shit. We're getting a new sibling. They always make us do this stuff for an Acceptance Day.'

Jerat's memory of previous Acceptance Days was hazy, though he remembered a feast and he remembered fearsome women in masks. He never noticed the beasts' strong smell as anything unpleasant – but perhaps the wives would. What did he know of wives? Anyway, the Teller Priest claimed that bad smells might carry contagion and being a wife was dangerous enough anyway without the risk of that.

It took most of the day to clean the Hall. The Hearth Guard insisted that all the children wash – even the parts that didn't show – and, in an unusual act of considerate care, heated the water first, putting it in the feast day cauldron that took two men to lift. Guardsman Lema cut Jerat's hair so that it formed an even curtain at a level with his chin and combed it ruthlessly to remove all the lice until his head stung and ached from her efforts. She rinsed his hair with nettle water to keep it clean. She was not gentle, but Jerat thought perhaps she had forgotten what it felt like, as her own head was shaved right down to the skin, to show she was a man-woman. Drannott said that meant she was barren, but if it were true, and

Jerat wasn't sure Drannott knew as much as he pretended, she didn't seem to care.

The Chief had provided all of the Brood Trove with new cloaks that the wives had woven. Jerat's was berry-red and green like the spring grass, the colours of the second quarter in the glorious, victorious Dependency of Lakeside. The cloak smelled of the imported cedar chest in which it had been stored. He loved the smell and the touch and the colour of it.

When all the Chief's Brood were dressed and cleaner than Jerat could ever remember them being, when tapestries had been laid on the clean dirt-floor, when the food cooked above and transported below had been laid out in lavish display, when the Teller Priest had arrived with his wild hair all neatly braided, then, finally, the Guardsmen manning the pulley lowered the wives down to the Hall in the large half-barrel that was kept for the purpose. The roof ladder that was normally used for conveying small items between the floors was altogether unsuitable for the wives, who needed to be treated with respect and honour, cosseted in the warmth and comfort of the Heart of the Home. The no-men, the gelded captives of bloody, now-forgotten wars, brought cushions and furs and heaped them on the ground and then the wives walked in stately procession into the Hall. Of course you couldn't see their faces, though Jerat peered. Each was cloaked in fur-lined finery and masked according to custom. He wondered what the wife of the second quarter looked like, behind her wooden mask of red and green, painted in a serene and unconvincing parody of a woman's face.

Technically she was his mother, so he knelt before her as he had been told. The hand that patted his head in blessing was surprisingly large and strong, the fingers blunt as a farmer's or a soldier's, though cleaner than both. He would have thought by the way the wives were pampered that they were made of fine Lakeside, bone-thin pottery.

When all the children of the Brood Trove had been blessed by all the wives, Jerat's father, the Chief, stood up. He was a big man, broad and barrel-chested and, it was said, still stronger than the biggest ox. He stood straight and tall for all that he was old and a grandfather many times over. He was wily too and had lived through more battles than even the Teller Priest counted, he had survived an assassination attempt from a grudge-bearing no-man who had not appreciated the forcible removal of his manhood, and had outlived four of his designated heirs. Jerat always had to fight the urge to hide whenever he saw him, which was often: the Chief was famous for his temper and his ruthlessness in battle. The Hearth Guard liked to tell the children of the Brood Trove about the time he had hacked a man's head from his shoulders with one well-timed blow. For some reason that made them all nervous of him.

Heron, a tall no-man much battle-scarred, handed Jerat's 'mother' a boy-child. The child was crying, his mouth wide and pink like the maw of a frightened animal. Jerat thought the child feared the strangeness of the mask that covered the face of his comfort-giver. The child pulled at it with plump baby fingers, but the woman's strong hand held it firmly in place. She waited until he'd calmed himself, though tears still ran down his face unnoticed like the rain, before handing the boy to the Chief. The boy looked lost in the big man's arms and stared at the children of the Brood Trove with mournful eyes, but he did not cry again. The Chief spoke to all of the Brood:

'This is your brother Roat, of my most valued wife of the second quarter. He has reached the age to put aside the place of ease in the Heart of the Home and take his rightful place of Acceptance within the Hall where he will learn the path of the warrior, that long walk to adulthood, and move from Brood Trove to Battle Horde.' Jerat's father smiled benignly at Roat who, unexpectedly, smiled back. Jerat noticed that Roat's teeth were as white and pointed as a young dog's. The Teller Priest mumbled a prayer and gave the child his blessing and the Chief handed the small creature over to Guardsman Hela's sturdy arms while Heron passed the wife of the second quarter a second child.

The child looked at her gravely. 'Mama?' he said quite audibly, and the masked woman put a long finger to his lips and hugged him hastily just once, before handing him to his father. Jerat did not watch as his father repeated his short announcement with the second boy, Rinat, clearly Roat's twin. Instead Jerat stared, fascinated, as the masked woman bowed her head and dug her sharp, red-stained nails into the soft flesh of her palm until the blood flowed.

After this brief ceremony the wives and the no-men all returned to the Heart of the Home, with more bowing. The women could not eat with their masks on and it would not be seemly to remove them in public, and the no-men could only eat when all else had finished because they were spoils of battle and not people any more.

The wives' departure was the signal for the feasting to begin. While the Chief joked and drank with the Guardsmen, a warrior among warriors, Jerat found a place sufficiently far from his terrifying presence and focused on filling his belly until it got so round and tight that it hurt; he ate greedily of the hot spiced boar and many types of salted fish from the store pit, and the flat-baked herb breads and honeyed apples and berries which were the feast-day fare. Then came the singing, when each of the Hearth Guards performed some ballad or trick; the Teller Priest told the story of the first harvest and Guardsman Hela proved once more that she could walk on her hands and balance an apple on her nose – but then she came from a very distant Dependency, a fearsome walk from the Chief's land, way over on the other side of the Lake.

It was full dark by the time the feast was over. A couple of the younger Brood were sick what with the stronger ale that they'd drunk and the rich food that they'd eaten, but Jerat was pleased that he was not one of them; he could at least hold his meat and ale like a real warrior. There had been no battle training at all that day and it was strange for Jerat to go to his bed without the familiar ache in his muscles and a new set of abrasions and bruises to keep him awake. Avet of the fourth quarter, his training partner, did not always fight fair.

This night, although Jerat made his bed as usual

from the sleep mat and wool blanket stored in the leather pocket of the quarter curtain, something else kept him awake. Someone had placed the small twins in his quarterage. They had been carefully swaddled and laid in separate hammocks slung between two sharpened stakes, driven hard into the dirt floor. Though, as usual, no one had said anything directly, he ought to have realised that they would stay in his section of the Hall for, like him, they came from the wife of the second quarter. It was unlikely that he and the twins shared the same mother – too many died giving birth and the position of Chief's wife was never a position that was vacant for long. Jerat had heard that his father took a new wife the day after the death of the old one, but he did not know if that were true as it was one of the Brood who'd whispered it and what they didn't know for sure they often made up. He did not know how many wives his father had taken and lost over the years – he wondered if anyone knew. His father counted himself a wealthy man, having twenty-eight sons and twelve daughters still living if you counted the twins, which might be a premature calculation, as their future at this moment looked decidedly uncertain. They had not looked much in his father's arms, these frightened children, but they counted as brothers, as rivals, as comrades-in-arms, or would do one day.

As Jerat lay in his bed in the darkness thinking of the night's events, the twins began to cry. What should he do? They might cry themselves back to sleep, wasting precious energy and body heat in the process. The air froze Jerat's breath, but he was used to it, used to the numbness in his limbs and the bone-freezing chill. It was not fair: they would be frightened and painfully cold. The four fires of the Heart of the Home kept upstairs hot as the height of midsummer when down below in the Hall it was always somewhere between pleasantly cool and cold-as-midwinter-river-ice. Sometimes, Drannott said, babies developed fever – separation sickness, they called it – and died in the first few weeks after their removal. There was an ancient saying he'd heard the old no-man Heron use: 'Removed from the heart of the mother, removed from the Heart of the Home, only the strongest heart survives, the heart with the beat of fire.'

It was strange how little Jerat had considered his own coming to the Hall – the years, or maybe the cold of its damp interior had numbed the shock of it. Once, long ago, his sister Moorat, now married to a Lakeside potter, had brought him to her blanket and warmed him with her own heat until he was big enough to sleep alone. He probably owed her his life. That memory, more even than the noise of the twins' gutsy screams, reminded him of what should be done. Jerat crawled out of his blanket. The impacted mud under his feet had not quite frozen, but chilled his numb feet further, even through his knitted socks. He carried the twins awkwardly in his arms one at a time and dumped them, squalling, on to his thin, quilted sleep mat. He brought their blankets and swaddled them tightly, then lay down carefully between them. They smelled of the Heart of the Home, of lavender bags, of scented wood and of the spiced tea the wives drank to make their birthings easier. He pulled them to him, one under each arm, and they snuggled close like rooting piglets and wiped their faces, wet with tears and snot, against his winter shirt. His warmth warmed them and his whispered words soothed them so that they slept, snuffling softly like the beasts. He did not. He was pinioned by the weight of their heads and was afraid to move to a more comfortable position in case he woke them and set them off crying again.

Their breathing sounded loud to him, so close. There was always noise in the great Hall, but the thick wool of the quarter curtain separated him from the beasts and the Hearth Guard and the children of the other quarters, and muffled their familiar sounds. None of the Brood were permitted to leave their quarters at night, so that the rivalry among the Brood brothers could not erupt into violence. Long ago, night had been the time for murder, so the quarterage rules had been imposed to keep the peace. There had been no children in his quarter since his own birth – the poor wife, or perhaps wives, of the second quarter had not much luck at breeding. These squalling babies were three winters old or they would not be in the main Hall to take their chances with the beasts and the cold, not to mention the Hearth Guard and the unreliable mercy of siblings. They were small for their age and missing their comfort-giver as he still, on cold nights alone in his quarterage away from the others of the Brood, missed his. He had been sickly and most unusually had stayed in the Heart of the Home, in the heat and care of his father's wives, the comfort-givers and the no-men, until he was five. He would have died certainly in the first fierce cold were it not for this small breaking of tradition, but as a side effect he remembered with longing his comfort-giver, the wife of the second quarter of his childhood. He doubted she were the masked woman he had seen that day. It was probably some other wife, his own dear comfort-giver long cold in the grave. Children never attended those funerals and the Guardsmen never talked of them in their hearing. He tried to recreate his five-year-old's memory, but the picture of her features would not settle in his mind. He remembered love. It was not a useful memory, but he treasured it anyway and eventually he slept, the warmth of his brothers' bodies a kind of comfort to him.

THREE

Jerat woke stiff and damp-chested from the heat of his brothers' heads and the slight saliva dribble from their mouths. The babies slept so peacefully that a more sentimental boy might have been loath to wake them, but Jerat's life to date had more or less cured his natural inclination towards sentiment: he was uncomfortable and it was time to get up and work. No light leaked through the solid walls of the Hall, but Jerat could smell the morning and hear the predictable stirrings of the Hearth Guard, the Herd and the Brood Trove – Jerat's other siblings. It was the beginning of a whole new day of labour, and a Chief's son never forgot that he was put on Lakeside to work and to fight and to live only at the Chief's pleasure.

Jerat got awkwardly to his feet, scooping the children off his chest as though they were puppies; the babes began to cry. The too-loud noise angered Jerat and he reached out to cuff the children quiet with the reflex aggression of one of the Hall dogs, but then

Keran, the door keeper and Horde leader, opened the great wooden door of the Hall and Jerat saw, even in the dim light, the terror and sadness in the children's filthy, tear-marked faces. He stayed his hand. They weren't puppies, they were his brothers.

'Hush,' he said, too harshly. 'No, please, shush,' he tried again more softly, putting his finger to his lips in a gesture long-forgotten and suddenly recalled. 'We don't want to make the others angry. Are you hungry?'

Two pairs of grave eyes watching him anxiously blinked away tears. The taller of the two, Roat, nodded firmly.

'You help me feed the beasts and then we'll eat. I'll show you what to do.'

The twins watched him without speaking. Rinat stuck his thumb in his mouth, then, hooking his index finger over his nose, began sucking loudly. Roat didn't move.

Jerat rolled away the straw-stuffed sleep mats and woven blankets, stowing them in their proper place, the large pocket of the quarter curtain that divided his quarterage from that of the others. When he pulled it back the boys could see all the byres of the beasts, clustered together in the centre of the Hall. The fragrant aroma of the sweet grass had definitely gone, and the boys wrinkled their noses against the stench of ordure and the strong smell of animal and human bodies. Rinat gave a startled cry: it must have seemed very crowded and confusing after the peace at the Heart of the Home. He slipped his hand in Jerat's – the child trembled slightly and his thumb was still wet, but Jerat did not recoil and a moment later Roat followed suit.

Jerat found himself leading both children by the

hand to the well outside in the Hearthyard, in the broad shadow of the Hearth tree. He liked the feeling it gave him, holding their small hands in his. Something that had hardened inside him in the five years of his exile from the Heart of the Home softened then, something that had been lost to him was found. It was no chore to wash the children in the freezing water of the well, to comb their light feather-down of baby hair, and to rub them warm with the blanket kept for the purpose. It should have irritated him, but it didn't, and by the time it dawned on him that, as the only child of the second quarter still living in the Hall, their care lay entirely in his hands, his hands had already begun to do the job.

Jerat tried to look back over his five long winters in the Hall. There had been a baby of the first quarter that had come to the Hall the previous summer, but it had died just after Placid, the biggest ox, had broken its leg. Jerat didn't remember much about it, though Guardsman Liley had cried so much her eyes were still red when she'd taught Jerat spear-throwing the next day, so perhaps she'd had the care of it.

The twins allowed Jerat to dry them and help them dress without complaint, even though he made them stand outside on the cold packed earth of the Hearthyard while he did it. No child of the Brood Trove grew up soft. If they grew up at all it was because they were hardy and tough – even so, all the Brood jostled for position as close to the cook fire as they could get without getting in the way of the cook. Keran was on cook duty on this memorable morning and the smell of corn porridge was making Jerat's stomach growl. Jerat liked Keran's porridge because he cooked it properly as he did everything else – he never let it burn.

'Oi, Jerat!' Guardsman Hela, the man-woman from afar with the gift for walking on her hands, called over to him and handed him new wooden bowls and spoons for the twins. 'Porridge is hot – have a care.' She said it casually, but he noticed that she watched him as he brought the babies their food. Heron, the old no-man, hovered too nearby. Neither Heron nor Hela intervened, though, not when the boys made a mess of their clothes, nor when Roat threw his food on the ground in a fit of temper, not even when Rinat burnt his tongue and cried for a good bit. Jerat did what he could, which was not much: he wiped them down and cleared the mess, washed their bowls and hugged Rinat to comfort him – then got on with the rest of his daily duties.

Later that day Jerat was given a small package of extra clothes for the twins – padded jerkins and hats with flaps to cover their ears. It gave him a strange adult sense of complicity with this current wife of the second quarter, to take these carefully worked clothes and dress the twins in this extra layer of protection. It seemed that this wife was determined that the babes should survive the cold that roughened and reddened and coarsened and chilled sometimes to death, and Jerat found he shared that determination.

It was difficult to train properly. When Guardsman Keran started the training exercises Jerat's concentration was badly affected by the need to check that the twins had not wandered away. Although they trained in the Hearthyard where they ate and cooked and lived for the greater part of the time, there was no barrier between the yard and the Hearthfields, and they were full of hazards, from the ill-tempered hound which bit anyone who got too close, to the river which was narrow, deep and treacherous at this point in its flow. Beyond the boundary of the Hearthfields was the wildness of the forest, and Jerat did not even want to consider what would happen if the twins strayed there. Jerat earned a clip with Keran's stave twice before he hit upon the idea of tethering the boys, like untrained dogs, to the Hearth tree. The twins did not appreciate that. Avet, Jerat's training partner and eldest son of the fourth quarter, was able to make many more hits than usual with his stave because Jerat worried that the twins might become entangled with the rope and somehow strangle themselves.

'You want to be a comfort-giver in the Heart of the Home, Jer?' Avet mocked. It was hard to fight Avet at the best of times as he had survived fourteen hard winters to Jerat's ten. He was a good head and shoulders taller, with the broadened shoulders of a warrior and the first shadow of a youthful beard darkening the red-brown of his jaw. Jerat usually relied on his own greater agility and ability to predict Avet's next move to avoid serious injury, though unfortunately he'd never learned how to avoid the non-serious sort: fights with Avet always ended the same way.

'Come on then, wife – you going to wear your skirts and your mask tomorrow, honey-touch?'

Avet got through his defences perhaps twenty times that first training day after his brothers' arrival. Jerat's ears strained to hear the babbling chatter of the twins, rather than Avet's breathing, which changed when he was about to attack and always alerted him to Avet's next probable move. The wooden stave was heavy enough to hurt, but all the bruises he sustained could not help him to marshal his thoughts and concentrate.

'Come on then, honey-touch, twitch your skirts at me.' Avet's expression was as irritating as his voice was goading. He hit Jerat a heavy blow on his shoulders which unbalanced him and caused him to trip over his own feet.

Serott of the third quarter started to laugh with such abandon that she dropped her practice stave, and she and her training partner Plueret of the fourth referred to Jerat as 'honey-touch' for the rest of the day. By the evening Jerat's whole body burned with his many bruises and with the heat of shame. When it came to lastmeal – served in the winter months in the centrespace of the Hall – he all but fell asleep with the babies in his lap, and Avet and Plueret began to sing some version of 'The Sad Wife's Lullaby', substituting Jerat's name for that of the sad wife. He began to feel his slow-burning temper flare, which he knew was what his brothers and sisters wanted. The Hearth Guard chatted among themselves of adult concerns, mended kit and traded stories. They only intervened in the many internecine squabbles between the quarters when the Chief's 'Brood brats' overstepped some invisible and unknowable line of their own imagining. They hadn't crossed it this night. Hela glanced quickly in his direction, but that was all, and Jerat was only saved from further torment and an embarrassing outburst of temper by the arrival of the Teller Priest.

FOUR

The children fell silent at the Teller Priest's entrance. He smiled and strode carefully into the packed circle of dogs and Guardsmen and Brood brats, crammed together in the centre of the Hall, sitting as close as they could get to the dying embers of the cook stove. The Teller Priest was a small man for a Lakesider – the largest of the milk cows only came up to his chest, so that he almost disappeared among them like a child – but what he lacked in stature he gained in presence. Wherever he was, all eyes were on him. His own eyes were the colour of cornflowers. Set in the creases of his weathered face, they were bright as gemstones.

'May Zerat, Lord of the Light, keep you, Teller Priest. You are welcome to our heat and light,' said Keran formally, as the Teller Priest hunkered down in the privileged place closest to the stove, displacing the ill-tempered dog as he did so. The children and other Guardsmen echoed the greeting.

'Zerat, Lord of the Light, keep you too.'

Jerat noted that the Teller suppressed a shiver and huddled into his thick, fleece-lined cloak, and Jerat wondered if he kept his own home warmer than the Hall. If he did, Jerat wondered if he might visit there some day. Jerat still remembered the heated winters of his earliest childhood with longing, and he hugged his small brothers to him more closely, as much for their living animal warmth as for that other thing that warmed him inside, but for which he had no name.

The Teller Priest came, like Hela, from some distant Dependency, and always conversed a little with her in their native tongue. This time their guttural conversation seemed to Jerat to include him, as they both glanced in his direction more than once before Hela offered the great traveller and wise one a share of their ale and the remains of their lastmeal. Avet and Plueret lapsed into respectful silence when the Teller Priest joined them: he was the dye-man, who knew the secrets of making dyes and stains and pigments that were the delight of Zerat; he was the healer who knew of herbs that made you sick, that purged you and made you well; he was the wise man who knew the lore of the Night Hunters, and some even said he had Hunter blood and could turn you into a fox, a bat or even a rabbit if the moon was in the right phase and the auguries were fitting. No one ever knew quite what the right phase of the moon was, so it paid to be cautious. Jerat was always cautious. It bothered him that the Teller Priest was not of the Hearth Guard or the Brood Trove; that he was not a wife or a no-man in the Heart of the Home. Jerat never knew quite what to expect of him – a trader with strangers, an outsider. The Teller Priest carried with him the scent of other places, heady but dangerous.

'I see the newest of the Brood is in safe hands,' the Teller Priest said after he had eaten his fill. Jerat shrank a little from the attention; he did not need more jibes about his newfound role as a comfort-giver.

Perhaps the Teller noticed, because he moved on quickly. 'These two remind me of the Great Divide and the twins of the clay – you must surely know that tale? Yes? Well, with your permission I will tell it again, and dedicate it to Jerat of the second quarter and his brothers. Twins should ever be seen as a sign of strong blessings, though it is not always so.'

Jerat loved stories, and although he was embarrassed to be singled out, he knew that in the failing light of the candle lamp his heated face would pass unseen by Avet and the rest. He saw Avet poke out his tongue, though, and make the gesture with his finger which made Plueret snigger. The Teller Priest took a long drink of his ale and began in the singsong Teller's way quite unlike his usual speech.

'On the first day of life when the earth was new and naked and had not yet laboured to bear fruit, that day the sky was pale and clear and had not yet troubled to bear rain-clouds and snow-clouds and the fruits of the air. In all the quietness of the first day lightning came and touched the womb of the earth to make it fruitful. In pain and violence the earth was rent by a quake so large it churned and ripped and toppled and tore the earth almost to death and made the highland of the Broken Teeth Mountains and the deep hollow of Mordant Lake. And in all the pain and tremors of birth, the earth brought forth the twin gods Zerat and Zeron, sired by fire and light and grown in the deep and secret places of the earth.

'For the first days the twins grew, and the earth laboured further to bring forth the trees and plants and good wheat to feed her children, and the sky laboured to bring blossoms of clouds to bloom and to shower the earth with cooling dampness to ease her pains and quicken the trees and plants and wheat of her bearing, so that in a few short days they grew, and Zerat was manlike in his strength and beauty and Zeron was like a woman in her strength and beauty and for a while they were happy. They swam in the hollow of the land which the sky filled with water for their delight. They played in the mountains of the land and learned how to make vessels of life from the good clay that bordered the lake. They made animals and birds and fish of all shapes and sizes, and the lightning and the earth together quickened them. Then as the twins' skills developed they made people of all shapes and sizes and the earth and the lightning quickened them too. But then the twins grew tired of such craftsmanship and began to quarrel over who was the best. Zeron delighted in the small people she had made with faces black as the night itself and she loved them best, and Zerat delighted in the large people that he had made with faces the colour of the sun on the yellow clay and he loved them best.

'The gods fought for three days and three nights. They fought with spears and staves made of the tallest Great Trees, the wood of which endures for ever; they fought with boulders from the rocks and flints of the high mountains, and they fought with fists and with feet and with nails. In their raging fury much of the land was despoiled and Zeron lost an ear and Zerat an eye and they both wept in their pain and frustration. Zeron lay on her mother earth and laid the torn place where her ear had been against the earth, and the earth blessed her with an ear to hear the music of the stars and the singing of the night winds. Zerat lay on his mother earth and laid the torn place where his eye had been against the earth, and the earth blessed him with an eye to see the tiniest movement of life in the forests and the smallest gradation of colour in the clay of the earth, and so they came at last to a truce. Zeron took the small people that she had made and claimed the night and all that darkness brought: the music of the stars and the night wind and all the crawling and the flying and the creeping things that she had made, and she called the people the Night Hunters and became the Goddess of the Dark, the earth's daughter. Zerat took the large people that he had made and claimed the day in all its bright and glowing colours with its many movements and with all its brave beasts and soaring creatures, and called us the Bear-men and became for us the God of Day. And this is the story of the Great Divide, and may it rest as true in your breast as it lay true on my lips.'

There was silence for a while after the Teller's words.

'The way I heard it Zeron tried to murder Zerat and used magic and evil sorcery to try to reclaim the day,' said Keran at last.

'That is one version of the story, yes,' said the Teller Priest, 'for magic lies in the songs of the stars and the Goddess of Night can use their powers. There are many variations – in some Zerat and Zeron promise to be reconciled when a daughter of Zeron should marry a son of Zerat, but the story I told you is the version I learned in my youth, and it still seems to be the truest.'

'Is it true that the Night Hunters want all the brightness and beauty of the day for themselves and try to steal any bright things they can find?' asked Keran.

'It is true that they do not weave or dye their clothes and so value brightly coloured things highly,' the Priest said.

Keran nodded, and Hela, who was next in command, said hastily, 'Thank you, Teller, for the blessing of your true tale this night. You will of course stay now that true darkness has fallen, and not risk walking in the Goddess's realm.'

'I'm sure I'd be safe enough, Guardsman Hela, but I thank you for your hospitality. It will be pleasure indeed to share your shelter against the full chill of the night.'

Jerat was certain this time that the Priest did shiver, because now the cook fire had burned out, the temperature in the Hall had fallen fast.

'Jerat, let me help you with your charges,' the Teller Priest said. Jerat was grateful. He was tired himself and did not look forward to the business of swaddling the children in their blankets and getting them to the sleep mat; they were sure to wake and cry and need taking outside to the soil pit.

The Teller Priest was deft and swift and strong for such a small, ageing man, and in no time he had helped Jerat to arrange himself on his sleep mat with the children again cradled in the crook of each arm. He did it so efficiently they did not even stir.

'How are you finding your new duties, Jerat?' the Teller Priest asked softly. Jerat was a little surprised to be asked such a question; in his experience it did not pay to think about what went on – it simply was, but he gave it grave consideration nonetheless.

'I don't know, Teller. I'm even worse at fighting Avet now with the babes to care for, but he always beat me anyway.'

'He is much older than you, is he not? The eldest of the fourth quarter.'

Jerat shrugged but then realised that the Priest would not see him in the darkness so added, 'The Chief says it's better to fight someone older than younger, for it will make me stronger if it does not kill me first.'

'That sounds like your father, and he has a point.' The older man chuckled, but it was a bleak sound. 'But know that you are precious, Jerat. I knew your dam before she was a wife of the second quarter and I know that she would be proud of you. You won't forget that, will you?'

'No, Teller,' he answered. He was uncomfortable with the conversation which mentioned that which was not mentioned in the Hall; those things that were to do with the treasured and never-to-be-spoken-of memory of the Heart of the Home and the lost mother of his infancy.

'Now, where is the warmest place in this icehouse of a Hall? I swear it is warmer in the Broken Teeth Mountains than here.'

'I think the only way to be warm is to sleep either with the beasts or with one of the Guardsmen, Teller, for the guest blanket is not as fine as it might be and smells a bit of the cow that gave birth on it last winter.'

'Goodnight, Jerat. I can see that very little gets past you.' The Teller Priest seemed to be struggling not to laugh, though Jerat could not understand why. Though he did a little later hear the clear sound of Hela's infectious giggle, before welcome sleep claimed him.

FIVE

When Nela woke it was dark and cool. The only light came from the camp fire. Someone had covered her in a blanket but left her, where she'd fallen, in the centre of the camp. Her back hurt and her legs were stiff. She stretched awkwardly. Everyone else was asleep. The only movement came from the bondsman tending the fire, the only sound his breathy singing.

She almost recognised the tune. Her stomach felt painfully empty; she had not eaten since breakfast, so, wrapping herself in her blanket, she moved closer to the fire. She felt a little unsteady, though whether from the after-effects of the fit or her peculiar experience, she did not know. She sank down beside the fire and tried to calm herself. Her youngest aunt, the one who had been least appalled by her fits, had tried to show her ways to restore her equilibrium once they were over. She hadn't paid too much attention at the time and had not known it for the kindness it was. Now she tried to remember what she should do, how she should slow her breathing and let all tension leave her body. It was quiet but for the hissing crackling of the fire and the gentle sound of the Findsmen's regular sleep-breathing and the half-heard bondsman's song. She tried to respond to the peacefulness of it, the endlessly shifting pattern of the flames, the luxury of being alone with her thoughts. She was even growing used to the pungent, faintly putrid smell given off by the burning timber.

The bondsman placed a plate of cornmeal porridge and some dried meat before her, still singing under his breath. She took it without looking at him, which was quite proper, but seemed strange in the quietness of the night: he had a very solid kind of presence for a bondsman. In the city one rarely noticed the large mass of indentured servants at all – perhaps this one lacked the talent for inconspicuousness mastered by the rest of his ilk. He was singing more loudly now, almost as if he intended her to hear.

He sang in the old tongue,

Shadows bloom as the Womanface rises
Earth grows sweet with the scent of the night
Hunt in the light of the
Beauty of Womanface
Fleet-footed, sharp as the
Lady's white light

Nela registered the song with one part of her mind as she ate her food. It seemed that despite the unpleasant and powerful aroma of the burning firewood she could still smell the lingering poultry stench of the

44

carrier coop and, in spite of the broad and starfilled sky above her, she could still feel the residual panic of being so totally enclosed in the small, dark space at the top of the ancient Tier House.

The hands that held her food shook slightly. To distract herself she listened to the bondsman's song. She could only translate the first stanza; the rest had too many unknown words. She recognised that this was a 'Great Song' that she had not heard before in so complete a form. The use of the word 'Womanface', the ancient circumlocution for the moon often identified with Zeron, suggested that the bondsman's version was very old indeed. She listened harder and with growing excitement. The bondsman was singing the ancient hymn of the evening as it must have been sung by the earliest hunter-gatherers.

She dropped her plate and it shattered on the dry ground. The bondsman was there immediately to clear it away and to hand her a replacement plate of food. She did not look at him, of course, nor did she acknowledge her foolishness in smashing the plate; instead she broke a greater taboo and spoke to him without giving him an order.

'That is the Evening Song?'

He did not answer. Bondsmen were beaten for answering back. He moved away to get rid of the broken pottery shards and Nela grabbed his tether and pulled. She did not pull hard, just hard enough to let him know that she was there. When he turned towards her he looked her full in the face and Nela realised she had made a terrible mistake. She dropped the tether as if it burned her.

The bondsman had an extraordinary face, strong and proud with even features and well-defined bones. His eyes were a very bright blue, the colour of the sea in the bay near Nela's home. Those eyes were not servile, not humble and not pleased.

Nela was so shocked by how much like a real man, a free man, he looked that she almost apologised to him, though the moment she thought about it the idea was ridiculous. Instead she repeated her original question.

'Your song – it was the Evening Song?' She was irritated that her voice did not sound as confident as it should, perhaps because she was still recovering from the after-effects of her fit.

'Yes. How do you know the language of my ancestors?' he answered softly, as though he knew her well and had spoken to her often.

Whatever else she had expected, she hadn't expected that, and she found herself bridling at his lack of respect. She glanced anxiously at the mounds of blankets which was all she could see of the men of her party. Fortunately they still slept.

'I have been collecting the old songs from the written story cycles in the Great Library at home, in Scraal, and from listening when I can . . .' She had not meant to go into such detail; a curt denial would have been better.

She looked away under his gaze when surely it should have been his place to lower his eyes. His open scrutiny was not acceptable. Not acceptable at all. Her aunts would have been scandalised. She took up her plate and finished her food. It was cold, sticky and without flavour but, according to her father, contained all the nourishment she needed. It was difficult to swallow it down but the bondsman anticipated this too and gave her a cup of sweet-leaf tea he had been keeping warm on the hearth stone. She tried to remain impassive, to re-establish the invisible barrier that should exist between the daughter of the Chief Findsman and the expedition bondsman.

The bondsman said nothing for a moment, though Nela was sure he had more to say. He refilled her pale china drinking bowl with more tea and said softly but assertively, 'You know that you cannot take the black stone away from here, that it belongs here and to move it would be sacrilege.'

'I know no such thing,' Nela answered with all the haughty dignity of her position. 'We came here to find evidence that this is the Lakeside of legend, the ancient homeland of my people. The Goodly Congregation of Licensed Merchants and Prince Helvennig himself, not to mention the Worshipful Company of Historical Archivists of Scraal, have invested vast sums in funding this expedition. If my father thinks that stone is evidence I'm sure that no right-thinking person could fail to trust him to do what is appropriate.'

She was conscious as she emphasised the word 'person' that the bondsman did not qualify. She did not need to meet the man's luminous eyes to know that he disagreed, nor did she need to examine her own reactions too closely to know that she did too. The stone she had held was not something cold and dead to be housed with the archivists or to decorate a palace, it was something warm and living and infinitely precious.

The bondsman did not say anything but continued to busy himself with whatever a bondsman did in the dead of night. Nela began to feel that she had behaved badly, not because she'd broken the taboo, but because somehow she hadn't been a very good Findsman. The servant knew the Evening Song and instead of carefully noting it down she had allowed foolish pride to get in the way of her Seeking after truth.

She cleared her throat. 'How do you know that song?' she said. He moved closer to her and looked her full in the face again when he answered.

'My mother taught me a song that her mother taught her and so on through the generations. It is the song sung every evening. I knew when I heard you speak with the stone in your hand that it was in the language of the song. All my life I have heard those words and never known what they meant. I would not have asked you – but you spoke first. Remember that.' He sounded almost belligerent but she ignored his agitation. She was not interested in him at all.

'Sing me the song again,' she demanded.

He obeyed. It was a strange tune, haunting and sad. The sound sent a visceral shiver through her, raised the hairs on her arm and filled her with a sudden longing for something just beyond her reach. She almost grasped the second and third stanza, but then understanding eluded her, slipping away like the strangely scented smoke from the fire.

'I can't understand it all,' she said at last, genuinely

regretful, 'but I will note it down and maybe I'll be able to translate it later.'

'You feel it though, don't you?' he said with his disturbingly direct gaze.

'What do you mean?'

'You know it is something more than a song – it has . . .' He hesitated, searching for a way to explain. 'It has a kind of a flame inside it.'

'And unfortunately the meaning is like smoke,' Nela moved closer to the crackling flames of the fire and spoke almost under her breath, 'and I think I will carry the scent of its smoke with me for some time.'

The bondsman nodded. 'When you learn what it means – you will tell me.'

It wasn't so much a question as a statement. Nela took a deep breath, inhaling the cloying scent of decay that emanated from the burning timber. How had she got to the point where she was being manoeuvred into negotiating with a bondsman?

'I'm going back to sleep now,' Nela said, hoping to end the conversation.

'You might find out more if you touched the stone again,' the bondsman persisted. 'There is magic in that sacred thing, old magic that may tell you.'

'I don't believe in magic. The stone is a historical artefact,' Nela answered stiffly, though she did not know how the stone had made her see what she had seen without magic. 'The stone is not something to be mauled and toyed with.'

'In your hands it is a door to another place – out of your hands it is merely a stone.' The bondsman watched her expression closely with what seemed to be his characteristic impertinence. Nela did not want her face to show her irrational desire to touch the stone again, to understand what was going on, to find out what happened to the woman in the carrier coop of the Tier House.

'The Chief Findsman will no doubt have put it somewhere appropriately secure,' Nela said firmly, and turned away to walk the chilly distance to her sleeping mat. She realised then that she had failed to deny that she wished to hold that stone again. She wasn't handling this situation well.

'Woman-who-is-not-a-woman!' the bondsman called softly.

Nela turned to see a small leather pouch in his hand. He put his hand to his lips to indicate that she should be silent, and beckoned to her. This was not seemly at all, not acceptable, not the kind of a behaviour suitable in a bondsman. Nela glanced nervously round at the sleeping men, then turned back to face him. The smile on the bondsman's face told her that he knew, knew that she could not resist the stone. Seeking out truth was her interest, her ambition, her reason for wanting to be there in this corrupted, putrefying forest. Wasn't knowledge, wasn't truth worth breaking the odd taboo for? Her father would be furious for so many different reasons that he wouldn't know which to be angry at first. If she accepted the stone from this man's hands she was not only consorting with a bondsman in a manner unbecoming to a Chief Findsman's daughter, but tacitly encouraging his dishonesty. More importantly still, she would be allowing herself to explore the implications of the artefact without the presence of a Findsman, indeed without a scribe of any kind. It was this last that made up her mind for her. She did not like the idea of her own father taking notes while she spasmed in an involuntary fit.

She did not smile back at the presumptuous servant – that would be to go too far – but she avoided flinching from his touch as he reached out his hand as if to give her the stone. But he did not give it to her, he held it slightly out of her grasp. Nela's heart was beating too quickly. She was afraid and excited and desperate to touch the artefact and be transported to that other place.

'Promise me you'll protect me,' he said.

'What d'you mean?' Nela was outraged. She couldn't help it – what was this bondsman doing, toying with her like her father might? She was a free non-woman while he was no one at all.

'Your father did not lock it away, but I have not taken the risk of borrowing this so that you can have me dismissed for theft. If you accept this from me, you and I are allies in seeking out the language and life of my ancestors.' He withdrew the bag and the stone so that she could not reach out and grab it.

'All right.' What was she doing – the Chief Findsman's daughter allied with a bondsman?

'Swear.'

'On what?' Her tone was scathing. The practice of taking oaths had long been outlawed when King Derant the Third had tried to put an end to oath killings. Nela had never made an oath and feared to, her vow which made her a new woman being regarded as something quite different.

'Swear by your own honour as a woman-who-is-not-a-woman, by your freedom from the Hearth.' He spoke very urgently, sure that such an oath would have meaning for her. He was right, but she did not know how he knew it.

'I swear by my honour,' she said simply, and accepted the proffered pouch and stone.

She emptied the leather pouch eagerly into her open palm. The dark stone glowed red with the reflected flames from the fire, but it was cold and hard in her hand. She felt no sudden shift in her perspective, no moment of dislocation. She felt nothing.

'This is not the black stone,' she said, disappointment making her voice as cold and unliving as the useless pebble in her hand.

'No, it is not, but I had to be sure that you were not some hysteric pretending to visions just to be important.' He took the stone that was not 'the stone' and, replacing it in its leather pouch, returned it to his belt.

Nela kept her temper with difficulty. This bondsman had the most extraordinary degree of arrogance. Outrage made her spit out her whispered words: 'And how, if I was making it up, did I know the language you claim for your ancestors?'

'You know more than I know of the meaning of the song "Black Stone of the Unmaking", and that is a song of my people, the hunters of old.'

Fury robbed Nela of the power of response.

'Here,' said the camp bondsman and picked up a pebble from the dark earth by the fire. 'Try this one!'

Their fingers touched as he passed the pebble to her; that was not done and she was embarrassed, and then she felt the warmth and weight of the stone in her palm and she no longer felt the heat of the fire, the discomfort of the servant's touch. She was elsewhere.

Six

I stand by a stream in the light of the egg moon and the night air is damp and cold. It makes me shiver and I want Mam and Moon-eye is staring at me and I know that she is looking stern even though her expression is hard to read and she is telling me to listen. It is very quiet – no people noises and few animals, just the stream burbling a kind of unending melody and the topmost branches of the high trees rustling a different tune like a counterpoint. The grass in the clearing blows too. If they are saying anything I don't understand it. I can hear the steady breathing of my teacher Moon-eye and my blood pulses hot and loud in my ears. I don't like people looking at me, expecting things of me, and I don't like it here. The damp earth smell is too strong and the water smell of weed and stones is so powerful I can taste it and it tastes like hunger. Somewhere there is a sudden fluttering in the bushes, a scuffling and a squeak – the death throes of some creature whose time had come and something else and I know that something else isn't hungry any more.

'Listen!' my teacher says in an intense whisper and I strain to hear something else that isn't just these ordinary noises but something more in the night.

'Can you hear it?' she asks and I try to think of something. I try hard but I can't and I shrug and I don't think she sees. What is there to hear that is special? Everything is as usual. I don't know what I'm supposed to be noticing.

Moon-eye seems as if she is made of shadow. She is never one to wear bright things from the Wandering Man's wares and she looks like part of the earth so that she can hide among the trees when strangers come, but even her soft earth-greens and browns are all turned to grey by the moon and when I look down at my own dress it seems wispy as clouds, as if I am a thing of dreams. Only her teeth are bright in the moonlight and the whites of her eyes glisten like a wet fish, shiny and beautiful and strange. Teeth and eyes and voice and the broken shards of moonlight, silver in the stream as the wind ripples the water – that is all I can see and it makes me shiver and not just with the cold, though the wind is lifting my hair and pulling at me like it wants me to notice something. I want my fireside and my mam's hand to hold. Here, all but alone, in the dark clearing where things I can't see and hear may lurk in the dark shadows of the bushes, there is nothing to hold but my stone, so I clasp that tightly. Eyes flick and teeth flash and the voice demands again, 'Listen . . .'

'But Moon-eye, I don't know what to listen for.'

Moon-eye's large grey-clothed body looms over me and her hand lightly brushes my hair.

'Child, you must listen for the sound of your heart and the pulse of the earth and make them beat together, for a Singer is grounded in the earth and a Singer lives according to the rhythm of the earth and can do only what that rhythm dictates.'

She sounds exasperated. Moon-eye does not like children much and has no gift for explaining, only for singing. She's not like Brown River or Daughter Green who showed me how to get the far berries without getting scratched and helped me take the bones from the fish all in one go, so you can see the shape of the frame inside them like the sticks that hold up our tent.

'Relax, little chick, you can't hear anything when you hold yourself so stiffly. You must bend with the wind or you will surely snap.' Moon-eye's strong sinewy hands that break the neck of a hare with a quick twist massage my shoulders.

Moon-eye is standing a little way away. She frightens me. Her hair hangs round her face and it's all blowing about so she looks like the spirit of a tree, not like a person at all. I want to do what she wants but I still don't understand what that is.

'Feel the earth's power travel up from the heart of the earth through the centre of your being, squeeze it upwards through your soul's core, through the womb of your life, then breathe that force out – that is how you must breathe from now on, always feeling the earth's strength running through you. Can you do that? You must do it all the time until you can make your breath come out in a steady stream as if blowing a feather and keeping it afloat.'

I nod. So she wants me to breathe in this long strange way all the time – even when I'm running around and playing and when we go berry picking and when I gather wood for the fire. I don't think I can do that but I don't want to say it, so I nod. Moon-eye looks at me with her funny eyes and way of seeing through my skin to whatever is underneath.

'Child, you are named Moon-stone for the gift of the Womanface that I sense in you and for the stone your father chose as your birth-name. That was an omen, but the right name is not enough to make you a Singer. You have to try. It's a gift, but not like a stone is a gift. You can't just own it, you have to struggle to make it work for you. It's like a fire that must be kindled and fed and tended, or like . . .' she stumbled, thinking of something else that singing was like, 'like making trews from a deer – you have to hunt it, skin it, scrape it, cure it, soften it, cut it . . .'

I yawn. I thought I understood what she was talking about for a moment, but now I don't. I don't see how singing can be like making trews at all. Anyway I'm too young to wear the trews of a hunter and if I never learn to sing, I will never get to go with my brother anyway. I can't hit the target mark from even ten paces with a stone or a throwing stick and Sky says I'm more hopeless than any girl he's ever known and worse than Hearth who is still suckling. I don't think Moon-eye can tell my thoughts because she doesn't say anything but that I must go to the stream and she must cut my hand to make the Singer's mark to show that I'm her acolyte now and must stay with her every day until I have learned the songs. I don't want this – I want to stay with Mam and Sky and Hearth and Dad and Butterfly, who is sick and needs me to help look after her. Moon-eye says I can stay in their tent until we move to the next stopping place.

She drags me to the stream and takes out her hunter's knife with the sharpest blade that Old Black Earth, our best knife-maker, ever made. I try not to cry. She holds me firmly, opens my hand and slices once across the palm. She cuts me in the shape of the waxing crescent moon, the fingernail moon for growth and promise, and it hurts, a sharp sting of pain that takes me by surprise. She washes my hand in the mud of the earth, in the moonlit water, and then she holds it to the wind to dry. It still hurts and I have to fight not to cry or gasp at the coldness and suddenness of the water and of all of it. But then she sings. It is a sound like honey, so sweet that it fills the air with sudden warmth and the pain goes away and she sings some more and I feel sleepy. She binds my hand with some cloth. It is not my best throwing hand – she must have known that.

'I have introduced you to the Womanface and you are marked for her now. Sleep, little chick. Tomorrow we will begin our work.'

And she picks me up in her strong arms and hums to me until –

Nela started awake in sudden fear. The stone was in the hand of the bondsman.

'What did you take it for?' She was disoriented – where had Moon-eye gone?

'You whimpered. I thought you were in pain.'

Nela hardly heard the bondsman speak. She fingered the place on her left palm where Moon-eye had carved the sign of the moon. She was surprised to find her own skin smooth and unbroken.

'Put the stone back where you got it,' she said, distractedly. She felt unsteady and confused. What was going on when she held that stone? She staggered back to her sleeping mat without acknowledging the bondsman further. All that mattered was the stone.

SEVEN

Jerat measured time by the twins' growing competence and his own rather complicated pride in them. By the time that Ro had survived eight winters he was as strong as an ox of the Herd, though a good deal wilder – and forever getting lost and having to be found. One time he had managed to climb halfway up the outer thatch-ladder to the Heart of the Home and Jerat wondered if Ro, like himself, secretly longed for the warmth and comfort of his lost comfort-giver. Rin was quieter, less robust; he made Jerat feel like a god among men, for only he and no one else (except sometimes for Guardsman Verre) could make Rin happy.

There were always changes in personnel in the Hall, new warriors of the Horde coming to serve their time with the Hearth Guard. It was expected that all men of fighting age would spend some time with the elite warriors who trained every day. After a time they went to their farms or back to their trades, though they would always remain of the Chief's Horde until they were too old and weak to stand and hold a spear. Some, like Keran or Hela, knew only warrior work and, if they moved on, retired to Dependency farms gifted to them by the Chief or worked in other Halls for older members of the Chief's Brood Trove. If they had family or a life beyond the Tier House, Jerat knew nothing about it, and if they went away for a few days on 'Chief's' business Jerat never questioned it. Quite a few of Jerat's Brood brothers had cleared wild forest land to set up Halls of their own with small Dependencies or taken over those of their conquered neighbours. The Brood members rarely stayed in their own Hall when they came of age but went to serve in their brothers' Hearth Guards, learned a trade or married. The web of alliances was complex and sealed with marriages, gifts and mutual support in times of war. Even among so much to-ing and fro-ing, the arrival of Guardsman Verre was something different; there was something special about Verre and everyone knew it. She was not a man-woman – her hair was long and tightly plaited, coiled around her head under a soft cap so that she looked like a man-woman, until you noticed that her head shape was all bumpy with plaits and not like Lema and Hela's egg-smooth skulls at all.

Verre was interested in all the Brood but took particular care with Jerat and the twins – and was the only adult who always seemed to know where they were. There had been no more children born to the wife of the second quarter in all that time, for which Jerat was quietly grateful, though a new sister came to the first quarter and a small boy came to the third but did not last the winter. Verre had tried to save him, even bringing in the Teller Priest and making all the Brood seek out roots and herbs to make poultices and infusions, but they all failed and the boy was buried in the 'Belly of the Earth', sometimes known as 'Zerat's pit', a trench on the edge of the forest. He was left there with little ceremony along with all the long-forgotten wives.

Verre was a good fighter, too, easily as strong as Plinket and probably as good as Keran. She was particularly good with a bow and helped Jerat a lot with this most difficult of skills. She also helped him tame the temper that from time to time got him in trouble with the Guardsmen. Jerat treasured the praise she gave him and the realisation that thanks to her help he was better with a bow than any of his Brood – better even than Avet.

Perhaps the most interesting thing about Verre was her attitude to the forest. In the glorious and victorious Dependency of Lakeside the forest was a place of fear and mystery that marked the boundary of civilisation. It was the grey-green shadow that threatened peace of mind, the wild land that had to be conquered, the haunt of night's creatures and all that thrived in the dark. Verre took Jerat into the forest too, and though at first he had been terrified out of his wits, she taught him how to live within it, mindful of danger but unafraid. She taught him to move silently and almost invisibly through its dappled shadows in order to track deer and other small animals. She was not from the glorious and victorious Great

Dependency of Lakeside, but had grown up among practical people for whom the forest was a good source of food. She was more than a little impatient with the tradition which kept the Lakesiders from the rich hunting and strange beauty of forest land. She always clicked her tongue disparagingly when anyone criticised her for venturing into forbidden territory, noting that their disapproval never prevented them from eating the meat she brought back. Jerat suspected that anyone else but Verre would have been shunned by the Guard, but somehow Verre got away with it and no one complained, even when she took Jerat with her, or at least not in Verre's hearing. Avet, of course, had plenty to say, but Jerat never told Verre that. Jerat missed Verre badly when she disappeared, as she was inclined to do for long months on end, and was frustrated that none of the Hearth Guard, not even Hela, would ever explain where she went.

There were other changes too. Jerat grew taller and stronger so that the gap in height and weight that had existed between him and Avet narrowed to the point where there was merely two fingers' worth of height between them, even though Avet now wore a wispy beard and was fully as tall and broad as Keran. But by far the greatest and most terrible change occurred in the summer after Jerat's fifteenth winter on the eve of the Festival of Longest Light.

The Chief had reintroduced the festival in the summer after the twins came to the second quarter of the Hall. The Chief's family, his Brood Trove, had grown to such a size that he had to make more of an effort to keep the familial connections strong and to influence the bloodline of his Brood. There were to be guests arriving from all the allied neighbouring Dependencies and the chance for the Chief's current crop of wives of the four quarters to turn their attention to the task of match-making for the Brood Trove, under his ever-calculating eye.

The festival was weeks in the preparation and almost all training had ceased so that the Hearth Guard and the no-men could erect tents and gather the tithe food from the surrounding farms and businesses of the Dependency. They also had to clean the Hall and brew enough small beer of sprouted-barley cakes, water, yeast and meadowsweet for the feast. Jerat enjoyed the change in the work, for one day was much like another in the life of the Hall. The business of wife-getting was of growing interest to him, so he listened when he heard Verre talking to Guardsman Hela in the confidential tone which always guaranteed his interest.

She was clearly outraged at the youth of two of the new Dependency farm wives who, in keeping with tradition, were helping the Teller Priest with the brewing.

'They're not much more than children – far too young to be wives. Those two little ones aren't even full grown – they're as slender as saplings and about as strong. Those poor girls – why did their fathers let them go?'

'For the nuptial gift, of course, Verre. Don't be naive,' said Hela.

Jerat was surprised to see Verre looking so upset. 'I doubt that one of them will live to see the next festival. And our little first wife here is already far too great with child. It is too soon for her . . .' She sounded troubled, and made the sign of Zerat to avert bad luck. Seeing Jerat watching her, she changed the subject. 'You go with Mirit and Tanit today to collect the tithe from the Near Farms, Jer. I'll look after the boys. I have to go away for a few days so I won't see them for a while.'

'You're missing the festival?' Jerat asked, surprise making him forget to address her by the honorific 'Guardsman'.

Verre smiled wistfully so that wrinkles crinkled the corners of her tanned face. They had been training hard outdoors over the previous few weeks and all of them had grown darker in the fierce sun.

'I have a contract to fulfil for someone – it can't be helped.'

Jerat was not sorry to leave the twins to her care. The break in their relentless routine had made them wild and reckless with happiness and they kept disappearing off whenever his back was turned, to play in the trees by the river, or explore the greater Hearthfields. Though they never ventured beyond the boundary enclosure, too much of his time was taken up with involuntary games of hide and seek. He had never raised a hand to them in all the years they'd been in his care, but over the last couple of days he had begun to wonder if that was a mistake. They were always good for Guardsman Verre.

It was not just the twins who were infected with wild excitement. Everyone was expectant that season; change was in the air. When Mirit, Tanit and Jerat walked the lengthy journey through the extensive Hearthfields of his father's land to the nearest Dependency farmholders, Jerat was greeted with a curiosity almost equal to his own. He had rarely been beyond the narrow confines of the Chief's Hearthfields, especially since he'd had the care of the twins: while the farmholders seemed to know a good deal about the Chief's Brood he knew less than nothing about them.

By midday the brothers decided to split up so that they could collect from more farms at once. Jerat was a little unsure of himself – he had his bow and a quiver of good arrows with him. He had left his belt knife behind, as its handle needed mending, but he was unconcerned by its lack as he had been issued with a borrowed elaborately decorated spear as a symbol of his status as a son of the Chief. He was proud to carry it, for he was not entitled to one of his own until he'd survived a full sixteen years. Keran, as a cautious leader of the Hearth Guard, was more interested in ensuring that the Brood brats were well protected than that the niceties of etiquette were maintained: there was rarely trouble when the harvest was good, but 'rarely' was not the same as 'never'.

Jerat enjoyed the freedom to walk his father's lands alone and was pleased, if nervous, to accept farmholder Barak's offer of sweet-leaf tea. They sat together in the cleared land of the Hearthfield outside the farmer's modest Hall. His home was simple, lacking a second tier for his wife and babes, so that it seemed that his wife lived, without ceremony, in the same one room as the beasts and the older children, separated only by means of a dirt platform, covered with a bright, woven rug. It was a revelation to Jerat that the children of farmholders grew up with their mother (if she survived their birthing) in the same room. The farmholder's ageing father also lived with him and took tea with them, squatting on the warm baked earth in the morning sun. The comforting smell of the beasts and their ordure, of cook smoke and sweat, wafted through the open door and mingled with the scent of the hot ground.

'Ah now, Jerat, Chiefson. They say that it's wife-hunting time at the Hall. Are you looking to get yourself a wife this midsummer? A big strong lad like you must surely be of an age.' He looked pointedly at the spear and Jerat shook his head, uncertain how much he ought to reveal of the Hall's business but concluding, rightly, that much of it was already known, carried by the servants and no-men of the Heart of the Home, and by the cowhands and ostlers who helped out in the Hall.

'Yes, farmholder,' Jerat answered politely. 'Mirit and Tanit of the first quarter, Drannott and Kellott of the third and Avet of the fourth are more than old enough to take wives. They were none of them fortunate in previous years.'

'I have a daughter of about your age,' the farmholder continued. 'She is beautiful and strong. I will fetch her for you and you must tell your Brood brothers, eh?'

Jerat looked momentarily panic-stricken until he realised that the farmholder was watching him with amusement. There was the sound of a giggle swiftly smothered and a flash of corn-coloured hair. Someone, presumably the farmholder's daughter, watched from the shadows of the Hall. Jerat peered inside but could see little.

The old man, the farmholder's father, spoke. 'You boys should leave the Tier House more often, meet the rest of us – help with our harvest a little. It is not good to be distant from your farmholders. You can tell your father I said so too. Remember that, Chiefson Jerat, if the Dependency should come to you. Dependency runs two ways – we need the Hearth Guard and the rest of the Horde's protection, but the Hall needs us too.' Jerat tightened his hand around his spear a little nervously, though there was no threat in the man's voice and no tension in the casual way the farmholder sipped his tea. 'Aye, there's change coming,' said the old man. 'Not many left of my birthingtide – your father and a couple of others. We won't see too many more hard winters, mark my words, and then . . .'

'There's good land over the Lake, they say,' said the farmholder gravely. 'And the winters are not as harsh, remember that, Chiefson Jerat. It's good farm land, not so far away from here that a bold man could not travel there, and not so much tithing either. Remember that if you should be chosen heir.'

Jerat looked at the older man in surprise. 'What do you mean?'

'Well, everyone knows that your father needs to declare a new heir soon. It's at least a season since Cariet of the fourth died. It's a wonder that he didn't choose a new heir straight away. He's getting long in the tooth, your father, but not soft in the head. Your father runs things the old way, but he could treat his farmholders better. He imposes too much on old loyalties – a new man, a new Chief could not do that.'

Jerat realised that at least part of what the farmer said was true. The Chief would have to choose a new heir soon.

'I reckon he'll choose a young one this time – harder to teach an old ox a new place to turn,' continued the farmer. 'Now let me help you load the bullock. I'll walk with you to the Tier House so I can bring the beast back.'

'I will be glad of your company, farmholder Barak,' Jerat answered mildly. 'And I would love to hear more of your daughter and of the lands across the Lake.' Jerat was not as attentive to the older man's words as he ought to have been – he was thinking about what would happen if he were named heir. The Tier House and the Dependency would be his – he would no longer have to tolerate Avet's endless needling. Jerat did not agree with the farmholder, though. He was sure his father would pick one of his older sons, one with the experience to run a Dependency and to hold what the Chief had won.

Jerat walked with the farmer along the rough track. He held the borrowed spear with pride, but he was neither alert nor ready for trouble.

EIGHT

It was dusk by the time Jerat got back to the main gateway of the Hearthfields: the doorway of the first quarter. Ro and Rin were there waiting for him, which made Jerat smile, though they seemed to have had the opposite effect on Avet, the duty guard. He looked irritated.

'Can I offer you some sweet-leaf tea or early ale at the Hall before your journey back?' Jerat asked Barak. Avet scowled as Jerat made the offer and banged his ceremonial spear against the ground, as though Jerat was planning to bring some enemy into the Hearthfields.

'I fear your Brood brother is less hospitable, Chiefson,' the farmholder said, his eyes bright and calculating in his sharp-jawed face.

'You are welcome if I say you are welcome,' Jerat said with more confidence than he felt, determined that Avet should not shame him in front of a farmholder of their Dependency. He made sure that the look he gave Avet was shorn of any hint of pleading. He made his face as hard as Avet's own. Ro and Rin stood close together, aware of the tension, as only children raised in the competitive atmosphere of the Hall could be. Ro had his stick with him, a blunted, cut-down spear, and he gripped it firmly as he glowered at Avet from under his long, straight fringe. He needs a haircut, Jerat thought irrelevantly. Perhaps Jerat might have backed down in front of the farmer, but he could not back down in front of the twins. His guest seemed to weigh the silence between the two youths before speaking with all the appearance of ease.

'Then it would be good to sit awhile and admire the view of the Dependency from your Hearthfields, and quench my thirst with your sweet-leaf tea or with your ale, if the Teller Priest has had a hand in its brewing.'

'Avet, this is farmholder Barak, who farms the tithe lands of the second quarter, and I have offered him welcome at the Hall as he brings his tithe to the Tier House and his loyalty to the Dependency.' Jerat used the formal language that he usually only heard at feast times and Acceptance Days: it seemed to him the appropriate way to speak to this farmholder at the traditional entrance to his father's Hearthfields.

Avet moved as if to block their way but Ro contrived to get in front of him, an expression of determination contorting his small face into a parody of a warrior's battle grimace.

'Out of my way, second quarter Lake-scum!' Avet grunted, and batted Ro out of his path with a powerful back-hand blow which caught the child across his nose with an audible crack and made it bleed. Ro did not cry, though he made a small startled sound.

'What did you say?' Jerat had forgotten the farmholder, had forgotten his duties as a host, had forgotten everything except the crimson slick of blood on Ro's frightened face. Jerat's voice was menacing. Everything around him seemed to disappear, to fade into non-existence until all he saw was the face of his enemy and his own borrowed spear.

'I didn't mean to hurt him,' Avet began, with a note of fear in his voice that Jerat had never heard before and scarcely registered then. Avet had his long knife in his belt and he drew it quickly. Neither Jerat's spear nor his bow was much use at close quarters, though he could use his spear like a stave if necessary. Rin handed him something and Jerat curled his hand round the handle of what his hands recognised as a belt knife, unfamiliar but of good weight and balance. He did not know where it had come from, but without taking his eyes off Avet, he accepted the knife from Rin's plump and clammy hand and gave him his spear and bow.

'You hurt Ro – now I hurt you.' It was hard for Jerat to get the words out. The anger that boiled in him had nothing to do with words, but was an inchoate rage born of a thousand small humiliations suffered in silence, the sly dig in the ribs and the outstretched foot at meal times, the accidental overenthusiasm at training. Jerat had learned to keep his temper and, with Verre's help, borne the thousand bruises from Avet's malice: now the fury that welled up inside him could not be dammed.

He thought he heard a voice say, 'Don't lose control,' but maybe by then it was already too late and his control lost, because the knife was unsheathed and the naked, well-honed flint blade was in his hand and he was hurling himself without caution or consciousness towards Avet. Avet dodged and held his own knife ready, but his eyes were wide and frightened and it seemed to Jerat as though he had plenty of time to reposition himself, to slice the sharp edge across Avet's arm so that the blood welled and then to jump back out of his way before he could retaliate. Avet came for him then, screaming incoherently while the blood ran down the exposed muscles of his knife hand. There was the hard painful sound of bone cracking as Jerat protected himself and made contact with Avet's forearm. Avet let out a cry of pain. They grappled for a moment, each trying to unbalance the other, and then gradually Jerat became aware of someone shouting his name. It was the Teller Priest.

'Jerat! Avet! Stop this now!'

Avet dropped his knife first and yelled at Jerat to do the same, but it took a moment for the sense of his words to permeate through the fierce focus of Jerat's anger. When he finally understood, Jerat staggered backwards away from his opponent, his legs suddenly trembling and unstable like a newly birthed colt. The Teller Priest was apologising to the farmholder, taking the spear and bow from Rin's hands and checking Avet's injury all in one moment. Jerat felt strangely light-headed but remembered to turn and apologise to the farmholder himself.

'There is no need,' Barak said. 'The boy brought it on himself – that is why I gave the child my knife to give to you. I would not see a man go ill-prepared into a necessary confrontation.'

Jerat did not know what to say but the Teller Priest came to his rescue.

'We'll keep this quiet, won't we, farmholder Barak? I don't know that we won't all live to regret such hotheadedness. Jerat, I am surprised you let your dog's temper slip from its tether in front of the twins. I thought you more careful than that.'

As Jerat turned round to draw the Priest's attention to Ro's injury, he noticed for the first time that he had gone.

'Where's Ro?'

'I think he was ashamed that he let Avet make him bleed. He ran to the den.' Rin looked shocked.

'I'm all right, Rin. I'm sorry, I shouldn't have fought in front of you. Thank you for giving me Barak's knife. You did nothing wrong.' Jerat, thinking Rin's expression was due to the violence he had witnessed, did his best to sound reassuring. He hugged the child against his hip, trying to ease the worried expression on his face.

'You see, it's all right, Rin. It's over.'

Rin shook his head. 'I think something's the matter with Ro.'

'What do you mean?'

Rin met Jerat's eyes gravely. 'I can't feel him here.' He patted his chest. 'I'm scared.'

The Teller Priest turned to Jerat. 'Run, Jer! Sometimes twins know things about each other that others cannot.' The Teller Priest's concern brought the bitter cold of winter to Jerat's blood, gave new strength to his weakened legs.

'Where is he, Rin?' Jerat asked, unable to keep the fear from his voice.

'In the water by the den.'

Jerat ran then with speed enough to make his lungs burst. He ran past the Tier House, past Verre and Hela who saw him and looked quizzical – he only had breath to shout 'Ro!' and they dropped whatever they were carrying and were running beside him, racing for the water. The boys had built a den in the low-lying branches of the trees that overhung the fastest part of the river. This time of year the torrent was so fast it was foamed with white spindrift, bubbling with eddies and unpredictable currents. The twins had learnt to swim like fish long before, but the river was treacherous. Verre got there first, screaming Ro's name over the rush and roar of the river. The spring melt had been heavy that year and there had been much rain, so that the river was still swollen even this late in the season. Verre was wading in the water, careless of its sudden cold and, in moments, was waist-deep in water. Then Jerat saw a dark head near the opposite bank and dived in, Hela close behind. They reached him together. Ro was not breathing. The river was pulling at him, dragging at him as if fighting to retain his body. Jerat was struggling to keep Ro's head above the whirlpool pull of the water, battling to get Ro's small, limp form to the bank. Once on the land Ro seemed to weigh nothing, but Jerat had to fight to drag himself out of the water, his own heart seemed so heavy.

'Get the water out of him!' Verre grabbed the child from Jerat's arms and turned him on his side. 'Get the Teller Priest, he might know something we can do.'

The Teller Priest was just behind and was swimming with powerful strokes across the river. Water was streaming from Ro's open mouth.

'Ro, wake up!' Verre was shaking him and more water was pouring out of his mouth and nose. She kept on shaking him but he did not respond and the water kept gushing out of him.

'I don't think he is alive,' she said at last, and looked back at the Teller Priest with desperate eyes. 'Can't you do anything?'

The Teller Priest was striding towards Ro, river mud and water dripping from his robe, and suddenly he was kneeling over the beached body of Ro, muttering the words to some song in a voice that was reduced to a rasp. Jerat scrambled to his feet, unable to move closer, and just stood watching, shaking with the cold, with the shock and with horrible fear. The Teller Priest's back hid Ro from his view and all he could think was that Ro was dead and that it was all his fault. If he had not got involved in that stupid fight with Avet it would never have happened. He stood there, unmoving, for a long time. Verre was sobbing uncontrollably nearby, a sound he never thought to hear from her, and Hela was holding her and hugging her as if she were Ro's age.

'He is breathing,' the Teller Priest said at last, 'but

he is not breathing strongly – it may be that his soul has already gone on and that by forcing him back I have done him a disservice. It is so sometimes.'

Jerat could not quite believe it. 'He is still alive?'

'He is hanging on. We should take him back to my Hall, away from all the bustle of the Tier House. We must keep him warm and I have herbs that might persuade his soul to stay a while longer. Help me carry him, Jerat.'

Jerat's hands were trembling so much that he had trouble picking Ro up. Ro's face and lips were bluish and his breathing was very ragged.

'Sorry, Ro, sorry, Ro, sorry . . .'

'Shh.' Guardsman Verre took Ro from Jerat. 'I'll take him. Don't worry, Jer, this was not your fault. He must have fallen and banged his head on the rock or somehow got sucked under by the current. He wouldn't be the first.' She held Ro easily in her strong arms, clutching him close to her heart as if he were still a babe not a boy of eight winters. Tears were still pouring down her face, but she looked hopeful. 'Thank you, Priest. I hoped that you would know what to do.'

'It's not over yet, Verre. He may not thrive, what with the cold and his soul having all but gone.'

She shook her head as if to shake away the thought and the risk that such a thing could happen.

'Come to Mama,' she said softly, under her breath, as she held Ro even more tightly to her. She spoke so softly that Jerat thought he must have misheard. 'You hold me steady as we cross the water and make sure I don't fall,' she added more loudly, though in a choked, strained voice.

Jerat nodded. He had stopped trembling. He hardly noticed the shock of the river's coldness. He held Verre by the waist to steady her, and Hela and the Teller Priest steadied him. All the way across no one spoke and Ro did not stir in Verre's strong arms. Above the roaring of the roiling water, all that Jerat could hear was the sound of Rin's wild, abandoned sobbing as he watched them bring his twin to shore.

NINE

The Chief Findsman regarded his daughter with irritation.

'I don't understand your irrational concern for this artefact. Yes, of course we will take it back with us. I suppose you may be listed on the Seekers lists as an Associate Findsman, but frankly, my girl, if this immoderate passion is indicative of your attitude to systematic Seeking then it would be more than you deserve.'

'It isn't about that,' Nela answered, knowing she sounded childishly sullen, and quite unable to do anything about it.

'Well, if you thought I was not taking your fit seriously, I can assure you that my first concern is always for the safety of my expedition, and that includes you.' Her father sighed melodramatically, playing to his small audience of Millard and Flear. 'I knew that it was inappropriate to bring you here. Young women, even young non-women, simply do not have the mental apparatus to permit the necessary kind of systematic approach. I should have left you with your aunts and their gossip in the sewing salons of Scraal.'

'Father, I feel that the black stone belongs here.' All she could do was to reiterate what she knew to be true.

'If Seeking after the truth of our past was about "feelings" no one would ever have discovered anything and the museums and collections in which you claim such an interest would be empty. This stone is the only significant discovery we've made. Go with Millard and help him dig by the felled trees. He may have more patience with your feminine fancies than I have.'

He swung away from her before she had time to protest. He had never mentioned the fact that her sex might make her less suitable for a Findsman's work before. She was too angry to wonder at the cause of his change in attitude, but smarted all day at the injustice of his accusations. She was utterly committed to Seeking and without her he would not have even guessed at the artefact's true value.

Findsman Millard smiled at her in a way she found as disturbing as her father's unjustified annoyance. She was a non-woman, by custom safe from the idiocy of courtship ritual and harassment. She did not need rich fools smiling at her as if she were some fashionable daughter of Scraal paraded in her finest clothes to snare a husband at midsummer.

She dug all day, trying to exhaust her temper along with herself, but all that happened was that her arms and back ached and her head pounded from the relentless brightness of the sun. Findsman Millard had at least the wit to stay out of her way and watched her with grave amusement from afar: that irritated her too.

Her mental irritation turned into a physical problem. As the day progressed a series of small weals appeared all over her exposed skin: the bites itched badly and made it impossible for her to sleep, even in the coolness of the night. She tried for a while but the heat of her furs only seemed to compound the problem. In the end she left her sleeping mat to sit by the fire and scratched her arms and legs so enthusiastically that they began to bleed. She wondered, as she scratched, if her father would ever let her handle the black stone again. She was confused, too, because from what she had learned the woman of the stone was not a settler living in a civilised Tier House, as her father thought, but a hunter, a primitive, of the bondsman's line.

She was distracted by the sudden hiss of metal against rope and the soft pad of bare feet on the earth. The bondsman was beside her. He gave her some tea which she took from him rather awkwardly. She had made a fool of herself talking to him before and she did not want him to think she was anything less than a Chief Findsman's daughter. His presence upset her composure; she fumbled the bowl and it fell to the floor, spilling hot liquid all over her, but at least this time it didn't break.

He tried to wipe her down and she leapt back when he touched her, as if he were a man presumptuously invading her privacy, not a bondsman doing his job. There was an uncomfortable pause before she said, 'I'm all right – just clumsy.'

She had spoken to him as a person again. She silently berated herself; she had not meant to speak out loud and now he might feel that she had invited him to break taboo and talk to her. She held her breath, but the bondsman said nothing. He went back to the other side of the fire before returning with more tea with which to refill her bowl. He did not look at her, but her peace was utterly destroyed. The bondsman ought to have stayed awake to tend her needs, but he did not. Perhaps he knew that she would not tell her father of his failure, for she had spoken to him and used the stone he gave her. She could not help watching out of the corner of her eye while pretending to stare into the fire as the bondsman lay down to rest. He lay, without furs or a sleeping mat, on the bare ground like an animal. It was not seemly to notice, but she did, and eventually she fell asleep where she sat, by the fire.

When she woke, far too hot, to the brightness of the late morning sun, someone had covered her over with her furs and laid a plate of food beside her. The camp was empty; her father and the other Findsmen had left for the day's Seeking. Nela was infuriated by that too; she didn't want to give her father any further reason to believe that she was not strong enough or committed enough to do her job. She started to duck under the perimeter boundary to go the lake to wash, but the bondsman stood in front of her and shook his head.

'What?' she said crossly, quickly checking over her shoulder that neither her father nor his men were close enough to see her speak.

'There are things in the lake that feed off blood,' the bondsman said, looking straight at her in his unacceptably impertinent way. 'Unlock my tether and I'll fetch you good water with which to bathe.'

Could he tell that she was smelly and filthy and needed to wash away the film of grit that clung to her? She felt doubly uncomfortable. It was never as hot as this in the city.

She shook her head. 'I can't.'

He answered her boldly with a freeman's look: 'There are things I know – stories and the like – that could help you, that would show him, your father, what a good Findsman you could be.'

She glared at him, though she ought not to have even looked in his direction. It was not seemly that even the bondsman should know that she was not respected as she ought to be. She licked her lips. She knew where her father kept the key to the heavily padlocked belt which kept the bondsman attached to the tether. It probably chafed in the heat, being of the kind of crudely cut hide leather that had a hard edge at the best of times.

'All right,' she said quietly. 'But have I your word that you will come back?'

'You're asking for a bondsman's word? We have no voice so we can have no words. I will come back. There is nowhere to go in this forsaken place.'

Nela found herself nodding – Lord of the Earth, what was she thinking of? She was fairly certain that no one would return to the camp at this time of the day. Her father was unlikely to check on her, but even so she found that her heart was beating very fast as she uncovered the Chief Findsman's strong box and, with the pin she used to secure her headscarf, carefully picked the lock. One of her aunts had taught her how, on the basis that a good wife knows her husband's business even if he chooses not to tell her. The black stone was there too, wrapped in a scrap of cloth. Since her conversation with him her father had obviously decided to secure it away from the other finds. Did he not trust her? She could not resist picking it up and slipping it into the artefact pouch that hung from her waist on a looser, unpadlocked version of the bondsman's belt. Loose as it was, she still bore blisters from its abrasions.

She contrived to unlock the bondsman's padlock without incident and without looking at the servant or touching him. Her hands shook but she didn't think he'd noticed. She found that she was braver and more daring than she'd thought, and that pleased her. The bondsman was as good as his word and she was able to wash in the water he warmed over the fire. She found less soiled clothes to wear: she surprised herself with her need to keep her aunts' rigorous standards of civilised cleanliness so far from the city. When she had finished changing she squatted next to the bondsman some distance from the cook fire which burned even in the heat of the day.

'Tell me what you know of the old songs and stories,' she said imperiously. She did not, of course, look at the bondsman – that way she could almost

84

pretend that she was not breaking the taboo. With her peripheral vision she could see that he had removed his tether belt and was rubbing some kind of leaf across the raw flesh of his middle.

'I know two stories by heart and fragments of others,' he said.

'Go on,' Nela said. She had taken out her writing materials ready to make proper Findsman's notes; in her mind that would compensate for her impropriety.

'Long ago the moon and the earth were one and of their union all creation was born. The earth favoured one people above all else and he caused the sun to shine upon them alone. But the moon, whom my people call the Womanface though you call her Zeron, the Dark Daughter, was angry at such favouritism. She withdrew to make her own light to shine upon those whom the earth, the Manface, did not favour, leaving her lover alone and always seeking to replace what he had lost. One day she will return to him, though no one knows when. Some think that when the day people and the night people are reconciled then she will return, but if the earth knows he has told no one.'

Nela wrote his words down carefully in the tiny, neat hand she had devised to husband the small amount of precious paper she had been given as a coming-of-age gift from her father. The bondsman took a sip of sweet-leaf tea, but pointedly did not offer her any. While he was free of the tether belt, it seemed he regarded himself as free of his servitude. He continued speaking.

'When the Womanface left him, the Manface was wracked with remorse, and granted one gift to the children he had not favoured, those who called themselves the Night Hunters; he granted each of them a small fragment of the song that called all creation into being. Thus they could sing to give strength to the forest, to help plants to seed in their season, and ease the birthing of young, and all such gifts gladdened the Manface and it pleased him that he had favoured the beloved of the Womanface. But a fragment of the song of creation was not a gift without its dangers. It was said that when a Night Hunter was ensnared and made to desire release, the power of the song grew, and for those in whose hearts the song was strong, the power was sufficient to force all of creation into a new pattern, shaped by their will to bring about their freedom from desire. And this is called the Magic of the Last Resort, for it was uncontrollable and brought into being by extremity, by need and not by choice. It was said that if you forced a Night Hunter to use the Magic of the Last Resort, in the moment of extremity when the world changed and twisted to the Night Hunter's will, you could wish for your heart's desire and it would come to pass. I heard that long ago many Night Hunters were captured and tortured to bring about the Magic of the Last Resort.'

Nela stretched her cramping fingers and said, intrigued, 'And did it work? Did they get their heart's desire?'

The bondsman, who had been relating these tales in a singsong voice quite unlike his normal rough diction, almost snarled. 'Findsman's daughter, do you think that the suffering of a Night Hunter could be justified if their magic worked?'

Nela found herself flushing. 'No! That is not what I said and it's not what I meant. For a moment I forgot it was just an old story and I just wanted to know if the magic was true.' She was annoyed by her own stupidity and by her own embarrassment. It did not matter what a bondsman thought of her. Lord of the Earth! She was a fool.

The bondsman calmed himself and answered, 'It is said that it did work once or twice, that the world was changed, bent and contorted from its normal course, and that the price for such wilfulness was paid in full.'

Nela could not help but seek a better answer. 'And is that what you believe?'

The servant was silent for a while. 'I think this place with its dead lake and its dying trees stinks of corruption and bad magic, but I'm an ignorant bondsman – what do I know?' He sounded bitter, and she did not answer, because it was true: how could he not be ignorant? His opinion should not matter, but he knew two of the tales of the Night Hunters which she had not heard before and that might well help her to impress her father. She got up and looked at the fire, her back to the bondsman.

'You had better put the tether belt back on – perhaps you need not relock it, and I will return the key.'

'And the black stone?'

She didn't answer. She was not required to account for her action to an indentured servant. Instead she returned the key to her father's strong box. She was less nervous this time, more confident that she would not be seen. She set out to rejoin the dig with her mind full of the learned treatise she could write on the creation stories of the Night Hunters. She would show her father just how much of the necessary mental apparatus she had. She would produce a work of such quality that the Company of Historical Archivists of Scraal would be obliged to bestow on her a full Findsman's rank.

TEN

They made a strange, bedraggled procession: Verre and Ro, Jerat and Rin, the Teller Priest and Guardsman Hela. When they got back to the Hall the no-man, Heron, wrapped Ro in furs and laid him on a sleep mat that they roughly secured to the ox plough so that they could convey him most easily to the Teller Priest's Hall.

'It's the Festival of Longest Light tomorrow, Verre, you cannot delay longer. I will see that you get word. For now he lives and Jerat and I will see to his every need.' The Teller Priest spoke kindly and patted Verre gently on the arm, in reassurance. Verre nodded with a kind of childlike obedience. Jerat thought she was still in a daze of shock.

She turned to Jerat to speak to him, but she hardly seemed to know where she was. Her voice was almost expressionless when she said, 'I have to go, Jer. I'll be back after Longest Light. The Teller Priest may be able to pass on any messages. What happened wasn't your fault – no one could care for him better than you do. Look to Rin. He needs you more than ever.'

Jerat nodded his reply, unable to speak for fear of weeping in an unwarriorlike way. Guardsman Hela walked away with Verre to the Hall. Verre didn't look back.

'I don't see why she should have to go,' Jerat said awkwardly. 'She doesn't want to.'

'No, she doesn't,' the Teller Priest agreed, lifting Rin to allow the grave and frightened boy to sit, precariously, on the broad back of the ox. The Teller Priest spoke gently to the beast and it continued to haul its slight burden along the rough pathways that led to his forestside Hall.

'Jerat, when you gain your spear you'll better understand how much of life is duty and obligation. Verre knows all about that, believe me – she will return when she can. You'll have to trust her.'

The Teller Priest's Hall was like farmholder Barak's – one room only but richly furnished with bright weavings and full of baskets of plants, roots and other yields of Zerat which were the raw materials of his craft. Seeing the expression on the Priest's face, the several no-men who laboured to make the dyes left their place at the fire and hurried from the Hall. Jerat would normally have been curious about the way the Teller Priest lived, but the sight of his brother's pale face rendered all other considerations meaningless. Ro's breath was shallow and the shadows under his closed eyes were dark as bruises, like death's finger marks. Jerat had to fight to control a sob that started somewhere in the pit of his stomach.

'Ro – he'll be all right, won't he?' Rin asked in a small, cracked voice. 'The Teller Priest will make him better.'

Jerat wanted to reassure Rin, whose own face looked almost as pale as Ro's, but honesty restrained him. 'I don't know, Rin. I hope so. We'll just have to wait.'

Rin thrust his hand into Jerat's and held it tightly. 'Let's get water and wood for the Teller Priest. That might help him.'

Jerat was quite sure it wouldn't, but he could not just hang around waiting to see if those eyes would ever open again, waiting to see if that pasty grey-brown complexion, the colour of the potter's slip, would ever improve.

That night Jerat slept next to Ro, with Ro in one arm and Rin in the other as he had done when the twins were babies. It was the first time any of them had slept away from the Hall. The weight of Ro's unconscious head on his chest was comforting. Its stillness felt like sleep, and the Teller Priest said it could do no harm.

In the morning when the Teller Priest opened the shutters and the early light of Longest Light poured like the spring stream over Ro's face, his eyelids fluttered. The Priest thought that was a good sign and sent Jerat back to the Hall with that news.

'I think he has moved from the deep darkness to the shallows and he will need to rest there awhile to give his soul the best chance of restoration and healing. You are needed at the Hall and you can do nothing here that Rin cannot do for me just as well.' The Teller Priest clapped his strong hand on Jerat's shoulder and Jerat noticed for the first time that the Priest's eyes were only at the level of his own chest.

'He will live, Jerat, but his soul had passed, however briefly, from his body and you must be prepared for him to be changed.'

'What do you mean?'

'He has hovered on the brink of death. No man comes back from that unchanged, let alone a child. The waters of the shore of death have lapped at his feet: it must not surprise you if he afterwards walks with a different step.'

Jerat couldn't think of anything to say to this so he simply said, 'I'll be back as soon as I can. Is there anything you need?' and when the Teller Priest shook his head Jerat turned reluctantly away to join the rest of the Brood Trove at the Tier House.

The day was going to be hot; already the wind was warm on his back and the shadows sharp. It struck him that he could have been happy but for his fear for Ro. It was unusual to meet any new people and there would be many at the festival, as well as brothers and sisters who had left the Hall; maybe even Moorat would be there, the sister of the second quarter who had more or less raised him. As he got nearer to the Hearthfields he could see the many people of the Chief's Horde walking towards the festival – some with animals to exchange and others with packs on their back with goods they'd brought to the fair. He felt excited in spite of himself, particularly when he saw a girl with long corn-coloured hair swinging round her waist and an elaborately woven cloak draped over her shoulders; surely that would be farmholder Barak's daughter. Jerat wanted to believe that Ro would be all right. It looked likelier now that he might live and perhaps that was enough to enable Jerat to enjoy the festival. Then the sight of Avet, his arm bound with a Teller's poultice of herbs and combed wool, dampened his spirits somewhat: what they had started the previous day was not yet over. Jerat checked his newly mended belt knife; it was not as good as the farmholder's, but he had honed it to a new sharpness and it would serve him if it had to.

'Jerat.' Avet acknowledged him with a nod. 'Is the boy recovered?'

'Not yet.' Jerat tried to keep his voice level. He did not want to fight Avet again, not now, not after what had happened.

'You are needed at the Hall – Keran has work for you.'

To Avet's credit he had managed to sound sincere in his question about Ro, and Jerat relaxed a little as he walked past. There was blood between them, but it would not flow again that day.

Keran needed Jerat to help with the preparations to bring down the wives from the Heart of the Home for the midday feast. Hela was there too.

'If you can get a message to Verre, tell her that Ro's eyelids fluttered, and the Teller Priest thinks that is a good sign!' Jerat said, suddenly aware of the gulf between his hope and the reality of Ro's condition, but Hela looked cheered anyway, so perhaps it really was good news.

The great door of the Hall had been opened so that the morning light spilled in, making the Hall look strange and unfamiliar: a bright pool of light surrounded by deep shadow. Its smell was different too. Jerat wondered if it was just the preparation for the festival which had made his home seem strange, or if everything was made strange by what had happened to Ro: he wondered if things could ever again feel safe and familiar.

Hela touched him lightly on the shoulder. 'He has survived, Jerat. Let that be enough for now. Don't borrow trouble. Could you clean out the barrel and line it with fresh wool for the wives?'

It was, of course, not a question, so he got on with his chores: they were numerous and, as the oldest of the brothers not yet of age, he had more to do than most. Much of the cooking was being supervised by the Hearth Guard with assistance from the Brood, so he had to help prepare the pits for the several fine heffers that would be pit-roasted whole for the feast.

When, at last, the time came for the arrival of the wives it was he, along with Hela and Draven, who had to lower the wives gently down to ground level. He got rope burn for his trouble and it did occur to him to wonder why they couldn't use the thatch ladder like anyone else would. His sisters could do it and Barak's daughter had looked lithe and strong enough to climb the roof unaided; why did the wives insist on being lowered down in a barrel? Afterwards, when he had assisted the wives and brought tapestry rugs and arranged them in the best position in the sunlight but close to the shade, he felt that he ought to have been allowed to join the older boys who were mingling with the guests and older members of the Brood as a preliminary to the serious business of wife negotiation.

He was not happy to discover that by then it was too late and the ritual part of the day had begun. Keran beat the large hide-covered drum that was used on ceremonial occasions or indeed any occasion where a loud noise was required. The Chief welcomed everyone to his Hall and, in the absence of the Teller Priest, said prayers of thanksgiving for the Longest Light and the time when Zerat ruled at his greatest strength. Everyone crowded around the entrance to the Hall, while keeping a respectful distance from the wives who sat quite still throughout. The first wife in her black and yellow sat awkwardly, in obvious discomfort, her dress so tight over her bulging belly that she looked like a plump bumble bee. Jerat found himself drawn as ever to the masked face of the wife of the second quarter, who was his nominal mother. She sat impassively, her strong hands resting in her lap. Although they had been painted with green dye to represent the verdancy of the earth at the time of greatest Light, their shape and latent competency seemed curiously familiar. He knew those hands.

He was distracted from his observations by the sudden appearance of the corn-haired girl who he'd seen on the track that led to the Hearthfields. She squeezed past him with a shy smile and seated herself almost directly in front of him so that his view of the wives was partially obscured. She had drenched herself in the scent of lavender, and the sweetness of her perfume and the lustre of her thick, fair hair made him unable to think for a while. When she turned to twist her hair over one shoulder she graced him with another shy smile. Her teeth were very small and creamy-white and she had coloured her lips with traded cochineal from the dry places, far beyond the Lake. It would have cost her father dear, but the reddened lips were a sign that she was available to marry a Chiefson: poorer women sometimes bit their lips or reddened them with berries to give the same message. He found her reddened lips fascinating. He sensed rather than saw the masked face of the wife of the second quarter turn his way and imagined the look that accompanied that deliberate gesture. He wondered how he could have failed to make the connection before, how he could have been so blind and foolish: the wife of the second quarter, resplendent in her robes of red and green, was none other than his friend and beloved teacher, Verre.

ELEVEN

Nela's father scarcely looked up from his work to note her arrival.

'You can work with Millard at the southern end of the lake,' he said brusquely, without enquiring after her health. Nela walked reluctantly to the lake and began the task of Seeking for artefacts in the stinking mud. She spoke to Millard only when she had no choice and, though they toiled all day Seeking something to justify the Chief Findsman's view of the importance of the site, they found only three pottery beads, a flint knife of inferior quality, lacking a shaft, and a quantity of broken pots.

'We should go,' Millard said at last. 'If this really is the cradle of our civilisation, we were lucky to leave it.'

'That doesn't sound like the opinion of a dedicated Findsman,' Nela answered sharply and with some surprise. She was herself disappointed by their lack of success in finding anything worth the effort, but she expected greater patience from a real Findsman.

'Well, there is more to being a Findsman than digging, you know. I'm more interested in the written records of later times and cataloguing our later, greater achievements. Scrabbling in the dirt is for dogs.'

'You'd better not let my father hear you talk like that – field work is his passion. Anyway, why did you come here if you hate "scrabbling around in the dirt"? It was all this trip was ever going to be.'

'I came for other reasons. There is more to life than work, Nela.'

She could think of nothing to say to that, at least nothing that did not involve asking more questions, and she was beginning to get the impression, from the intense way in which he was staring at her, that she was not going to like the answers.

They worked in silence for a while, then Nela found a fragment of something that could have been a brooch. It was in poor condition and was in every way typical of the commonest kind of cloak pin, found in all parts of the country and not dissimilar to those worn now in rural districts.

'Let me see.' Millard was next to her in a moment, his breath on the exposed skin of her neck, his plump, rather too smooth fingers eagerly touching hers to take the find.

'Hey, Findsman, it's only a straight-pin ceramic brooch – nothing to get excited about.'

He held on to her fingers for too long and she felt uncomfortable under his scrutiny.

'You must have a care that you don't burn – the sun

is strong this close to Longest Light,' he said softly, standing so close to her she could see the bristles of new growth on the parts of his chin that he normally shaved. She could smell the rancid stench of animal fat with which he greased his red-dyed beard: it was scented with some herb, but the mixture had not travelled well. Back home in Scraal he probably bought it fresh each day from Layden Bridge, the spice and balm market.

'I'll be fine,' she said firmly, taking a step backwards, and twisting away from him. 'Are you going to log the find? I'm sure it's unimportant, but we'd better do it right – the way my father likes it.'

He followed her with his eyes; he made her skin crawl.

'If you were mine I would not make you slave under the hot sun – you would have a fine house in the city and enough bondswomen to wait on you that you would need never soil your hands if you did not wish to. You must know I am of good family with a long lineage.'

'And I am a non-woman,' Nela answered shakily. 'I have had fits since I was a child and I have chosen to be a non-woman. This is where I want to be and I would like someday to be a Findsman in my own right.'

'Don't be ridiculous! Women are unsuited to such work – there has never been a woman Findsman!'

'And you are not listening to me, Findsman Millard. I am a non-woman. I cannot be courted or married. I seek to earn my own living in my chosen field and that is in Seeking after ancient truths. I would be happy to be the first non-woman Findsman. Unlike you I do at least enjoy the work.'

She found that her heart was beating very rapidly after her little speech and that her words had not come out with quite the fluency she'd hoped. She had not noticed how hot she was, but was suddenly aware that her tunic was soaked in sweat. She wiped her face with the back of her hand and then, on realising that her hand was black with mud, regretted it. She was glad of her lack of hair, although the new growth stubble itched a little in the heat; with all that had been going on she had forgotten to shave for a couple of days. The mud of the Lakeside smelled of the slimy weeds which choked it and made it stagnant and foul. The stench and the heat exacerbated her discomfort and suddenly the world swam and blackened and she fell.

She came round to find Millard's plump arm around her shoulders and his breath on her face. He smelled of the spiced wine he kept sipping from his hip flask. He was trying to force some of it through her lips.

She spluttered and spat out the sweet concoction so it dribbled down her chin; her aunts would not have approved.

'Leave me. I will be all right in a moment. Did I fit?'

He nodded. She hoped, unkindly, that he had been shocked by the sight of her writhing around. She hoped that he had been disgusted by her antics. Obviously, she had never seen herself when the fit was upon her, but by all accounts it was a frightening sight. Her aunts had almost drowned her once – the first time it happened, when she was a little girl. They had feared that it was some kind of possession by Zeron, the Dark Daughter of the Night, or one of her ilk.

She pushed Millard's flask away from her.

'Do you have some water?' she asked through lips that were so dry they felt twice their normal size. While Millard went to get some from the bondsman, she had time to collect her thoughts. Millard was not the kind of man to risk her father's displeasure by making advances without his approval; therefore her father must have given Millard permission to begin this clumsy attempt to get closer to her. Would her father be greedy enough for money to permit his only daughter to be sold for a good bride price? Unfortunately, she did not need to think too deeply to come to the conclusion that he would not hesitate to do so if it enabled him to pursue his ambitions. Her father was capable of ignoring any number of unpleasant facts when he chose, like the fact that few people believed that the trip to Mordant Lake was worth the effort, or that his only daughter had elected to become a non-woman and thus could not legally be married off until her hair had grown down to her shoulders again.

Milllard returned too quickly.

'Are you feeling better now, Nela? Do you need me to fetch your father?' Millard said with an unctuous tone that she found deeply unattractive. She shook her head.

'No, but I do need to know what is going on. Has my father suggested that I am marriageable in spite of this?' She took out the metal pin which secured the

101

headscarf covering her bald head and saw him wince at the ugliness of it. Her skull was not a beautiful thing, carrying with it many scars from accidents caused when unexpected fits had brought her into collision with heavier objects.

'Nela, it is not what you think,' he said, looking quickly away. 'I had talked to your father about the possibility of courting you even before you took your vow, so it was actually quite proper.'

'No one spoke to me about it. I took that vow honestly – I wanted to be a non-woman. I am not free to marry until my hair has regrown and, as I intend to shave it every day, *that* might take a while.' She watched his already high colour intensify.

'Your father is right – you are a wilful, ill-managed girl, but the agreement I had with your father takes precedence over this non-woman vow. Your father accepted a bride price sufficient to cover the costs of the expedition. There is no further issue. I would have preferred to woo you in a more romantic way, but what is agreed is agreed.'

Nela felt her grip on reality begin to waver.

'The trip was paid for by Prince Helvennig, the Merchants and the Archivists of Scraal,' she said with more certainty than she felt.

'And chiefly by my own father – the most prominent member of the Goodly Congregation of Licensed Merchants.' Millard paused to let her take that information in before continuing, 'Your vow as a non-woman will be regarded as invalid according to the law, as it was made after your father and I had agreed your marriage.'

Nela tried not to faint or fit or do anything to make herself look more foolish than was strictly necessary. The ground was wet this close to the lake and she buried her hands in the grey mud, as if to anchor herself to reality.

'I don't understand,' she said at last. 'Why did my father let me go through with my vow? And why in the name of all that is holy did you want to marry me?'

TWELVE

There was no opportunity for Jerat to seek Verre out and confront her with his discovery. Perhaps she already assumed he knew. He should have known; a mask and a heavy robe should not have been an impenetrable disguise to anyone but a very young child.

After the ceremony of welcome each of the wives disappeared to walk through the Hearthfields and visit the stalls and tents of the visitors, accompanied by the masked wives and no-men of the other Dependencies. It was a time of trade for more than just wives. Jerat ought to have socialised with the festival crowd. He ought to have met the older members of the Trove, the brothers and sisters of the Tier House whom he knew more by reputation than anything else. Many a night he had laughed over the Guardsmen's tales of Hirat and Barit and those other boys and girls who had lived the life he lived in the Hall before him. Last festival he had been too shy, too cowed by their confidence and strangeness to speak much. He would have liked it to be different this time. He knew that somewhere among the horde of people these older members of the Brood Trove laughed and drank ale in their boyhood home, but he could think of nothing but Verre. He was so distracted that he did not notice for a whole half heartbeat that a beautiful corn-haired girl was speaking to him.

'You're the one my father told me about, aren't you? I think I saw you when you came to our Hall,' she said, smiling as though she knew something he didn't. She probably did – probably everyone did.

'Did you?' he said, absently.

'You are the brother of the boy that nearly drowned.'

Jerat looked at her again more closely and detected the slightest echo of farmholder Barak in her even features, though the lineaments of her face were infinitely preferable to his.

'Yes,' he said. 'I'm Jerat.'

'Chiefson Jerat,' she corrected with another knowing smile. 'Is your brother all right?'

Jerat shook his head. 'I don't know yet.'

'Oh!' She seemed momentarily crestfallen, as if she would have liked a happier ending to the story her father had obviously related to her. 'I'm Lirian, and I think my father wanted . . .' She didn't finish, but blushed in a rather unexpected way and played with her lustrous hair. 'Is it true that the wives of a Chief's household never go out except at festivals?'

Jerat shrugged. Where once he would have answered an unequivocal 'yes', his discovery that

Guardsman Verre was also the wife of the second quarter had confused him utterly. Lirian was beginning to look impatient. He did not know what she wanted from him, but it was obviously something more than he was giving.

'I don't know much about the life of the wives,' he said at last, when it was clear she expected some reply. 'We only see them at festivals.'

'And what of the other wives – the wives of the Brood Trove and the Hearth Guard – they don't have to work the fields, do they?'

Jerat shrugged. 'We don't talk about it.'

'What do you mean you don't talk about it?'

Jerat felt uncomfortable. It was difficult to describe the life in the Hall – it was all he knew. Guardsmen did not talk of their life outside it, or even of what went on within it in the Heart of the Home. It made Jerat cringe inwardly even now to discuss that which was not discussed – the hidden life and death of wives.

'I know that the wives of the Heart of the Home spin and dye and weave to make garments for the Brood Trove – their children,' Jerat said, surer of his ground on that issue at least, 'but that is all I know.' It was clear that Lirian did not think his knowledge amounted to very much.

'Do you want some spice bread?' Jerat remembered belatedly that he had been instructed to be hospitable to all the guests of the Hall.

Lirian took some from him with hands, he noted, that had been scrubbed to rawness. 'And do the wives cook?' she said, eating coyly from behind her hand, though her teeth were perfectly nice and did not merit elaborate hiding. Jerat thought back to the smells of his early childhood, the constant warmth and the bubble of cook pots and a memory of a tall woman with busy hands and the spice scent of her skirts.

'I think so, for the babes I suppose, but the Hearth Guard cook for themselves and for us.'

'An easy life, then,' Lirian said caustically.

'I don't know,' he said, softly. 'They seem to die a lot.'

'Only the weak ones,' Lirian said, firmly. 'Father says my dam only died because the cold got her, and that the wives of the Chiefsons are cosseted and waited upon when their birthgiving time comes.' She blushed and Jerat found himself blushing too. 'I beg your pardon – you must think me very . . .'

'Scared,' said Jerat with sudden understanding. Lirian's eyes welled with tears and Jerat kept talking as if he hadn't noticed. 'Who are you supposed to be marrying?' The question was out before he had time to stop it, and he was suddenly sorry that he was not yet quite of age.

'Avet – the one you fought with.' She lowered her eyes.

'Oh, well, he is strong and will make a good warrior. If you are to be married to him it will be easy for you to find a place in any Horde, and he will be granted a fine farm Hall to hold and plenty of no-men to farm it. Then he can build a Hearth Guard for himself, and perhaps he will be a Chief one day of his own Dependency.' The words stuck in his throat, but he made himself say them anyway – for Lirian, who looked so scared and unhappy. Her eyes were green, like the tithe-offering jade necklace that the Chief wore round his neck.

'But it will take time, all that,' she said softly. 'And I may not live to see it. All I know for certain is that I will have to go wherever he goes, and when I die it will be far away and I will be buried in a place I don't know, and Father will not put flowers there or offerings at harvest like he did for my dam and each of his other wives and my brother.'

Jerat wanted to comfort her as he might have comforted Ro or Rin, but he was not sure how to behave with someone who was neither Brood Trove nor Hearth Guard. Besides, she was prettier than any in either.

'You won't die for a long while yet,' he said with no cause but kindness, hoping that by saying the words with such certainty he could make them come true. 'Anyway, we will all be split up and have to move to new Halls when the Chief dies. None of us knows where we will end up – scattered throughout Lakeside, fighting for another Chief's Horde no doubt, living in some strange Hall as Hearth Guard.' He did not much relish that prospect himself, he wanted to stay with Ro and Rin and Verre for ever, but he forced himself to sound cheerful. 'We may meet at Longest Light in some other place – who knows?' It struck him that he was deeply grateful for the fact that he was a boy and that even should battle come, his chances of survival were probably better than those of Lirian if she became a wife. But Verre had survived and he was sure that the twins were her own flesh. He would have liked Lirian to know that, but he could not possibly tell her.

'It is different for you, Chiefson Jerat,' Lirian said, and he saw a strange look in her quickly averted eyes: a kind of wildness he'd seen only in the eyes of a Herd beast before slaughter. 'And I don't even know how to bake spice bread,' she added with a rather forced laugh.

'It's good isn't it, the bread?' he said, grateful for the chance to change the subject. From the corner of his eye he saw Avet giving him a look that would sour milk. Jerat wished that he had injured him more thoroughly so that he could not take this girl to wife, but then he rebuked himself for such a thought. At least Avet was young and handsome, and that might be a good thing for Lirian. Jerat found that he did not like that thought any better.

'I have to go, Father is calling me.' She half raised her hand in a gesture of farewell but then looked embarrassed and let her hand drop.

Avet held his injured arm like a weapon and his face was hard when he saw Jerat.

'Don't sneak off – you're needed back at the well,' Avet snarled, but Jerat noticed that he was careful to keep his distance. Jerat would dearly have loved to hit him again. He could not look at Avet's face without seeing Ro's as he had looked when Verre had carried him from the water. Jerat grunted some kind of reply.

As he neared the Tier House he became aware that all was not well. He was uncomfortable with so many strangers in the Hearthfields, but it was more than that. Guardsman Hela looked strained and was shouting orders at two other Guardsmen. She did not smile when she saw Jerat.

'There's trouble, Jer. It's the wife of the first quarter. Her time has come, but it's too early. All the wives are out, taking care of the guests. Please find the wife of the second quarter and then you must run to get the Teller Priest. Tell him the problem – he'll know what to do.'

Jerat had seen Verre walking with a woman in a green mask – a Chief's wife of some other Dependency. He raced away and in spite of the unaccustomed crowds and the strangeness that came with the scent of so many people and the confusion of noise and tents, he spotted Verre easily by her walk. He suppressed unexpected anger at the sight of her in her red robes and the ridiculous mask that had kept her identity secret from him for so many years, and ran to her side.

'Revered wife,' he began, and he saw that the eyes behind the mask were wary. She knew that he knew. 'Guardsman Hela has need of you.'

'Is it the first wife?'

Jerat nodded and he thought he heard Verre mutter a Guardsman's curse under her breath. She said something in an unknown dialect to her companion who visibly tensed and then they both turned to hurry towards the house. They did not run – they were too burdened by their heavy ceremonial robes – but they moved more quickly than he expected, their masks inclined towards one another as though they still conversed urgently together.

It was hot and tiring to run back to the Teller's Hall the way he'd come in the cooler morning. Rin was there in moments to greet him, and by the paleness of his face Jer knew that there had been no further improvement in Ro's condition. Jerat hugged Rin reflexively, felt him struggle to keep his sobs under control. Members of the Brood Trove did not cry much, but Rin was still young enough for it to be permissible.

The Priest's face when he too emerged into the sunlight was no more optimistic.

'The first wife?' he asked quietly, and when Jerat nodded he added, 'I feared it would be so, it is too soon for her to be breeding again. Her first child nearly killed her, this second will be her death.'

'Is there nothing you can do?' Jerat asked, thinking that it could be Verre and Lirian as easily as the unknown first wife, struggling under that death sentence.

'I will do what I can, but it is probably too late. It is too late to get a Singer, anyway. Stay and care for Ro – just watch him and keep him comfortable. We wait now. That is all that we can do.' With those cryptic remarks and stopping only to pick up his cloth bag, the Teller Priest was on his way.

Jerat allowed Rin to lead him inside to the strange stillness of Ro's face, quiet as a corpse. But for the almost imperceptible movement of his chest Jerat could believe him dead. The sight made Jerat want to weep, though he was well past the age where it was permissible.

THIRTEEN

Nela did not know why she had asked the question. Clearly Millard could only want to marry her because of her father's status as Chief Findsman; money alone could not buy that, for all that it was a rather precarious privilege. There were far too many people plotting to undermine her father's position for his continued incumbency to be certain. Nela did not now know how to deal with Millard's answer and looked around for some excuse to walk away without having to listen to it. Too late. Millard was already answering.

'I wanted to marry you because by all accounts you are intelligent and independent and would have no particular interest in running my home. My father insists I marry, and the last thing I need is a woman to destroy the happy life I have built for myself with my work and domestic arrangements. If you will refrain from bothering me you will have, as a married woman, an allowance from me which you would be free to dispose of as you might wish, and some freedoms – not least from the demands of your father.'

Nela was about to protest that she desired no freedom from her father, but knew that it wasn't true. Instead she started to laugh.

'Well, thank you for not pretending you've fallen in love with me.'

'My dear non-woman, I know you are not stupid, and the contract was agreed before I'd met you.'

Nela nodded, understanding all the things he didn't say. She was not beautiful and her illness was a serious handicap, in so far as she would be regarded as cursed by the ignorant and as one possessed by the Dark Daughter by the superstitious. It was not a bad offer as such contracts went, but it was not what she had dreamed of; it was not becoming a Findsman in her own right.

'I am grateful for your honesty, Findsman Millard,' she said with as much dignity as she could muster, 'but marriage even to such an accommodating and generous man as yourself was not what I had in mind. If you will excuse me – I don't feel well,' she whispered, oppressed by his certainty as much as by the humid heat of the day and the miasma of decay that lay like invisible fog over the Lakeside. Millard seemed to understand her need to be alone, for he said nothing as she quickly tidied away her equipment and returned to the camp. She squatted next to the blistering heat of the fire and tried to persuade herself that the sick emptiness in her stomach was no more than hunger. She had not wept since her mother died and was for a moment surprised by the dampness on her face. A contracted marriage had never been part of her plans; her father's betrayal was a cold stone in the pit of her stomach.

The bondsman was at her side offering sweet-leaf tea within moments. Perhaps he dared not risk ignoring her in the day, when he might be observed. Nela did not want him to see her tears, but it was probably already too late. She wiped her face with her muddy hands and then, realising the hopelessness of that, allowed her tears to fall unchecked.

Silently the bondsman slipped his tether belt and disappeared from the cordon, returning a little while later with a bowl of lake water which he warmed with hot stones from the fire's circular hearth. Heating the brackish water made it seem cleaner somehow and Nela washed her face with silent gratitude.

'He wants to marry me off to Millard,' she said into the fire.

The bondsman did not answer for a long time; then he said, 'You would not be more free married?'

'I would not be a Findsman,' she answered.

The bondsman had a small supply of leaves with him, and when he lifted his shirt to rub them on his stomach, Nela could see the weeping sores where the tether belt had abraded his smooth skin. She looked away, repelled and disturbed by the sight, and he replaced the tether belt.

'Why do you want to be a Findsman so much?' the bondsman asked, apparently unconcerned by her repulsion.

'I want to understand the past, find things out for myself, be respected for myself.' Nela did not look at the bondsman but out of the corner of her eye saw that he nodded, as though he understood.

'And are you going to use the stone again?'

He had not forgotten, then, that she had it in her belt pouch. She had not forgotten either; its slight weight was a kind of a comfort.

'I don't know,' she said, though even as she said it she knew it wasn't true. She was frightened by the strangeness of the experience, but intrigued too; there was no doubt that she was going to use the stone again.

They sat in silence for a while and then the bondsman got to his feet and busied himself with preparing food and, though Nela was ashamed of her impulse, she could not help but watch him covertly. In spite of the restricting tether he moved as gracefully as the wild cat her mother had tamed and kept from its kittenhood in Nela's childhood home. The servant was clean-shaven as all bondsmen were, forbidden to wear the beards of manhood that were coloured and plaited to denote status. His face had the elegant proportions of an ancient statue, sharp-boned but delicate, and Nela, for a small subdivision of a moment, almost regretted her plainness and her stubbled skull. But then if she had possessed anything approaching the bondsman's striking beauty she would have been married in childhood for a substantial bride price and never even had the chance of becoming a non-woman: plainness for Nela was something of an asset. Unfortunately, it had not saved her from Millard. What could?

FOURTEEN

It was dark when the Teller Priest returned from the Chief's Hall. Ro had not stirred all day and Jerat had tried to keep busy cooking up summer vegetables for lastmeal. Jerat knew by the old man's expression that the wife of the first quarter had died and went outside to meet him so as not to disturb Rin who was dozing by his brother's side.

'By the time I got there it was too late. I had told her that she should have let me get her a Singer, though in truth it was a little late in the day, but she would not. She was a true Lakesider, set in her own ways and unbending as a Great Tree. Well, she died for it.'

'What d'you mean, a Singer?'

'A Night Hunter, of course.'

'Here? You know them?'

'They are real people, Jer, not creatures of legend. Yes – I know some and their skills are very great – few of *them* die in childbirth, as their babes are not as

116

large as ours. I have known the old Chief Singer of the Long Hill Summer People and the Bear Caves Winter People a long time. I asked if she would sing for our women too.'

'And did she?'

'In secret – her people have little more time for us than we for them. She was fearful of what her tribe would say if they found her consorting with "Bearmen", as they call us, but she has been a friend to me over the years and I hope I have been a friend to her. Moon-eye – that's her name – saved the wife of the second quarter, and if I'd found her early enough she might have been able to save the first wife too.' The Teller Priest sighed. 'Anyway, the first wife is already buried now and your father, never one to ponder overmuch on his decisions, has chosen a new wife of the first quarter and so it will all go on again. May Zerat smile on her.'

Jerat could not say anything for a long time. He had to put this new information into a kind of order – he did not seem to have the right kind of space in his head for these new thoughts.

'Teller Priest,' he said, as it seemed to be the time for secrets and arcane knowledge, 'why did no one tell me that Verre is the wife of the second quarter?'

Even in the near darkness Jerat could see that the Teller Priest gave him a sharp look.

'It is not my story to tell, Jerat.'

'And is she the one who let the singing servant of Zeron, the Dark Daughter, sing for her?'

'I don't think I can –'

Jerat would not let him finish, before demanding

another answer. 'Tell me, Priest, is she Ro's dam?'

Perhaps he looked more fierce and dangerous than he intended, perhaps the Priest took pity on his ignorance, because he sighed and said, 'Yes, and yours too, Jerat. She is brave and tough and has broken many unspoken rules to watch you grow. It is only because she is a clever advisor to your father, the Chief, and a good manager of the other wives, that he has not put her aside. He has been very angry with her too often and I have feared for her life.'

Jerat did not know how to respond. The comforter of his earliest memories was Verre; the same Verre who was the companion and advisor of his youth. Compared to that amazing truth, the fact that she had risked her soul with the Night Hunters seemed as nothing. Verre was his dam, his true mother. He could not take it in.

The Teller Priest left him alone with his thoughts for a moment while he went inside to check on Ro and Rin. Jerat followed a little while later.

'Does everyone know – that Verre is . . . ?'

The Teller Priest shrugged. 'Keran and Hela know, of course, and some others of your father's Horde remember her from the time before she was married. She came to a festival here long ago. What others know I cannot say.'

The Priest's answer did not make him feel any less of a fool and so Jerat changed the subject abruptly.

'Who has my father chosen as his new wife – am I allowed to know?'

It was not the most important thing on his mind, but he did not want to talk about Verre or Ro. His chest was packed tight as the wattle and daub of the Tier House with feelings for which he had no name.

The Teller Priest looked old in the firelight – old, sad and weary.

'I suppose in a night of such truth-telling you may as well know the rest. Farmholder Barak's daughter is old Chief Galet's granddaughter. She is beautiful and young.'

'Lirian? But she is my age and to be wed to Avet.'

'You have met her, then?' The Priest smiled tightly. 'She was born soon after you. I was there to bless her birth as I blessed yours, and I fear that I will be there at her death too.'

Jerat shivered. He was outraged, filled with a righteous anger that took him by surprise.

The Teller Priest contrived to look both sad and amused. 'But the nuptial gift is better from the Chief and she will have a comfortable life for as long as it lasts,' he said. 'There is nothing you can do, Jerat. Lakesider customs will not change in my time, nor in yours, of that I'm sure.'

Jerat could think of nothing to useful to say. He tried not to think about Ro and Lirian and the dead first wife and Verre, his mother.

The Teller Priest had taken out his pipes and was playing a complex melody, full of melancholy. He put down his pipes regretfully.

'I can never quite remember the Singer's songs – this pipe is the closest one in timbre to her voice that I've managed to make, but it still lacks something.' He stoked the fire. 'I think that Ro will wake tomorrow or the next day and then we should know.'

It was a long time before Jerat answered and when

he finally spoke it was with a kind of grim determination.

'Could the Singer who serves Zeron, the Dark Daughter, make him well?'

'You mean could she restore his soul if it has gone? I don't know, Jer. I don't think so. That would take more than music, perhaps the Magic of the Last Resort.' He smiled grimly.

'And is there such a thing?' Jerat's voice was eager. The Teller Priest shrugged.

'There are old tales, not much spoken of these days. Most Tellers no longer know their telling. It is said that if you trap a Night Hunter you can have your heart's desire.'

Jerat straightened up, eager and alert.

'It's ancient lore, Jerat, I wasn't being that serious. According to these stories Night Hunters have a power deep within them that is unleashed only in rare and terrible circumstances. One story has it that if a Night Hunter desires anything with his whole heart then he could be forced to remake the world to fulfil his desire. In that story a Night Hunter, trapped against his will in a cave, made the whole mountainside disappear so that he could be free. They say that like a wild animal that would gnaw through its own limb to escape a trap, a Night Hunter cannot but use whatever magic lies within to be free. I don't know if that can be true, because in winter the Hunters live in caves and, though they don't build Halls as we do, I don't know why they would be so frightened of being trapped.'

'It isn't true, then?'

'I don't know, Jerat. Sometimes the oldest stories have wisdom in them, but I don't know of anyone who has tried to trap a Night Hunter. It is said that anyone who catches one and forces them into the Magic of the Last Resort may make a wish and have it granted. If that were true, I'm sure your Chief would be trapping Night Hunters regularly.' He smiled and then added more seriously, 'Moon-eye will never talk of it and, to my mind, if there is such a power it must be an evil thing to bend the earth out of shape at the desire of one person. I should not have mentioned it.' He shook his head as if he was angry with himself. 'What I was trying to tell you was that whatever magic lies in the songs of the Singers it is not evil. What has happened to your brother may be the will of Zerat and to change that would be evil. Moon-eye explained to me that she could not save a woman who had not the strength to bear a child, but she could help one who was weary and frightened. Their songs accord with the will of Zerat – follow the grain of the world, work with the weave of this world's fabric. The Magic of the Last Resort, if it exists at all, runs counter to that.'

It occurred to Jerat that he would not care if magic ran counter to the whole world, distorted the warp and the weft of it – if it saved Ro and kept him safe.

FIFTEEN

Ro did not wake the next day, the day that the Teller Priest went to perform the burial and mourning ceremony for the first wife and the child who died with her. He did not show any signs of waking the next day either when the Longest Light festivities moved into their final phase. Jerat was, however, commanded to attend their father at the Tier House.

'I don't understand why he wants me there,' Jerat complained.

'I imagine he wants you as a witness to the acceptance of a new wife,' the Teller said calmly. 'There's no need to look so scandalised. It's always done very discreetly and in the privacy of the Heart of the Home. She wears the mask and cloak of her predecessor, bows to the Chief, each of her fellow wives and the representatives of the Brood Trove and Horde, then takes her place at the cook fire. I then say "The household is once more complete" and we eat spice cakes and that is it. It is scarcely a ceremony at all, because to all outward appearances nothing has changed. Your Spear Day is not so far off, so you are of an age to take this role and represent the Trove. It is a sign of honour. At least you should be grateful that the Chief remembers you. He has been known to lose track of the eligibility of his sons from time to time – which often causes trouble.'

Jerat tried to take this in. How many such ceremonies had he missed – how many times had a wife died only to be seamlessly replaced by another wearing a dead woman's mask and a dead woman's cloak? No one ever spoke of any of it – not the deaths, not the marriages, not the ceremonies. The whole business of birth and death was kept apart from the Brood Trove like some arcane secret of Zeron, the Dark Daughter.

Jerat's feelings on the matter did not matter – the Trove were disciplined above all else; Jerat had always obeyed the Chief in the past and he would do so again.

Dew still dampened the summer grass when he arrived, and the Hearthfields were still full of the small tents that their many guests had brought with them from their distant Dependencies. The cool morning air was full of the scent of cookfires and barley cakes and the subdued chatter of people coming to terms with the day. All the visitors made the familiar environs of home seem so strange that it almost seemed as if he had arrived at a new place. Perhaps the place he thought had been his home had never existed except in his imagination.

Guardsman Keran left the cook pot he was tending

when he saw Jerat and moved to greet him almost as if he were an equal, so that to Jerat, struggling with new knowledge and new understanding, it seemed for a moment as if he might even have become a new person.

'Jerat, you are wanted above. What news of Ro?'

'No change – he sleeps still.' He would have liked to have blurted out his fear that Ro would never wake, but he was conscious that to do so would not seem manly. Avet emerged from the Hall just as Jerat was about to ask why he was required above in the Heart of the Home, which he had not seen since his banishment from the women's place so long ago. He was conscious of Avet's scrutiny and hoped that he did not show the discomfort he felt: he did not know what was expected of him. A crowd was beginning to gather round the cook fire; the Trove bombarded him with questions about Ro, and the rest, the outsiders, looked at him curiously so that he felt himself colour under their scrutiny and his hand unconsciously sought his mended knife now hanging at his hip.

'You are expected, Jer,' Keran reminded him with a hint of rebuke. Nervously Jerat followed the Teller up the ladder to the Heart of the Home, followed closely by Avet, who only added to Jerat's acute discomfort.

The smell overwhelmed him with memories of his infancy. The air was scented with herbs and the three remaining wives of the quarters were dressed in their masks and finery; the light through the shutters shone on the bright wool of their garments and on the lined face of the Chief. Something about the old man's face made him very afraid and Jerat's anxiety deepened. He stood where the Teller indicated in a cluster of older men of the Brood Trove, along with those brothers who had just come of age: the twins Mirit and Tanit, Drannott, Kellott and Avet. From this position Jerat was better able to see the other man present who squatted opposite the chief. It was Barak, the farmholder of the second quarter, the man Jerat had escorted to the Hearthfields, Lirian's father. For one ludicrous moment Jerat wondered if the old man had come to complain about Jerat's behaviour the day of Ro's drowning, but it soon become clear that something altogether graver was underway.

'She is your responsibility. We had an agreement – find her or else . . .' The Chief did not shout; he did not need to. Fury was evident in every crease of his face and in the rising colour of his neck.

'Now wait a moment.' The farmholder wagged his finger aggressively at the Chief. 'We had an agreement, but it was always on the basis that Lirian was amenable. I'm not a father to send my daughter where she does not want to go. I will gladly repay the nuptial gift. It is not what I want, but I am an honest man, as you yourself have good enough cause to remember.' Barak's voice was strained and Jerat scarcely dared breathe. The air in the room was warm and felt charged with portent like the heavy stillness of the air before a storm. The Chief glanced round the room; Jerat had to struggle not to flinch from his look.

'Where has your daughter gone?'

'I cannot say.'

'Find her or I will! And when I do – she dies. No

one reneges on an agreement with the Chief of this Dependency. Oath-breakers are not accepted here.'

Jerat sensed rather than heard a sudden communal intake of breath. He did not know for sure that this was unusual, but it seemed as though it was unexpected. His eyes sought the wife of the second quarter. If she noticed him she gave no sign, but her hands, resting on her lap as decorum decreed, were bunched into fists and her knuckles were white. He did not know what that meant.

The Teller Priest stepped forward with his arms raised, as if to intervene, but the Chief gave him one quelling look.

'Not now, old man – I will have none of your womanish counsel today. That is my word. Bring her back by tomorrow, Barak, or you will live to regret it – but not for long.'

The farmholder did not reply. His face was a mask as impenetrable as those of the wives. He did not bow except to the Teller Priest.

'There will be much regret over this,' he said simply, and left.

There was a pause, a strange ominous silence, and then the Chief spoke.

'He will not bring the woman back.'

'He is kin to Chief Galet of High Ridge – and Galet will not tolerate the murder of his granddaughter,' the Priest answered matter of factly.

'Do you think I don't know that! Do you think age has blunted my wits, Teller? I know Barak, he was once part of my Horde – he has land here that I gave him for his courage and his pride. I wanted children of his bloodline to strengthen my Brood Trove. I am not a fool. And because I am not a fool I will not tolerate oath-breaking. No one breaks trust with me, not even Barak! He has until tomorrow, but we must ready ourselves for war.'

That sentence chilled the marrow of Jerat's bones. The old man could not be serious. He was surely not so hotheaded? Jerat was almost old enough to fight this war, if it came to that – fear and excitement vied for precedence in his heart. He saw his mother look at him and at the Chief. He noticed with shock that the old Chief's rheumy eyes were damp with tears.

Sixteen

It was quite clear that Jerat could not return to the Teller Priest's Hall to care for Ro. Keran's eyes were stern and stony after he came back from speaking with the Chief, and he appeared to have forgotten all about Ro when he sent Jerat to take his turn training with the others. Everything had changed again: the bright tents that cluttered the Hearthfields were swiftly dismantled and the festival guests were disappearing as swiftly as smoke from the cook fire. By noon only the Chief's own Hearth Guard and members of the Brood Trove and their descendents remained. That alone amounted to a fighting force of around eighty trained fighting men and five men-women. This corps also included Heron and a couple of the other no-men who had been with the Chief so long that their loyalty could not be doubted. The Chief placed lookouts around the Hearthfields, while others combed the Dependency, looking for Lirian. There was no sign of her, of Barak or of his old father to be found. Someone had burnt Barak's Hall to the ground, though no one was sure whether the deed had been done by Barak himself or by one of his neighbours angry with him for precipitating such trouble. Whoever was to blame, the Chief appeared to take it as a declaration of hostility.

'Barak saved the Chief's life once in a skirmish at the far north of the Lake. The Chief built him that Hall and gave him his lands as a gift of thanks. He treated Barak as if he were part of the Chief's own Brood, and this is how he is repaid.' Keran's explanation, delivered in a hard, tight voice that was so uncharacteristic of the quietly competent Guardsman, made Jerat reassess the Horde leader. Keran, whose hand had steered the running of the Hall for all of Jerat's life, was paler and grimmer-faced than Jerat had ever seen him.

When all the work was done and evening came, the Hall was full to capacity with the entire Brood Trove and the Hearth Guard drinking the Teller Priest's ale, eating the remnants of the festival food, shouting and laughing as though the threat of war was nothing. Jerat tried not to draw attention to himself; all the arguing and speculating about what Barak might be playing at was overwhelming. When almost everyone had agreed that either Barak was a fool, or a brave man ill-used, and large quantities of the Teller's ale had been drunk and pronounced remarkably fine, the Trove returned to their traditional quarterage.

It was another strangeness Jerat found difficult to bear. He sought out a spot near the quarter curtain away from the feet of the biggest men and closest to his old Brood sister Moorat. She was with child, which made Jerat frightened for her, but her voice was as cheerful and soothing as ever. He hugged her carefully so as not to press against the bump of the soon-to-be-child. She was not the wife of a Chief, but of a potter, and was herself a recognised craftsman; as a member of the Chief's Brood Trove she had a right to stay in the Hall and she was determined to exercise that privilege, perhaps to be with Jerat. Jerat feared it would be for the last time. Most of the Brood brothers were scandalised that she should choose to sleep among them, with-child as she was, and not as a guest in the Heart of the Home or even with their own wives and babes in the tents they had brought for the purpose. However, knowing Moorat of old, no one bothered to argue with her.

Jerat told her all about Ro and Verre and he found himself struggling for self-control. He didn't understand why Lirian had run away; surely marrying the Chief could not be so bad, old though the Chief was? He could not imagine that marriage to him could be so objectionable that dying would be preferable, yet, even as he posed the question, he found that the thought of Lirian in the mask of a wife, sitting by his father, made him feel strangely uncomfortable. Moorat let him prattle on, as she always had, and patted his arm as if he were still a babe.

'Are you scared, Moorat?' Jerat asked suddenly.

'Of war? No – our Battle Horde is the best. If we have to fight we'll win, even against Galet's mob.'

'No,' Jerat said, groping for her hand in the darkness so he could hold it as he had long ago. 'No, I

mean about you. Aren't you scared about your babe?'
It was a bold question, touching on the things that
were ever left unspoken.

'Yes,' she said, without hesitation. 'I would rather
take my spear and my bow into battle than face this,
but Zerat decreed that a wife should risk her life to
bear every new life as a warrior risks his to defend it.'

'But Moorat . . . why?'

Her quiet whisper sounded amused. 'Why did I let
myself get with child? It's like the story of Zerat's love-
curse – when that falls on you you have no choice.
You'll understand one day. I'd half expected you to
already.'

Jerat felt himself colour. He did not like the
implication that he was somehow backward or
immature, though he was beginning to feel that he
might be both.

'I think I would have liked to, you know, be with
Lirian,' he said haltingly, though he knew Moorat
would never mock him, 'but she was chosen for Avet.'

'Poor Lirian!' Moorat said. 'She was a fool to run.
The Chief will kill her, and if he doesn't do it himself,
one of our boys here will. She offered too grave an
insult and the Chief cannot go back on his word. I am
sorry for Barak too – he was a good man.'

Jerat noted the past tense, and realised that as far as
the Horde were concerned Barak and Lirian were as
good as dead, and war all but declared.

The next day was hot and still, with a terrible
heaviness in the air, as if the whole of Zerat's realm
waited on Lirian's return. The men the Chief had sent

out returned when the sun was at its highest, when the men and boys, the men-women and girls of the Brood Trove, sweat-soaked and red from training, finally took their rest in the cool of the Hall: there was no sign of Lirian. Everyone thought it likely that she had crossed the Lake. A Lakeside fisherman claimed to have lost a coracle to thieves, but as he was an old Horde hand who'd served with Barak, he was not believed. He was fortunate that his age and the men's respect for his service in the Horde kept him safe from anything more serious than a gentle roughing-up.

The Chief would wait until the next day to formally declare war on any who harboured Lirian. It would be days more before all the Dependents who owed service to the Horde could be assembled and provisioned for the journey. There were not enough boats in the Dependency to take the whole Horde across the water, so the entire fighting force would have to take the long land-way round the Lake to Galet's Dependency. It would take time to be ready, but by the time the weather broke and the promised storm came, as if Zerat himself signalled his agreement, everyone knew: war would come.

Guardsman Hela had set off early to see the Teller Priest on the Chief's business, and she returned as the rain began to pelt against the packed ground outside the Hall. Jerat was about to stand his turn manning the Hearthfields defences. Hela's face was tight and anxious.

'What has happened to Ro?' Jerat almost knocked her over with his eagerness for news.

Her eyes were wary, watchful, old.

'No change, Jer.'

Jerat's stomach felt peculiar and he found it hard to concentrate on Hela's words.

'How soon . . . ?' he began.

'How soon do we march?' Hela finished helpfully. Her dark eyes crinkled and she smiled a tight-lipped smile. 'I imagine the Chief will name a new heir today – it is well overdue. Everyone will drink too much ale – always assuming there is enough left after last night's excesses – and we will march after that.'

'Hela, this is very sudden. I don't understand . . .'

'It's the Chief, Jer. He is old and worried that if he looks weak even for a moment . . .' She shrugged. 'His family is too big; there is not enough land to go between all the Brood. Your father needs more land on which to settle you all. He was always at war when he was younger – that's why he has so many of you running Dependencies elsewhere. He has conquered most of the good land this side of the Lake. He wants to go to war again before he dies and he's had his eye on old Galet's land a long time – Lirian is the perfect excuse. We're lucky we've had so many years of peace.'

She hurried off, stiff-backed, towards the Tier House, to talk with the Chief and assist in the preparations for war. Jerat heard his Brood brothers talking and was shocked to discover that Hela too was a child of a child of Galet, cast out by a high-born husband when she could not bear a child of her own and denied her place in Galet's own Guard. She knew the land, but if she fought against Galet she fought against her own. Why did Jerat not know that? All his childhood he'd never wondered much about anything, never questioned why things were as they were. Now everything was about to change.

He turned his thoughts to the Heir-naming. Like the rest of the Brood, he had fantasised about sleeping upstairs in the Heart of the Home, with the Hearth Guard and the Brood Trove below him. He'd dreamed of being Chief and owner of the Hearthfields, recipient of the tithes of the Dependency and defender of the land. He was eligible to be named as heir – all the Brood Trove were, from Hirat who was a grandfather himself and had lived almost forty summers, to the newest babe born of the wife of the third quarter who had not yet been brought down to the Hall. Jerat felt that he knew the elder members of the Trove. He knew them through the memory stories of the Hearth Guard that had kept him and his Brood brothers amused on winter nights. Hirat, the eldest of the first quarter, would be a good Chief. His courage as a child was one of Guardsman Hela's favourite stories, but he was probably too old.

It was a long walk to the boundary of the Hearthfields, the fortified heart of the Dependency. The thorn thicket which marked the boundary had been augmented earlier in the growing season by the huge timbers of a Great Tree felled by lightning. When Zerat sacrificed a tree like that, it was thought to be auspicious to use it for defence, and this one had been cut and sharpened to make a wall almost as high as a man on the high bank above the ditch that lay outside the wall. Some of the wood had been kept back to make weapons, but the bulk had gone into this additional barrier so that the whole of the Chief's extensive Hearthfields would be under Zerat's protection.

It was still raining hard and the earth had turned to mud as Jerat walked along the flattened ridge behind the wall of wood. The other brother of the second manning the ramparts – a tall man, probably Ferat – was too far away to engage in conversation. Jerat waved an acknowledgement and Ferat set off back towards the Tier House. The rain was a grey curtain separating him from the noise and restless activity of the rest of the Brood. He was glad of it – so much had happened so quickly he needed peace to think. Would the Chief perhaps name him heir? It was not a realistic hope and in his heart Jerat knew it. The Chief was unlikely to name any of the younger Brood Trove as heir.

Jerat had not thought too much about what would happen when his father died – it had always seemed a distant and unlikely thing, but now it struck him forcibly that when the new heir took over, the Heart of the Home, the Hall and even the carrier coop would be given over in their entirety to the new Chief: the wives of all four quarters, the Brood Trove and the fighting Horde would have to find homes and work in other places, on other Dependencies or in the wilds, if they were not asked to remain and swear Dependency. He and Ro and Rin, Verre and Hela and Keran – all the people he cared most about – would be Hearthless. The Chief was old, but strong, he reminded himself, and vigorous as ever. With luck the heir would not need to claim his inheritance until Ro and Rin were already of an age to leave the Tier House and find a place in another Horde. May Zerat grant them all such luck – Jerat didn't want to think about the alternative.

Jerat checked the fortifications which were the responsibility of the second quarter and stopped at the section marker. This taller timber pike had been skilfully carved by the same long-dead craftsman who made the masks of the quarters. It had been recently repainted under the Teller Priest's direction with both the colours of the second and the third quarters intermingled: green and blue and red and orange interlocking circles, stripes and dots, so that the red of the original wood was lost under the elaborate design. He patted it – for luck – as he had every time he'd done a duty there since he was a child.

Who would the Chief choose to rule this familiar land after his time? Let it be someone who would be good to Ro and Rin. He heard the long yodelling cry of Keran calling everyone back to the Hall and the ceremonial drum thumped its message like thunder. It was time for the Heir-naming.

There were too many of the Brood Trove to sit comfortably in the Hall. Instead the more than eighty direct descendents of the Chief sat outside, cross-legged in a circle in the rain, along with their wives and husbands, so that the circle enclosed the whole of the Hearthyard. The Chief sat, flanked by the ranks of his Horde, with a wife at each quarter of the circle's circumference. In the place of the first wife a crossed stick had been dressed in the robe of the last incumbent and her mask hung emptily from the top of the pole. It made Jerat shiver. The baby of the third quarter mewled and was hushed by the masked woman in the blue and vibrant orange of that quarter. The Teller Priest stood just a little behind the Chief with the ceremonial drum he used sometimes to give rhythm to their songs at night. He looked distracted, withdrawn, and did not seem to see Jerat slink into his place beside Verre. She was impassive in her mask of red and green, a carved wife, wooden as a child's doll in among the offspring of the Chief. Rin sat at her other side. Jerat thought she must have had to fight hard not to hold that small hand in her own. Rin was scared. Jerat saw his beloved Moorat take the small boy into her arms.

Jerat had been one of the last to arrive, so almost as soon as he squatted in his place the Teller Priest began to beat a rhythm on his drum – not yet the tattoo of war but the steady rhythm that announced that the Chief would speak.

'My fair family,' he began, 'my Brood Trove, that is dearer than land and wives and herds and riches! I have seen fifty-six summers and survived as many winters, and the time has come, and perhaps is overdue, to name my new successor. For those of you who think your time in the Hall is too long past for memory still to recall you, I want you to know that your names are carved in my heart, your wives' and children's names are carved in my heart and I remember with joy the birth and Acceptance Day of each and every one of you.'

The Chief's eyes met the gaze of each of his children

in turn, in a silence that stretched longer than Jerat could hold his breath. When the Chief met his own eyes he felt suddenly frightened; the Chief looked old and fierce and half-demented, not the solid figure Jerat thought would live for ever. The realisation struck him that this old man expected to die before too long and did not think he'd see these, his children, all together again.

The old man's eyes moved on and Jerat found himself shaking. The drum beat began, starting quietly with a steady rhythm, then each moment growing louder and faster until it reached a crescendo of noise. It stopped when the Chief spoke again.

'I have outlived four of my heirs and it grieves me that none of them lived to take over my land, but I am blessed with many strong sons, so that I have had to think long and hard to weigh and measure the length and the breadth and the depth of each one of you to decide who will guard best my lands, who will serve best the Dependents, who will go on and make this Dependency greater still. I have at last decided that when I die the care of all will fall on this man's shoulders. I name as heir – Avet of the fourth quarter.'

There was a sharp intake of breath, for Avet had only just survived twenty winters, and many of the older Brood brothers looked very unhappy. Avet himself looked stunned and struggled shakily to his feet, helped by others of his quarter who had begun to cheer and beat their hands upon their earth and their feet on the packed ground.

Jerat could not at first accept what he had heard. Avet! Someone of his own birthingtide! His enemy,

Avet! Jerat felt sick and prayed earnestly to Zerat under his breath that the Chief should have a still longer life, for if he did not Jerat's would not be worth living.

SEVENTEEN

Nela ate her supper in near silence, as far from Millard as was possible; it was not nearly far enough. Fortunately, everyone appeared too preoccupied with the failure of the day's labours to produce anything worthy of their efforts. They all retired early after a short and uncompanionable evening. Nela couldn't sleep. The stone in her artefact pouch was weighing on her mind. She ought to have put it back. She had thought about it and changed her mind; the exploration of the stone should be done properly, systematically, with a scribe and a Findsman witness; it was not something to be explored alone but for a bondsman. Besides, when her father found it missing she would be his first suspect, as he knew she did not want it moved from the Lakeside.

She waited until all the Findsmen were snoring and then crept with as much stealth as she could manage towards the strong box. She was startled when the bondsman laid a hand on her wrist. She was about to cry out but he placed his hand over her mouth. Was he going to kill her for the stone? Nela started to panic and tried to kick out and scream.

'I'm not going to hurt you, non-woman,' he whispered, somehow managing to convey exasperation even though his words were scarcely audible. Nela stopped struggling and, feeling rather foolish, nodded her head to show that she'd understood. The bondsman released her.

'Here.' He handed her the pebble in its leather pouch that he had pretended was the black stone. Would her father know the difference? It lacked the warmth of the true stone, but a cursory glance in the strong box would not reveal the substitution.

She let the bondman's hand briefly brush hers as she opened her hand to receive it and, while the bondsman stood watch, picked the lock of the strong box and placed the pebble inside. It felt as though her heart were beating in her throat, and her hands were shaking, as much from her encounter with the bondsman as from the inappropriateness of what she had done. Before this dig she had never been anything but her father's conscientious, if argumentative daughter: she did not know herself in this newly reckless guise.

The bondsman gave her a drink of sweet-leaf tea – he must have noticed her shaking. She managed to drink it without smashing the china bowl, and it helped a little.

'Thank you,' she said, as much for the false stone as for the tea. She still did not look at him. He knew her weaknesses too well, this bondsman, understood her greed for understanding.

'My name is Moss,' the bondsman said by way of acknowledgement. It had not occured to Nela that he might have a name. Her father always called him 'bondsman', and what he might have called him in a busier place with more servants she did not know; this servant had been recommended as tough enough for this trip by another eminent Findsman and bought especially for the journey. Discomfited, she did not respond to his introduction, but instead took out the real black stone in all its living warmth and held it in her hand. The moment she held it, it was as if she disappeared.

I can't believe it. The tree is blackened, blasted by a force like lightning, but it was just a note. I only sang a note. I know it was a note of deepest anger but surely even that could not cause this. I touch it and the tree is hot and smells charred. I mark my face with the black soot, rub it into my palm so the mark of the moon shows more clearly. I do not know what I did to do this, but the need to know is very strong. I will try again. It is a long time since those first lessons with Moon-eye. Breathing the right way, standing the right way, thinking the right way, making my whole self an instrument for the production of sound is now the only way I breathe and stand and think: I am Chief Singer of the Long Hill Summer People and the Bear Caves Winter People for the Night Hunters hereabouts, and it is my voice that tempts the deer from its hide and holds it, trapped in a dream, so that the hunters may kill it. It is my voice that soothes the pain of childbirth and lights the death path of the dying. It is my voice that calms the tribe in lean times and gives sharper sight to the women at their gathering. How can it be my voice which blights the tree and causes it to burn?

I do not know what I did that was different. Was it the fury in my thoughts, fury with Sky for his ridiculous raids on the Bear-men? Or was it the difference in the way I sang the note, the extra resonance, a hint of dissonance? I make the note come again, louder and stronger like a cracked bell so that it offends my ear, rigorously trained to detect the tiniest slippage of pitch. I cannot go against the rhythm of the earth, that is what Moon-eye taught me, and do I serve the earth now? The Womanface cannot see me yet. It is not yet her time – is it my will then that makes the tree bloom fire and blacken as if from lightning within? I am shaking and have to sit down. The wanton destruction makes me sick and at the same time makes me want to dance, exultant. I hope the Womanface will not be angry, nor the earth – but if I cannot go against the rhythm of the earth, this too must be part of a Singer's gifts. It must be part of what a Singer should do. I press my stone hard between my fingers so that I will remember what I have done today and what I have felt. It is to be hoped that Sky, my ever-angry brother, never finds out about this, at least until I have worked out what this is good for, this fearful power to destroy. I touch the smouldering bark of the second tree – a sapling only. There is no life left in it. I have not brought death in this way before. It is a serious thing, so I mark my face and my moon mark on my hand again with the soot and dedicate this new power, lent to me by the long-suffering earth, to the Womanface, my Lady.

But then I look again at what I have done. My head is beginning to ache with the strain of it. Do I want to remember this? This sudden sense of loss, as if my voice has grown a spear within it. I do not want to remember this. I let my fingers loosen their grip on the stone and let it fall.

Nela let the stone slip from her hand so that it lay in her lap, but the scrap of cloth she had been holding in her other hand was burnt almost to nothing.

The bondsman was looking straight at her, an expression of horror on his face.

'You sang something – what did you do?' he whispered.

'I don't know,' she answered, meeting his eye in shame and confusion, before letting her gaze drop first. She shivered. This was more than a dream memory: this was like some kind of possession.

EIGHTEEN

'But you can't do that!' Jerat could not hide his fury, but both Verre and the Teller Priest were looking at him, unmoved.

'Yes, Jer, I can, and I'm probably the only person who can – I thought you might be grateful.' Verre spoke in the decisive tone she had always used with Rin and Ro when they were very young.

'Grateful! To be left behind with no hope of glory – left to tend the Hall with the babes and the no-men, and you thought I'd be grateful!'

Verre's face was strained – her hair was plaited so tightly to her head that it looked painful; she grimaced as she fastened her cap over it. She was in battle dress, woollen trews in deep ox-blood red and a thick leather fur-lined waistcoat, far too hot for the weather, that offered good protection against spears. She had painted her face in the colours of her quarter as if her true face had become the mask that she wore on important occasions. She adjusted her kit for a minute: the sling she carried at her hip in a small bag next to her sheathed belt-knife, the quiver of good arrows she carried on her back, along with her bow. She looked grim beneath her make-up: Guardsman Verre, nothing more. Eventually she faced him.

'Jerat, you are my son and I care for you as I care for Rin and Ro, children of my body as well as of the quarter. Do you not know how rare it is for a woman to see her children grown to boyhood? I would like to see you live to manhood too, and I will not risk you in this war. There is no glory in this fight – just an old man seeking more land on the pretext of a lost bride. Don't be fooled.'

She spoke quietly, but the part of Jerat that had begun to ache when Ro was injured hurt now with a stabbing pain. It was the first time she had admitted to him that she was his mother – the first time she had admitted her care for him. He feared he would weep again like a child. She reached out to touch his head and, with her competent Guardsman's hands, pulled his head towards her so that it rested on her shoulder. She smelled of the comfort-giver of his memory and, as she embraced him as she had when he was a child, he felt like that child again. They stayed like that for an unmeasured time: Verre stroked his wolf's mane of light hair and then suddenly pulled away as Keran's commanding yodel informed the Hall that it was time to muster.

'I have told the Chief that without you Ro will die. Keep him safe for me, Jer, and Rin too – I am so glad to have lived to know you.' She smiled so that the paint of her face cracked slightly around the lines of her mouth, but it was already ruined in any case by the furrows of cleaned skin ploughed by her tears. She didn't speak again, but turned to join the assembled men and did not look back.

Jerat wiped his face on his sleeve.

'I know she wanted to protect me, but all she's done is shame me,' he said in a dull, choked voice. 'I may survive the war but what will my Brood brothers think? Who will take me to their Hearth Guard if I hide behind my brother's illness?'

The Teller Priest shrugged. 'I don't know, Jer, but on this one thing Verre was immovable.' He glanced quickly at Jerat. 'Perhaps I should not tell you this, but you know that Moon-eye sang at your birth – I told you that, didn't I? Well, in the moments after you were born she said to me that you were blood-marked,' the Priest said dramatically, as though such a title ought to mean something to Jerat. It meant nothing.

'So what is that supposed to mean?' Jerat continued to watch Verre as she moved to an honoured place behind the Chief and Keran, listening with only half an ear to the Teller's recollections.

'Among the Night Hunters it means that you are both marked for greatness and marked for death-giving – to be the death of many is not seen as such a good thing among their people and Moon-eye was very disturbed, but your mother was very proud. She has told me that if you are marked to be a great warrior she could not prevent it, so if she could prevent you from fighting in this war then this is not the war you are destined to fight in.' The Teller Priest smiled crookedly. 'Your mother thinks her own way on every subject. You should be proud of her, she is no fool and her judgement is as sound as her instincts. And her instincts must be good or the Chief would not have her protect his left side in a fight. She is as extraordinary in battle as she is as in life.'

Jerat finally tore his eyes from the army of his brothers and looked dully at the old man.

'So I'm to be a great warrior, am I? That's a story to soothe a child, Priest, and I am not that any more. When do *you* leave?'

The Teller shook his head. 'Verre has meddled in my life too. The Chief has left me in charge of Hearth and Hall.'

'But who will do the battle rites?' Jerat was aghast.

'I sang the ritual of the painting of faces for the blessing of Zerat which the Chief believes will guarantee victory. As for the rest, one of your brothers has picked up a little lore here and there; the death song is short enough. He, Travit, will take my place.' The Priest's tone was dry, and it was clear that he was as little impressed with the arrangements as Jer himself. 'Perhaps we should be grateful that all women are not as strong as Verre, or what would be the need of a Chief? Come on! Let's watch them go from the upper field: we might as well make ourselves thoroughly miserable.'

They walked together in silence to the highest point of the Hearthfields, from which vantage point they could see the hundreds of men, loyal no-men and men-women march out. The Chief's fine horses, too small to support the height and weight of a full-grown

Lakesider, followed behind, laden with the supplies the Chief had put away last winter and the early harvest. It would be a lean winter if the Horde did not return victorious in time for main harvest.

They were a fine sight, the great, strong men of the glorious and victorious Dependency – many with their faces coloured like Verre in the shades of their quarter. The men limed their hair so that it stood stiff as corn away from their heads, making them look larger and more glorious even than usual. Avet walked at his father's right hand holding the decorated spear that had been given to him when his beard had begun to grow, when he had lived sixteen winters. Jerat was ashamed of the envy that rose like bile in his throat: it tasted as bitter. Their way was lined with those who were left behind, those too old or too young for the fight, and the new wives and women with-child – their eyes dark with knowledge of their own battle to come. The Brood Trove were running around whooping in a frenzy of excitement, waving sticks as spears and yodelling the battle cries they had learned from Keran. Even Rin, quiet and withdrawn as he had become, lost himself in a wild ecstasy of yowling and whooping to see so many of his Brood brothers all together and dressed for war. It was for him, as it was for Jerat, the biggest crowd he had ever seen.

'I should be there. He should have chosen me as heir.' Jerat spoke softly but the Teller Priest had sharp ears.

'Did you think he would?' The Priest could not keep the surprise from his voice.

'No, not really, but I think I might have dreamed of

having the Hall. You know, of living in the Heart of the Home – in the warmth and the spices, of having the Horde at my calling. Foolish things.'

The Priest did not answer for a moment – just squinted at the marching men, humming a little under his breath as if in blessing. When his strange half-heard song was done he answered Jerat.

'You would have been a good choice, but the things that would have made you a good Chief are not things the Chief recognises. Avet is a bully, and that is one kind of leader – your Brood brothers fear him, young though he is, and that might be a good thing. I can see why the Chief chose him, but it was not what I advised.'

'You advised?' Jerat was shocked and his voice betrayed it, but the Priest only grinned.

'You have friends in high places, Jerat, Chiefson, when your friends are the noble Teller Priest and the revered second wife. Between us we have tried to keep you safe. It would not be surprising if Avet ends this battle with a spear of our Hearthfields in his back.'

Jerat thought about that as the column of the Horde became just dust in the distance, a faraway sound of feet and hooves.

'I should get back to Ro. Should I bring him back to the Chief's Hall, do you think? I will be too busy to travel daily to your Hall with all the extra work that will be needed,' said Jerat.

'So shall I. I will also be staying at the Chief's Hall while the Chief is away – as steward of his affairs. Take Heron and bring Ro here."

The Teller Priest patted Jerat awkwardly on the

back, which was something of a stretch as Jerat was already much the taller.

'It will be all right – you will be the oldest of the Brood brats and life will be easier.' If he'd hoped to make Jerat smile by his use of the Guardsmen's term for the Trove he did not succeed. Jerat did not register his words. The Teller carried on, 'There are things I can teach you that you would like to learn. Trust me. This is for the best.'

Jerat nodded and managed a rather strained smile, but his mind was busy, thinking of Verre and the battles to come and of Moon-eye's words that he was blood-marked for greatness and for death-giving.

NINETEEN

The days that followed the departure of the Horde were strange days for Jerat. Once the wives and young children of his own elder siblings had left for their own Tier Houses there were at least fewer people to feed. There were also far fewer people to tend the Dependency farms with all the men away, and Jerat found himself running between farms helping to deal with problems about which he would normally have known nothing. He was the oldest of the Brood Trove left behind and so he took over the running of the Trove, kept them training and running errands, keeping the Hearthfields and their defences in order, gathering firewood and the wild strawberries that were in season, doing all that needed to be done, under the watchful eye of the Teller Priest who noticed everything but said nothing. Quiet Rin became Jerat's shadow as Jerat shadowed the Teller Priest. The Chief's wives had voluntarily abandoned the Heart of the Home to lend their labour to the farms from which they came. Jerat did not see them leave and would not have recognised them in any case. They too were young and not yet with child and had preferred to spend their precious time in the sunshine rather than in the cosseted dimness of the Tier House.

Jerat felt the emptiness at the Heart of the Home in his own heart. The four fires of the Heart of the Home were ashes: the only Hearth fire was now the common cook stove in the Hall below, and the only Chief the Teller Priest.

They moved Ro to the Hall and the Teller Priest arranged a rota so that each of the Brood Trove spent time sitting with him, singing to him or talking to him so that his soul might be tempted back from the shadows by the promise of all the good things that life offered.

Jerat took his turn, and though it pained him to see his adventure-seeking brother still looking so pale and ill, it helped to talk to him, as if he could hear.

'I should be there – when the Chief dies no one will take me into their Horde if they think I'm too young and weak to fight, and Avet won't have me here, I'm sure.'

At Avet's name Ro began to stir and his eyes flickered open.

'Avet!' Ro said, in a voice that was little more than a whisper. 'Avet – dead?'

'No! Avet is alive and Ro, so are you. How do you feel?' Jerat reached forward and hugged his brother but Ro frowned slightly.

'Jerat killed Avet?'

'No, Ro. I fought Avet, but he is well. It doesn't

153

matter, I thought we had lost you!'

He helped Ro to a sitting position. Ro seemed confused, but he was speaking; he was alive. Jerat ran outside and bellowed for someone to fetch the Teller Priest. Rin appeared from somewhere in the Hearthyard and was at Ro's side in a moment. He ran into the dimness of the Hall and flung himself at his brother with an abandon that was rare for him.

'Ro – you can speak!'

Ro's eyes were filled with tears and he nodded. 'I speak, Rin,' he said wearily, as though it cost him much effort. 'But I dreamed – bad dreams. I feel wrong – all wrong.'

The Teller Priest gently separated the weeping twins and examined Ro calmly. He checked his body carefully, then, looking intensely into his eyes, asked him questions. Jerat hardly dared speak for the conflicting emotions that fought within him. Ro could speak – that was wonderful – he had woken and recognised Jerat, but with every passing moment it was becoming increasingly clear that he was not the same lively, daring little brother who had fallen into the water scant days ago. The Teller Priest gave Rin some broth from the pot with which to feed Ro and took Jerat to one side.

'Will he be all right?'

'It is as I feared,' the Teller Priest said gravely. 'He came too close to death to be carefree as he once was and he has paid the price for his return among us.'

'What do you mean?' Jerat felt his spirits sink and he was almost afraid to hear what the Teller Priest might say next.

'His wits may recover somewhat, but I think his body has been permanently harmed. He will need much help if he is to walk again – he has little control over his limbs and I fear he will always depend on others for his welfare.'

'But he is back with us. He is alive!'

The Teller Priest nodded, though from his expression it was not clear that he thought that a good thing.

'He is my brother, Priest, child of my mother, Verre, and I will always look out for his welfare. Do not worry, he will not be a burden on the Hall – I will see to him.'

The Teller Priest touched Jerat lightly on the arm. 'There is no need to speak so fiercely, Jer, I know you will care for him well. What I fear, I fear for Ro himself. We may have done wrong in bringing him back to us. Death has some claim on him now – he has been touched by the unknown and he may find it difficult to stay with us. I only speak of what I have seen before.'

'Could a Singer help him?' Jerat's mind was racing, desperate to find a way to bring back the brother he had lost, not just some shadow child, for ever marked for death.

'I do not think so, but it is too early to be sure: only time will tell, Jer, and for now I declare a day of celebration for the return of our wanderer from the shores of death. Let us be glad for what we have, not sorry for what we may have lost.'

They celebrated by slaughtering a good many

chickens and birds of the forest and one of the no-men who was gifted in the seasoning and preparation of feast meals took charge: it was a welcome change from corn and vegetables and trapped hare. For a time Jerat was able to rejoice in the return of Ro. When Ro smiled it was as if the bright boy of the past returned to them and Jerat would feel unreasoning hope blossom, but then a shadow would seem to pass over Ro's face and a sadder stranger sat in his brother's place, looking out from his brother's eyes, and that made Jerat afraid.

The Teller Priest insisted that the Brood Trove worked to the same rota as before, only this time helping Ro to walk up and down the courtyard in front of the Hall, but his legs did not work as they once had and he seemed happier to be half carried. Jerat could not watch him resist the Teller's attempts to help him without pain, but he made himself scold Ro and join with the Priest in the fruitless task of persuading Ro to walk unaided.

Rin said nothing, but whenever Jerat's back was turned he carried his twin to wherever he wanted to go, and it seemed to Jerat as if Rin, the weaker, quieter brother, seemed to grow in strength and vigour as Ro weakened. As the days passed it became impossible to deny that Ro had declined, even from the first day of his recovery from the death sleep. He spoke less and less and the darkness and strangeness that lurked behind his eyes grew deeper daily. Rin alone could make him smile and let the old Ro shine briefly as a cloudy sunrise on a winter morning.

Jerat could not control his anxiety. He slept little in

his quarterage, but lay awake listening to Rin's steady breathing and the disturbed mutterings of Ro, who seemed even less content at night than in the daytime. For many nights Jerat lay beside the restless Ro, stroking his brow that was sticky with sweat and uttering calming endearments under his breath, as he thought Verre might have done had she been there. He missed her and was sure she might have had some instinct for what Ro needed, might have been able to find a way to calm his evident nightly distress. But for all Jerat knew, Verre might be dead, and he was alone with all the responsibility of the Hall and the Brood on him. It seemed as though the night truly belonged to Zeron, the Dark Lady of nameless malice, and that with the dying of the sun's light all hope was leached from him. He became certain that the war would bring them no victory, only a wealth of corpses; that the harvest would fail or wither in the field for lack of men to bring it in; that the Brood Trove would all fall prey to the sickness that afflicted Ro, that injury to the soul that so disturbed Jerat and filled him with unreasoning fear. In the daylight when he was busy about the Hearthfields, talking with the Priest and encouraging the Brood in their tasks, he was able to deal better with his fears, but still no news came of the battle. The carrier coop remained empty and the Heart of the Home cold, and Jerat did not know what to do about any of it.

TWENTY

It was Findsman Millard who found them – Moss and Nela sitting together like friends.

'Nela, what do you think you are you doing?'

Nela was suddenly very aware that Moss's hand was close to hers, close enough to touch, though Moss had made no effort to do so. She withdrew her hand involuntarily and, wrapping the stone in the folds of her cloak, swept it away under the folds of her trews.

'Findsman Millard,' she said with more composure than she felt. 'I did not know you were a night prowler.'

'And I did not know you were given to consorting with servants. I am at a loss for words.'

'I was thirsty – this bondsman brought me something to drink. That is all. You are quick to think ill of me, quicker than I might have hoped, after our earlier conversation. What we talked of requires trust – it seems you have little enough trust in me.' Nela managed a tone of injured innocence. Long experience of observing her father's approach to argument had taught her that attack was often the most effective first line of defence, and she tried to rearrange her features into a semblance of outraged righteousness rather than guilt. Moss had quietly edged away and returned to tending the fire.

'No you don't,' said Findsman Millard firmly. 'I am not a fool and I won't be treated like one – you are up to something and I have a good idea of what. Your father has been carefully hiding the artefact, but I'm sure a watchful servant might find it, or a sensitive daughter with an affinity for such things.' Millard watched her closely and Nela felt hot and uncomfortable.

'Shh! Couldn't we talk about this in the morning? I don't know what you are talking about. I'm sorry, but I'm not feeling well. I'd like to go back to my sleeping mat now.'

The hand on her arm was stronger than she had expected.

'No, you don't! Not until you tell me what is going on, or I'll have your friend here dismissed from service. Don't forget, sweet Nela, you are sworn to me by binding agreement and it is to me you must answer for your conduct.'

Nela was very conscious of Moss's eyes on her, although he pretended to be busy. Millard seemed equally unconvinced by his show of activity.

'You, bondsman. Come here. I want her to know that I am serious.'

Moss kept his eyes lowered in accordance with Millard's expectations of a good servant and skirted the fire to stand next to Nela. Moss was a small man, though sturdily built: he contrived to make Millard with his soft richman's body look coarsely made and over-large. Millard did not seem aware of this unflattering contrast and reached out to slap Moss around the ear. Nela acted on an instinct she did not know she had, a recklessness she had never before allowed herself. She slipped the stone from the protection of her cloak and, as it touched her skin, hung on to her own identity for all she was worth. It was a foolish thing to do. Before when she touched the stone she had been at the mercy of the random memories for which the stone was a repository, but this time she called to mind the destructive power of the woman of the stone, and the stone remembered. She sang two or three strange discordant notes and flame bloomed along the tunic of Millard's outstretched arm and he screamed. Moss, with admirable presence of mind, pushed him to the floor and rolled him against the ground to extinguish the blaze. The smell of burnt cloth and flesh was strong. Millard groaned.

Nela, shaken, slipped the stone back into her cloak and hid it quickly in her artefact pouch, an inadequate hiding place, before rushing to his aid. Moss looked severe, and flashed her a look of such anger that she was quite taken aback; she had expected gratitude at the very least.

'Let me see, Findsman Millard,' she said as she checked his arm, and Moss rushed to get cold water from the water jar. Millard's arm was blistered but it was not as badly burned as it would have been had

Moss not acted so swiftly. It did not seem as if the flame had penetrated too much of his skin.

Suddenly the Chief Findsman was there, his hair awry and his beard partially unplaited.

'What is going on here? Why are you awake at full night?'

Millard groaned, incapable of answering, as Moss sliced away the sleeve of his tunic with a knife and gently poured the cool liquid over the burn.

'What happened here?' the Chief Findsman demanded.

'I think it was a spark from the fire,' Nela lied. 'You know how this strange, dead old wood spits and burns erratically.'

Her father seemed content to accept that explanation.

'Sweet-leaf tea and a restorative,' he ordered, and Moss bowed and hurried to fetch them from the supplies; the rope at his waist rasped as he moved from one part of the camp to the other and Nela found herself thinking of the weals on his own skin formed by the abrading leather of his belt.

After Millard had drunk the tea and enough grain wine to dull the pain, the Chief Findsman returned to his mat. Nela guessed that he did not wish to be seen in such an undignified sleep-befuddled state for any longer than was strictly necessary. When Nela's father was gone Millard returned to the subject of their earlier discourse.

'I know you are up to something, Nela, but I am a reasonable man and I will not tell your father about your dalliance with the servant so long as you do not oppose our agreement.' There was an edge to his voice that made her reassess Millard. He would be a more dangerous enemy than she had imagined.

'There is no dalliance, Findsman Millard. He gave me a drink when I was thirsty, that was all.'

His smile was wolvish. 'And what would your father with his love of status say of his plain, mad daughter consorting with servants – would he be tolerant?'

Nela winced at the careless insult. So, he thought her plain, and he had no qualm about insulting and humiliating her; she was becoming less sorry by the moment that she had burned him, until she caught Moss glancing at her. She dared not meet his eye in Millard's presence, but Moss turned from her in such a way as to make the chance of even a glance impossible; bizarrely she felt as if she'd let him down, and she was unaccountably ashamed.

'My father would not believe such ill of me as you seem all too keen to accept,' Nela answered.

'No? He believes you dangerously unstable, with your unfortunate predilection for fits, and he will believe anything I tell him in exchange for your sizeable bride price. There are places in Scraal where people can be cared for when they are not in their right mind.' The underlying threat in his voice was unmistakable.

'I am a non-woman and I will not marry you.' Nela knew she did not sound as confident as she would have liked, but she was shaken by her ability to call upon the power of the woman in the stone as much as by Millard's threat.

'No, you are not. You were my betrothed before you took that vow.'

'We'll let the lawyers in Scraal resolve it, then, shall we? I made a sacred commitment which my father should not have permitted if he had already betrothed me, but I had not accepted any such betrothal!'

Frustration, fury and fear made it difficult for her to keep her voice low and she felt rather than saw Moss's swift glance in her direction. In truth she had no idea whether her father had the right to accept a bride price for her without telling her – it was not usually done but that did not make it illegal. She touched the stone in her artefact pouch. She could have killed Millard. She did not know how she had commanded the stone into bringing forth the one memory she could use and she did not know if she could do it again, but what she did know was that she was not powerless in the face of her father's scheming and this spoilt man's manipulation.

She added in a quieter voice, 'We will talk about this again, but I do not want to marry you.'

'You forget, sweet Nela, that what you want has nothing to do with it. I have paid for you and I will have you as my wife and you can accept it and cooperate – my demands on you will be trivial. You may even keep your servant if his attentions please you – I am not interested in what you choose to do for pleasure, but I need a wife for my own reasons and you are that wife. If you do not cooperate I can make things very difficult for you and for your "friend".'

Nela felt herself grow cold and her heart seemed to stop its rapid beating. 'What do you mean?'

'Perhaps it was the bondsman who caused my arm to burn – perhaps he pushed me in the fire. It happened too quickly for me to be sure, but as I think of it, I'm sure that must be the explanation, and a servant who harms a freeman can be killed with equanimity in any way that best suits the crime.'

On the other side of the fire Nela felt Moss's own stillness. She did not know what to say, though now she thought of it, she knew that what Millard said was true. Bondsmen were put to death all the time for more minor infringements of the laws of Scraal. Nela had promised on her honour as a non-woman to give Moss her protection. What could she do?

'That had nothing to do with Moss. He tried to help you,' she said with as much authority as she could muster.

'Moss – you know that bondsman's name? Nela, this just becomes more and more charming.' He smiled a predator's smile which she had never seen before that day. 'There are times, my sweet Nela, when all one can do is to acquiesce gratefully to the inevitable. "Moss", I would like some more restorative now.'

Nela could not attempt to meet Moss's eyes as he served her odious future husband. She wanted to cry and would not permit herself. She touched the stone, warm and dangerous, in her artefact pouch. She was not powerless. She should remember that.

TWENTY-ONE

Twenty days after the Horde had left the Hearthfields there was still no news of their fate. Jerat became a man, reaching his sixteenth summer after the tenth day of their absence.

What should have been a day for rejoicing and feasting was instead a grim little celebration clouded by uncertainty. The Teller Priest did his best, but all the good spears had gone with the Horde, as had the Horde's flint-maker and the ceremonial painter. Nonetheless the Teller Priest contrived a manhood spear of sorts from some of the sacred wood from the lightning tree. Some of the old men of the Dependency came as witnesses and drinking companions for Jerat's Spear Day. It was good of them and they did justice to the ale the Teller Priest had brewed for the occasion. Heron and a couple of the no-men were also invited to swell the ranks of drinkers, though it was not customary. The men who had once been warriors bowed to him and whispered charms from their own long-lost Dependencies to bring him the fortune in battle that they had lacked.

Even so, Jerat longed for the company of Verre and Hela and Keran, the Chief and even those older members of the Brood Trove who could welcome him into their shared adulthood. He wanted them to know that Jerat, Chiefson of the second quarter, was at last a man, but most of all he wished with all his heart that he knew that Verre was alive and that she would live to see him carry his spear as a man.

The lack of news worried even the children.

'What can have happened to the carrier birds?' Rin fretted. As a babe he had loved their gentle cooing and always watched their comings and goings with fascination. Now his interest had a greater urgency.

'The people of High Ridge must have shot them, I suppose – it would be difficult, but not impossible if they were on the lookout for the birds.' Then, on seeing Rin's lip tremble, Jerat added hastily, 'Or perhaps they just lost their way – some are quite young, they may have got confused.'

Ro, sitting in the shade, propped against the outer wall of the Hall, laughed unpleasantly.

'They dead, Rin,' he said. 'Chief dead too.'

Jerat felt his blood flow like ice in the river, and shivered.

'What do you mean Ro? How can you know?'

It was a dark stranger who looked out of his brother's eyes.

'I know,' he said simply, and Jerat believed him.

'And Verre?' The words were out before he could stop them.

'Not Verre,' Ro answered. 'But many others.' He pulled a face and briefly looked like Ro again. Jerat, who was about to put his arm around him, drew back when Ro said flatly, 'I see them at night. They call to me.'

'Whatever do you mean?' Jerat looked in vain to see his little brother in the small broken figure who spoke so bluntly of death and whose toneless voice so frightened him.

Ro looked at Jerat wearily. 'I belong with them and they call for me.'

'Oh, Ro!' Jerat said, and this time did not allow himself to be repelled by the coldness in Ro's voice. He held him in his arms and hugged him until gradually the boy responded and began to cry, ordinary childhood tears.

'My poor, poor Ro, and it's all my fault,' Jerat murmured, and held Ro until the sobbing ceased and the child, warm and vulnerable again, fell into an exhausted, natural sleep in Jerat's arms.

Rin had run to find the Teller Priest, who arrived a few moments later.

'He sees the dead in his dreams,' Jerat whispered over the sleeping child's head. 'Is there nothing you can do to help him?'

The Teller Priest squatted down beside Jerat in the pool of golden afternoon sunlight, a light that touched everything with almost sacred significance. He stroked Ro's hair gently so as not to wake him and shook his head.

'It is not a sickness, Jer. Ro has left part of his soul on death's shore and he knows the faces of all others who walk there. I have heard of this – it is in one of the tales – and there is no cure but death itself. He is not wholly with us.'

'I will not let Zeron, the Dark Daughter of the Night, take him.' Jerat had trouble talking because of the choking presence of some powerful emotion he did not know how to fight. His words came out in a savage whisper.

'The Dark Daughter does not own death, Jerat – it will come to us all, and we have brought Ro back from the brink when we ought not to have done. We hold him here against nature, against the will of our own Zerat as much as anything else. I don't think we served Zeron's will when we did it.'

'I will not give him up.' Jerat was fierce. 'I will not give him up to death. I will find a way to make him whole again. He is my brother.'

The Teller Priest sighed. 'Jerat, be careful. You cannot bend the world to your will. Some things must be accepted, like rain at harvest and sour milk. It is my mistake. I should have let him die.'

'How could it be right to have let him die?'

'He is paying a price for living that he might not want to pay.'

'I thought you were a priest, not just a dye-man and trader! Don't talk to me about price! This is my brother we're talking about, and I will make him well.'

The Teller Priest did not speak for a while but softly stroked the hair of the sleeping child.

'There are things a Teller Priest cannot do and there are things that even a Chief's son cannot do, and for us both there are things that we should not do.' He smiled and got to his feet. 'And there are things we both have to do. Put Ro down, Jerat. There is work to be done.'

Jerat reluctantly manoeuvred his sleeping brother off his lap, irritated by the hint of rebuke in the Priest's manner. Though he went about his business, he could not forget the darkness in his brother's face or his claim to know that the Chief was dead.

Each morning after a wakeful night attending his brother, Jerat asked Ro to tell him of the dead, and each day Ro listed in a dull voice the names of all the fallen – those who'd died in skirmishes with their enemy, those who had been killed for attempted desertion and those who had died in fights over women or plunder, and even those women who had died in childbirth in the surrounding areas and an old man who had died in his sleep in a farmstead half a day's walk away. From Ro's dull delineation of killings Jerat was able to deduce quite a lot about the fate of the Horde. They had engaged several times already, but lost fewer men than their opponents. Jerat knew that because Ro listed the dead of old Galet's men, a long list. Jerat was grateful their names called no faces to mind.

On the sixth morning after Jerat's discovery of Ro's terrible gift, Ro was particularly subdued.

'What have you seen?' Jerat asked abruptly – in these conversations he tried to forget that he spoke with a child, his own beloved brother. He dealt with what he was told by imagining he spoke with some ancient truth-speaker of the kind that figured in the Priest's stories. He did not know if the conversations upset Ro – it was hard to tell, and Jerat did not want to think about Ro, he wanted the information too badly. He needed to know if Avet still lived, for if he had died there was some hope for them all, a distant chance of holding his quarter together. If Avet took charge of the Hall they would all be sent away, and Jer was sure that Avet would not permit Jerat the comfort of caring for his brothers; he would take pleasure in dividing them, and without Jerat to care for him what would happen to Ro? Each morning he whispered his request in secret while Rin slept, and in a voice so low that even the sharp ears of the Teller Priest would not know what he did. Jerat knew in his heart that the Priest would not approve of his questions any more than he approved of Ro knowing the answers.

Ro's eyes glinted in the dimness of their quarterage where little of the dawn light infiltrated the sturdy construction of the walls and bolted door. Jerat always wanted to ask after those he knew and most cared for but he made it a rule that he should wait for Ro's response. In the moment between question and answer his guts always twisted with dread in case Ro spoke of Verre or Hela or Moorat. Each morning he had to fight down his agitation and fear – each day it seemed to get worse.

'I saw Lirian,' Ro said, his usual toneless delivery tainted with fear.

'Lirian? The girl this war was all about – why, is she dead?' Jerat asked, unable to suppress his relief that the first name Ro had spoken was not one dearer to him.

'She told me on death's shore that they came for her, Avet and others of his quarter. They come to Chief Galet's Tier House all drunk on plundered ale and full of themselves but the Chief will not give her over to them. He curses them and his Teller sends vicious curses to doom them all but Avet ignores it. He laughs in Galet's Teller Priest's face and steps forward to fight the Chief, but Galet is old and another comes in his place, a big man, a head taller than Avet. He is Heneien, Lirian's cousin and Galet's chosen champion. They fight until the sun goes down and all watch. In the beginning everyone is shouting and making a noise but then the shouting stops and all are silent as Avet kills Heneien little bit by little bit and the brave man's blood stains the Hearthfield. Then, though weary, Avet, gory still with her cousin's blood, drags Lirian from the Tier House by her beautiful hair. She weeps and cries out for help and for mercy but no one dares stand in Avet's way because he has killed Heneien. Most of the women try to run and to take the young of Galet's Brood Trove with them. There is much screaming and the women do not get away. Avet's Horde make them watch as Avet kills Lirian.' Ro paused and continued in a calmer voice. 'She was no Chief's daughter, no Brood brat schooled to pain and combat: she knew nothing of weapons or self-defence. She did not even raise her belt-knife against him. Avet killed her slowly, bit by bit, like he killed Heneien, so that her blood flowed by the flicker of firelight and her screams filled the Horde with dread. He did it out of respect for the old Chief and out of envy because she was not his.'

Jerat remembered the beautiful lively girl he had spoken to at the festival and felt a sudden choking sense of loss.

'Avet shamed her and made her suffer before the Horde,' Ro said.

Jerat, who did not want to hear any more, heard himself saying, 'And who else did you see on death's shore last night?'

'Chief Galet with his throat cut,' Ro said, 'and –'

'How many?' Jerat said quickly, before Ro could list all the names, for if it had been anyone else Jerat knew, the name would have been first.

'Fifty men, two men-women, a no-man and a stallion,' Ro said, his voice dull and emotionless.

'Not Hela?'

'Not Hela.'

'Were they of Galet?'

'Yes,' Ro said, and Jerat almost rejoiced because it sounded as if the Horde were victorious and that those he most loved still lived. Then the great door creaked open as the Teller Priest let in the sun, and Jerat saw what he could not have known from the dull calm of his voice – Ro was terrified, his eyes wide in a face grey with suffering.

'Zerat forgive me! What have you seen, Ro?' Jerat asked softly, his need to know suddenly evaporating at the horror he saw in the boy's face. He hugged Ro to him.

'Blood and hurt and men and women in bits,' the boy whispered.

'Poor Ro, poor Ro. I'm sorry I made you tell, Ro, I'm sorry – forgive me.'

'You must stop this.' The Teller Priest pulled back the privacy curtain so that sunlight almost blinded Jerat and his eyes watered in the brightness. 'You are forcing him to remember dreams that were better forgotten. It is not kind, Jerat.'

'They are not dreams, Priest. I am sure he sees truly.'

'That is often the way with dreams, Jer. But even so, if you love your brother you should let him be and let the morning drive away the night fears. It is wrong to force him to remember and, if you let him, he will forget as you forget your dreams. I can't believe you want knowledge more than you want his peace of mind.'

'I need to know if Avet lives, if Verre lives.' Jerat knew that he sounded stubborn, awkward, selfish, but he could not help himself.

'You will see both soon enough. The Horde saved one carrier bird at least. They have victory, though the Chief is dead, as is Galet and his granddaughter, the reluctant bride, Lirian. Avet is leading the Horde home – they will be back within ten days.'

'Then it is all as Ro told me. He really has walked the shores of death in dreams!'

The Teller Priest was silent for a moment.

'It is as I feared: he pays a far higher price for his life than most would want to pay.'

Twenty-two

Nela waited until Millard had collapsed into something between sleep and stupor, then got quietly to her feet and crept to where Moss tended the fire. He looked up as she approached.

'What did you do?' His tone was hard.

She hesitated before she answered; it was not easy to explain. 'I don't know exactly, but I used the stone to do what the woman of the stone once did, and I made flame grow.'

'I don't think you should have used the stone as a weapon.' He did not look at her but stared instead at the heart of the fire so that the light played on his face like demons of Zeron dancing.

'I did not mean to,' she began, but that was not true – she had meant to use the stone as a weapon, and so she finished less dishonestly, 'I mean – I intended to do something to save you – I did not know what.'

Moss nodded. 'I thank you for the thought, but I

am in serious trouble now. Millard could have me killed – though I would imagine they wouldn't pass sentence until my usefulness here is over.' He sighed. 'I don't understand what you did.'

Nela was anxious to explain. 'I remembered how the woman of the stone made the tree burn and somehow it just happened. I did what she had done. Do you think the woman herself is somehow trapped here in this stone? That she helped me?'

It was not a happy thought. Nela reached for the artefact pouch containing the stone. Although she tried to touch it only through her cloak, by mischance her finger touched its warm surface and she felt herself disappearing under the burden of memory: she flung herself to the ground, certain that she would otherwise fall. And then she saw another fireside through another's eyes.

The Wandering Man is at our fireside wearing the unusual mix of clothing that marks him out. His skin is dark as mine but he wears woven cloth like the Bear-men's and something that shimmers like water when he moves, something that is the colour of the sky and is called 'silk'. He claims it is made by worms, but I know he is teasing. I want to touch it to see if it feels like water, but I am afraid of him because he wears other things too – linked bones and rare polished stones and fine pottery amulets, made to look like living things, and many finger rings of some hard stuff that is not bone but made in the earth in faraway places. He wears his long hair in many braids and it grows to his knees, which is the most hair I have ever seen on one of us Night Hunters.

He calls out my name at the fireside to sing a song of celebration for a journey ended, which though it is not a song of power requires a feat of memory and makes me nervous. It is hot by the fire and in the shifting flames my family sitting round the open fire seem strange and far away, but I plant myself in the ground as Moon-eye taught me and concentrate on the magic of sound and I draw it out from the belly of the earth up and through my own belly and let it out as easy as breath itself. I do it right – I know I do, and it makes the space by the fire sad and happy at the same time, which is hard. No one speaks for a long time, and I am afraid that I have done wrong, until the Wandering Man turns and dips his head at my mother as a mark of honour and says that he has a gift for me of great value. He says lots of other things – complicated things like the words of the oldest songs full of curly sentences that get tangled up in themselves, and only after a long while grow clear with a plain meaning. I grow tired of all the words and stop listening, watching instead the way the flame lights the liquid stuff of his garments and I can watch the way the shadows fall in the flowing folds of fabric for ever. I sit by the fire unnoticed while he talks to my mother, and then everyone is looking at me again and I wonder if he has asked me to sing again and I missed it. I stand with difficulty because my foot has gone to sleep. He asks me to give him something to hold the gift he has for me, something that is precious to me, and I can't for the moment think of anything.

'Have you no special finger ring or brooch that you treasure?' he asks me, and though I have a small shell brooch that Sky gave me, that does not seem to be what he is asking for. Then I remember the stone, the polished stone I have had since before birth, the thing for which I was named, which I have always held when I am afraid, and I dig it out of my pouch and give it to him. He takes it from me, smiling, and moves away. My mother comes to me and pats my hand and says in her soft voice that I love to hear because it has a special kind of happy music in it: 'You sang well – you will be the best Singer the tribe has ever had, perhaps that our people have ever had. You are truly touched by the Womanface.' Then the Wandering Man returns and hands me my stone, wrapped in a scrap of the beautiful blue silk, and I can't believe that I can touch the silk at last and I stroke its smoothness in amazement, until the Wandering Man laughs and says that the gift is what lies within. It feels as though all of my assembled tribe forget to breathe and crane forward to see the thing that I'm holding. I slip my stone clumsily from its cloth and hold its rounded shape as I always do in the palm of my hand. I smile because it is my special stone and I am about to put it back in my pouch when the Wandering Man stops me.

'It is your stone and it is not your stone. Long ago I collected water from a sacred spring far, far from here. All things washed in that water have a kind of special life. I have washed your stone in that water – that washing is my gift to you. Your stone has a kind of life now and it remembers all you have known while you have held it, it knows all that you are and it will keep all that you are safe inside itself, ready for when you have need of it. It is a thing of such preciousness but a thing that none but you and yours can use. You must sing a note to waken it and then this stone will be yours for ever.'

I have never heard that any thing could make stone live, but I can tell by the way my mother and Moon-eye are standing, rapt and anxious, that this is true and important. So I hold the pebble in my hand and think. Every thing has its own special note that holds its secret shape; it is its true name and finding it is part of the Singer's art. Moon-eye has taught me many of the secret names of our home walks but there are others that I have to find for myself and this is one. It is true that even holding my stone I know that it is different and I am different for having it, because to have a stone made to live by the gift of the Wandering Man is a very special thing and Sky will punch me harder for it and some of the girls will pinch me, and I will have to try not to mind because one day I will be a great Singer and that is a powerful thing and I have to be humble for it is the gift of the Goddess, the Womanface herself, and given by her.

I try not to panic and to keep breathing as Moon-eye has taught me, breathing from the heart of the earth, and I listen as Moon-eye taught me. I cannot hear the crackling fire or the movements of the tribe, the old ones' coughs and the shuffling of limbs. It all fades away and I hear only what I need to hear and the stone yields to me its name. And when I sing it I can feel the hairs rise on my neck and my skin feels like fire and the sound I make is loud enough to ape the thunder. The stone burns my palm like the heart of the fire and I smile and the Wandering Man smiles too.

TWENTY-THREE

Rin saw them first, the distant line of the returning Horde. Jerat was busily organising the feast of return and victory so could not run to them as Rin did. He was arguing with old men about the number of animals roasting in the many pits in the Hearthfields when they arrived. People of the Dependency kept coming throughout the day as news as the imminent arrival of the Horde had travelled through Lakeside. Jerat wiped greasy hands across his face and paused to listen as the Horde met those left behind. He did not want to see Avet and face what had to be faced. He had been thinking of what he would have to do all the long days since he had learned of the Chief's death. He did not want to do what had to be done.

The Teller Priest greeted the victors with proper dignity – Jerat could hear the singsong voice he used for formal occasions. The words 'joy' and 'victory' wafted his way and he heard the Horde and waiting crowd roar as the Priest had intended. Jerat turned from his duties to look for Verre. Seeing her again was the only joy he was likely to find that day. He found her easily among the assembled fighters, the painted remnants of her quarter's colours still evident on her face, though much overlaid by grime. She looked essentially unchanged, though her upper arm was bandaged with a scrap of cloth and her eyes were weary. Her face lit up when she saw him.

'Jerat! You have grown – how like a man you look.' Jerat winced at the reminder that she still thought him a child, that she had forgotten his Spear Day, but this was not the time to argue – he had news for her, though whether it would please her or break her heart he did not know.

'Ro is awake,' Jerat said. Verre smiled a wide smile of surprise and joy, grasped his hand briefly in a warrior's embrace and rushed away to find Ro. Dare he follow? Someone from the Dependency was sobbing quietly as they realised that not all the Horde was complete. Jerat turned and ran after Verre to explain about Ro. After what she had gone through it would be better if she did not face that alone.

Ro and Rin were together in the cool of the Hall: the only people not outside greeting the triumphant Horde. Suddenly Jerat felt that perhaps he ought not to be there at a private moment. The great door was only slightly ajar so that he could see Verre standing in a narrow wedge of sunlight while he stayed, hovering, in the shadows. Rin, seeing Verre, left his brother's side and fell into her arms, sobbing.

'My love,' Verre said and her words came in a kind of a sob. She hugged Rin and let him cry on her shoulder until he had done and then turned him gently aside to go to Ro.

'Ro! My Ro!' She picked him up, in spite of her injured arm, and held him to her in a fierce embrace, and Jerat could see that for the moment Ro was more like the boy he thought they'd lost than he had been since his waking.

'Verre! I've been so frightened!' Verre and Ro did not need Jerat to explain anything – they were alive, that was all that mattered.

'Jerat, come out of the shadows. I would have all my sons with me. I didn't think I'd see any of you again.'

He felt a little foolish lurking in the doorway as if he had no right to be there.

'Oh, my boys,' she said softly, and held them all tightly, though blood seeped through the dressing of her arm and she was clearly exhausted. She held them as if by will alone and the remaining strength of her arms she could keep them from ever being parted. After her experience in the war with Chief Galet, it seemed that she no longer had the energy to pretend to be other than the true mother of Ro and Rin. The boys responded as though they had never doubted that she was theirs. Jerat stayed with them for as long as he could, but he could hear Avet speaking and so he hurried reluctantly outside to perform his duties as feast organiser.

Avet waited until the greetings were over before announcing the death of the Chief. He had changed, Jerat could see that at once. He looked older and less arrogant. The Horde shushed the crowd when he began to speak, so it was clear that they, at least, accepted him as leader.

'In accordance with the wishes of the Chief, our father, the Hall, the Herd, the Horde and the Brood Trove are mine. I hereby free the Horde of all obligations, and the wives of all four quarters may be free to remarry. The youngest of my Brood brothers may stay until such time as they are ready to join the Hearth Guard. Zerat has given us victory and the lands of Galet of High Ridge Dependency have given us many riches, many no-men to serve in the Hall, many daughters of Galet to serve as new wives for those who have given the Horde of their best. In the morning the Priest will reconsecrate the Heart of the Home, and those of you wishing to serve me in my Horde will make an Allegiance of Dependency.' Avet's eyes sought out the Teller Priest, who nodded. 'For now, take your ease and eat, for our good Priest has prepared a feast to welcome home the brave men and men-women of our Dependency.'

There was the anticipated, necessary roar of appreciation and Jerat felt only the slightest resentment that his part in preparing for the feast had not been acknowledged, though it was impossible that Avet could yet know his part in maintaining the Hall. The smell of roasting beef filled the air, and new-baked bread and the Teller's ale: he took some satisfaction from that.

Jerat waited until Avet had finished eating and had drunk deeply of the good late summer ale before approaching his Brood brother. Avet was surrounded by the younger brothers and men of the Horde who were busily trying to remind him of their right to take a wife from the plundered women of Galet. Jerat carried his plain spear as proudly as he could to the place where Avet was seated.

Avet's eyes gleamed with old malice when he saw Jerat and the spear.

'Avet, Brood brother, Chief,' Jerat began reluctantly, and those of the Brood Trove and the Horde, filling the broad space outside the Hall, all stopped their drinking and their chattering to look at him.

'Jerat,' Avet answered evenly. 'You have come with a request for a wife?'

Jerat felt himself colouring, and the men laughed more raucously than the poor joke merited. It had always been so with Jerat's father, who had always believed himself one of the most amusing men alive on the strength of the Horde's sycophancy. Jerat could see more clearly that the old Chief had picked the one son of all the Brood who most resembled him.

'I have come to beg a favour,' Jerat continued with difficulty. He had more pride than he had realised, and even in his imagination he had not expected this to be so hard. He took a gulp of air. 'I have come to humbly request that Ro, Rin, myself and Guardsman Verre be allowed to remain in this Hall as part of your Hearth Guard.' There, he had said it. There was a long pause, during which Jerat's face seemed to burn like the flames of the cook fire, and then Avet laughed.

'You think me a fool?'

'No,' Jerat stuttered in startled reply.

'Well, surely only a fool with a gut full of too much of the Teller's good ale would let an old enemy sleep in his Hall, armed as one of his trusted Hearth Guard? Only a fool would let a veteran fighter and brothers loyal to an enemy remain under his roof.' There was muted laughter from someone of Avet's coterie and Avet gave the man a look of irritation. 'There is blood between us, Jerat – blood we share and blood you spilled. I think you know which blood I count as dearer.' He paused. 'I tell you what a wise man does. A wise man sends his old enemy to a Hall and a Dependency far away – to assist in running the lands of Galet, perhaps, and he sends one of the much-loved Brood brothers born of the same quarter still further afield, and the veteran fighter somewhere else, perhaps to the Horde of Chief Larace in the farthest reaches of Lakeside, and the weakest of the Brood brothers he keeps close by, vulnerable and dependent, as hostage to the good and loyal behaviour of the rest.'

'That is a refusal, then,' said Jerat, trying to fight the urge to lower his spear and plunge it at Avet's heart. He stayed his hand. If he should die in some pointless vengeful gesture Ro and Rin would lack his protection.

'That, dear Brood brother, is an emphatic "no" – take yourself and your excuse for a spear of manhood from my sight. You will leave in the morning.'

Jerat bowed stiffly and backed away. To keep from trembling he gripped his spear until his knuckles were white.

Verre met him by the cook fire. She took in the expression on his face and the crude spear in his hand in one glance.

'Jerat, I am sorry that I had forgotten that you had

come of age. I have nothing to give you that is my own, but here, have the cloak of the wife of the second quarter. I will not let Avet's bride have it because I wove it myself and have worn it too long to give it to anyone but you.' She smiled and he accepted the richly coloured thick woollen cloak with something like awe.

'It is better than my spear,' he said wryly.

'Don't judge a spear by its decoration, Jerat,' she said, and took it from him, hefting it above her shoulder. 'It is not beautiful, it is true, but it is well balanced.' She inspected the haft. 'And it is carved, if not well, then powerfully, with many symbols of magic that the Teller Priest knows and a few others I haven't even heard of. I hope you were not ungracious.'

Jerat felt ashamed. 'Perhaps I was not as grateful as I might have been.'

'Do not underestimate the Teller Priest, Jerat – he is wiser than many people realise. Even the old Chief knew that, and for all his faults he was no fool.' Then she added sadly, 'The Teller Priest was right about Ro, too. I can see that he's a shadow of the boy he was, a darker, sadder shadow: he is much changed.'

'I asked Avet if he would allow us to stay here together,' Jerat said, switching from that very uncomfortable subject abruptly. Verre laughed without humour.

'You could not have expected him to say yes. He will send us as far away as possible. He will keep near him only those he can dominate, and you will never be one of those. He is enough like his father, and his dam too, come to that – I never liked her.'

'What will we do?' Jerat asked for a moment, allowing his uncertainty and vulnerability to colour his words. Verre shrugged her reply.

'We could try to find work as part of a distant Hearth Guard – I have many contacts, but no one will take us as Ro is now.'

'What if I told you he could see the dead – or at least those who had just died?'

Verre put her hand to her mouth in involuntary horror. 'Zerat's heart! Tell me that isn't true.'

Jerat looked anguished. 'It was why I knew you were safe and how I know the names of all those who you killed – Ro saw them all while they waited at death's shore.'

Tears sprang to Verre's eyes. 'My poor, poor Ro. You must not tell anyone else of this, Jerat. Too many people would think him cursed or touched by Zeron, the Dark Daughter, and want his death. Promise that whatever happens you will keep silent about this.'

Surprised by the vehemence of her reaction, Jerat promised. It seemed Verre, his mother, the former wife of the second quarter and veteran fighter, had even less idea of what to do next than he did. He, at least, had an idea, though a desperate one. He returned to his job of supervising the preparation and serving of the feast, wondering if he dared to do the only thing he could think of to save Ro and keep the wife and children of the second quarter together.

TWENTY-FOUR

Jerat's first instinct was to run; to take Rin and Ro and leave. Verre would come with him, he knew, and perhaps they could find a place somewhere far away, safe from Avet's malice. In these early days of Avet becoming Chief his control on the Dependency would be weak and it ought to be easy to leave the lands under Avet's nominal control without him noticing. The problem was he could not run straight away, as he felt obliged to help the Teller Priest in readying the Hall for its new Chief and, in any case, if he were to put his plan into action he could not leave the Tier House for several days.

After the meal when everything had been cleared and most of the Horde had established a place to sleep, and all of the Brood Trove young were sleeping, Jerat assisted the Teller Priest in readying the Heart of the Home for use. They lit the new fires in the pottery stoves. They were of the most innovative invention, of clay so strong it could withstand the heat of the cook fire, and formed to carry away the smoke out through the roof and keep the Heart of the Home warm and clean of any foulness. The Priest chanted a song in a sonorous bass, which he claimed would bring good luck, and they swept and oiled the wooden floor until it glowed golden as honey in the lamplight.

'Avet will bring his new brides here tomorrow,' the Priest said conversationally, as though Jerat was not about to be made Hearthless, as though his world had not been turned upside down. 'And I believe there is a babe too.'

'Not Avet's?'

'No, one of the most beautiful of Galet's grand-daughters had the care of her sister's child – everyone else in the family being dead. As a sign of good faith Avet has agreed to raise it as his own, the first of the new Brood Trove.'

'I wish this was not happening. I wish things could be as they were before Ro's accident,' Jerat said. He wished too that he could have had the ownership of such a Tier House – he knew now, after his time as steward with the Teller Priest, that he would have made a good Chief – but he said nothing of that.

'Everything changes – that is a condition of life, Jerat, and a wise man changes too, keeps pace with the times. It is foolish to wish life other than it is.'

'Will you stay and work for Avet?'

'He will not ask me. He knows that I am a friend of yours and for some reason he fears you above all of the Brood.'

'Why? I have only just come of age.'

'You have bested him too many times in spite of

your youth. He is no more a fool than his father, and perhaps he sees the fire in you that burns sometimes in your eyes – your passion. I know what you did today – it was bravely done, if fruitless.'

'I have to find a way to cure Ro – then at least we may find a place somewhere together.'

'I've told you, Jerat, if your ears would hear me – there is no cure but death for what ails Roat.'

'So you say,' said Jerat without conviction. He ignored the sharp look the Priest gave him and followed the old man down the thatch ladder. The scent of oiled wood and spices still lingered in his hair.

'Do the Night Hunters still hunt in this part of the forest?' Jerat asked. In all his trips with Verre he had seen so few signs of them that he feared they might have changed their hunting grounds. From the ladder of the Tier House the treeline of the mountains could be clearly seen, and it was the most natural thing in the world to ask about that which so interested the Teller Priest. It seemed that he too was glad of the change of subject and answered eagerly.

'They do not stay in any place long – they have their seasonal camps. At this time of year they live closest to us, and at the egg moon – that is an auspicious time for them – they will hunt in a large group for deer and boar.'

'How?'

'Oh, they have bows which are quite as good as ours, but at the egg moon they use the song of the Singer to enchant the beasts and will take many back to their camp for the feasting.'

'Is that what the old Singer told you?'

'Moon-eye? Yes. They have a new Singer now, a young girl whose power is strong as the moon herself – or so Moon-eye says. The girl was once her acolyte, and Moon-eye is very proud of her.'

'Is she dangerous?'

'You should know better than to listen to all the folk tales that the ignorant claim for truth. The Night Hunters are gentle people, they take only what they need from the land. They think us greedy and cruel for making the earth bear barley for us year after year. They think we will exhaust the earth. Their power is all to do with preserving the bounty of the ground: no one should fear that.'

Jerat listened, but his thoughts had already moved on.

'Avet wants to split us up. I will stay near here to keep an eye on Ro – would you take Rin wherever you are going, and Verre too? I could follow you later – when I find a way to cure Ro.'

The Teller Priest gave Jerat a searching look.

'There is no cure for Ro – but I will take Rin with me as an apprentice. I will take good care of him, Jer, don't worry, but I will have to leave soon, before Avet has time to throw me out and take my dye stuffs. I buried the most valuable of my trade goods, but Avet will expect that. I will speak to Verre tonight. I'm sorry, I do not think I could manage Ro too, even with your help. Avet will kill you if you stay here – perhaps you should move on anyway, and find a place in a Hearth Guard of your own choosing. You are a good fighter, they tell me – maybe better than Avet, if less ruthless.'

'I am unblooded, thanks to Verre, and I will never leave Ro.' Jerat spoke angrily. He was surprised by the Teller's unexpected pragmatism; he had expected more loyalty from him. 'Will you leave me word of where you will go?'

'I will travel east – as I've done before, staying in all the major Tier Houses along the way, telling my tales and trading my wares and maybe working for a season when I choose. It is the life I've always lived, before I settled here. It is a good life and I think it will suit Rin, if not Verre.'

'When Ro is well I will find you and take Rin back.'

'Jerat –'

Jerat did not want to hear the Teller's opinion again so he interrupted.

'I need to see Verre for a moment. Zerat keep you.'

Verre was with Hela, a little apart from the drunken men. She quickly realised that Jerat wanted to speak to her in private and, leaving Hela to rejoin the Horde, walked with Jerat across the Hearthfields.

'I have spoken with the Teller Priest. He is leaving to take up his old travelling life. He will take Rin, and you too if you will go with him. He is leaving soon – in a few nights, I think,' said Jerat.

'What of Ro?'

'I have not given up hope that he might be whole again. Anyway, I will stay here near the Tier House, hidden – maybe in the forest so I can keep an eye on him. Will you stay with Rin?'

'Jerat, Avet will kill you if he finds you here. You go with Rin and the Teller – he has much to teach you that will be of use. I should stay with Ro. I know the forest well and Avet is wary of my fighting skills – he is less likely to have me killed should I be discovered.'

'Rin needs you, Verre. He needs you to teach him how to be a warrior, to learn how to be of a Hearth Guard, all the things you taught me. I will come and find you when Ro is well again. Don't worry, I'm not so easy to kill – and anyway, I will stay out of the way of Avet. Trust me, Verre. I can do what is needful.'

She touched his face, briefly, sadly. 'I have been luckier than you can know to see my children. I cannot bear to see you hurt, but you are a man now and I cannot protect you from all that means. I will go with Rin if that is what you want, but I do not think Ro will ever be well again.'

'Thank you, Verre. I will be better for knowing that you and Rin are safe, and when Ro is fit we can all offer service with some Hearth Guard and earn the gift of a Hall of our own.'

It was the egg moon, and the light from it illuminated Verre's sad smile.

'You dream, Jer,' she said chidingly as she might have done to a young boy. 'But I will pray to Zerat to keep you safe. Don't do anything foolish. You go back. I want to walk awhile.' She turned away from him and something that might have been tears glistened on her cheek; it was hard to tell, and he'd rather not think of Verre's tears – he had to be strong and brave and decisive as he had never been before. He had no time to weep.

When Jerat crept into the curtained sleep space of the second quarter, he found his spear, his bow and arrows, his sling and small bag of shot and the cloak that Verre had given him, and woke Rin.

'Rin, I need you to help me. Be very quiet!'

Rin did not question Jerat, but rubbed his eyes and unwound himself silently from his blankets. They both glanced at Ro, but since the war had ended he slept better, his nights less disturbed by dreams of the dead. Rin carefully placed his blanket over his brother's exposed legs and followed Jerat into the open.

'Can you get me some rope from the byre without being seen?'

Rin nodded, his face watchful and serious.

'Find me a good length. I will explain later. I'll meet you at the gate of the first quarter as soon as you can get there.'

Jerat fastened the cloak around his shoulders. He was grateful for the brightness of the moon, because what he was about to do was risky and foolish in the extreme and doing it in full darkness would have been more than foolish.

He waited for his brother at the gate as they had agreed; he felt sick with apprehension. Only the fear of what would happen to Rin without Ro, whom he loved above all else, could persuade Jerat that it was right to drag Rin into this wild, desperate scheme.

'What are we doing?' Rin asked, excitement and fear evident in his breathless whisper.

'We are to go into the forest to bait a trap.'

'In the forest at night?' He sounded terrified. 'But it's too late to hunt, and anyway it's the time of the Night Hunters and the Dark Daughter, not us.' Rin was clearly dismayed, and Jerat did not think what he had to say next would reassure him.

'Rin, we are going to try to trap a Night Hunter. When I give the word you are going to run through the forest making as much noise as possible.'

Rin nodded furiously, probably out of desire to please, but his small body was rigid with tension.

'It will be all right, Rin. The Night Hunters will not hurt us. The Teller Priest says that all the stories about their evil nature are untrue. You trust the Priest, don't you?'

Rin shrugged and clutched his sling and bag of shot more tightly. He must have gone back to get them when he got the rope. Rin was no fool either.

'We will need to walk quietly and keep alert. Look for some sign of the Hunters and stay close until I tell you.'

'Why, Jerat? Why do you want to catch one of the evil ones?'

Jerat took a deep breath of the sweetly scented night air. It was cooler than the day, but not cold, and it smelled of all the things that he loved, the animals and the earth and the forest itself, and he realised with a sudden sense of loss that even if his scheme were to work, he would be an exile from all this for ever. He was as mad as old Brood brother Dravot, who, according to the Teller's tales, had lived four full turns of the year with an axe through his skull.

'I want to catch a Night Hunter because only one of the Dark Daughter's friends can make Ro well.'

Rin said nothing for a moment and then said softly, 'I don't think anyone can make Ro well – not as he was before.'

'I think a Night Hunter can, and anyway I have to try – what kind of brother would I be if I had an idea of how I could make him better and I didn't at least try?' Jerat was speaking more loudly than he should and he stopped abruptly. 'I'm sorry, Rin. It's not a good plan, I know, but it's the only plan I have. We cannot find a place anywhere with Ro as he is and I cannot imagine that Avet would be kind to him if he stayed here. We need to do something.'

'Is it true, then? Avet will send us away like the Brood brothers are saying? He'll separate us?'

'I think so, Rin. I think it's true, and I don't want that to happen, but this, what we're doing now, is a chance for us. It may not work – probably won't work, but whatever happens it is a secret and you mustn't tell anyone about it, not even Verre or the Teller Priest.'

'Or Ro?'

'No, not even Ro.'

He did not like to admit it, even to himself, but Jerat was more than a little afraid of the changed Ro and his ability to meet the dead – it put him too close to Zeron, the Dark Daughter, and if she were to know what they were doing she might very well not approve. The Dark Daughter. Jerat did not want to think of her or the offence he might be causing – who knew what such a being might do to wreak revenge? He pushed that thought from his mind.

They walked on into the deeper darkness of the forest. Thanks to Verre's early training both of them were able to track quite well, though Jerat was the more practised. Jerat had little idea of where the Night

196

Hunters might be, and as they walked aimlessly into the darkness without any tracks or knowledge to guide them, Jerat began to feel that his efforts were as pointless as he'd feared.

They spent the night searching for signs of the Hunters, but there were none. Rin had grown silent and fearful as they walked further into the forest. Distantly a wolf bayed and something scuttled away from them in an urgent rustling of undergrowth, too quickly for Jerat to be able to tell what it was.

'Can we stop, Jer? I'm too tired. Can we just rest?'

They had come too far to go home, and as they approached the heart of the ancient forest it became denser and darker so that even the bright silver blades of moonbeams could not pierce the foliage, and the low branches of the Great Trees grew gnarled and intertwined so that every step was a risk. It was dangerous to go on and dangerous to stay where they were. Jerat was tired too and he feared that Rin might lose an eye to the thorn thickets and spear-sharp branch tips.

'We can rest, but I think we should not rest here. I'll help you climb,' he said with as much confidence as he could manage – he did not want Rin to know that he was afraid. Jerat lifted Rin on to the lowest branch of the nearest Great Tree – its girth was greater than that of ten men and its height lost in the canopy of leaves. Rin was agile but tired, and Jerat watched him anxiously until he disappeared from view. Jerat was heavier but not so heavy that he could not still manage to haul himself up to the mid-level branches where each bough was broad enough to comfortably seat a grown man. Rin's teeth flashed a grin in the darkness.

'You took your time – you must be getting old and slow,' he said in a whisper.

'Well, I'm here now. Are you all right?' Jerat was too tired to banter.

'I'm cold.'

With some difficulty, because he was not comfortable with heights, Jerat managed to tie Rin and himself to the branch and cover them both with the warm woollen cloak. He did not know what dangers he might encounter in the forest trees, but he was determined to be ready for them. He forced himself to alert wakefulness, craning his neck to see the flint sparks of Zerat that were the stars. Above him the treetops swayed in the wind and the tree was alive with the whisper of leaves, speaking some language he didn't understand, by turns angry and confiding.

He woke with the dawn. He was ravenously hungry, thirsty, and, as was rapidly becoming clear, lost. He climbed higher, sending unknown birds scattering like seed corn until he reached the highest branches. Distantly he could see the smoke of the Tier House and wondered if Ro was afraid they had run away without him. Verre would know, though, Verre would know that he would never do that, and Ro would know that he was not dead – so they could give each other comfort. He had little enough comfort to offer Rin – no food, no water and the promise of a day in the forest: for Jerat was determined that he would not give up his quest after only one night. He hoped that the Teller Priest would wait for Rin's return before setting off on his new life. Jerat had not counted on taking Rin away from the Hall for more than a night. Anxieties crowded his thoughts and he pushed them all away. He had to be singleminded and courageous if he were to achieve his goal; he would be both.

They found plenty of berries, safe ones that Verre had given him as a child, and they ate those and drank from the swift-flowing stream. The berries only took the edge off their hunger, though they ate them all day and by the evening both of them had stomach cramps. They might have caught a rabbit, or even a small bird, but Jerat had no appetite for uncooked meat and he was loath to light a fire.

They spent the day looking for signs of the Hunters. In one place they found the remains of a burnt-leather cook pot and a trace of ashes, which had to belong to Hunters as no Lakesiders but Verre roamed the forest. After that they confined their searching to a broadly circular area around that site. When night fell and the forest was again filled with strange shadows, Jerat almost gave up hope. They had seen no further signs of the Hunters in any direction and Rin was almost too exhausted to stand. Then Jerat spotted something in the moonlight – a small shred of cured leather impaled on a branch. There was no way of knowing how long it had remained there, but perhaps not too long. The winds had been strong in the night and would perhaps have blown such a fragment of fabric away. He walked cautiously on before deliberately catching his red cloak on a thorn so that one thread became tangled on the branch. Disappointingly, the red was less bright in the moonlight, leached of all colour, like blood washed away, but he hoped that perhaps the Night Hunters saw things differently and it might still bait his trap.

He walked to a small clearing a little way further. It was bathed in the eldritch light of the Dark Daughter of the Night, Zeron, and there he carefully arranged the cloak in the semblance of something carelessly lost, though who could be rich enough to lose such a thing was beyond Jerat's imagination. He shivered. His stomach was a tight knot and he did not know if it was from fear or hunger. What if they did catch a Night Hunter – what if the Priest were wrong and it attacked them? He was shaking as if he had a fever. Gaining control of himself with difficulty, he gently pushed Rin into the bushes and followed behind. He scooped a handful of the mulched leaves and droppings that littered the ground and rubbed it on to his skin and Rin's, hoping to disguise their own odour with ordure – then they settled themselves to wait, again. As Jerat had already said – he had no better ideas.

TWENTY-FIVE

Jerat and Rin did not have long to wait. Within the space of heartbeats something walked towards them. Jerat held his hand over Rin's mouth. Rin's eyes were dark pools of panic, and Jerat feared that he would forget the discipline Verre had taught him and cry out. It took effort for Jerat himself to stay still, though it was the urge to crane his neck out of his hiding place that he had to fight. He was afraid, but so desperate to see a Night Hunter with his own eyes that waiting silently was agony. The something coming towards them walked noiselessly, like a shadow, or perhaps like one of Ro's dream-dead. It brought with it a faint scent of otherness, a musky, animal smell that was not unpleasant. Jerat tried to peer through the leaves without moving, straining in his eyes to see detail in the poor light. The creature was small, no larger than a child of the age of Acceptance, and dark as the earth. It was no child though, that was clear – its form was slender, fine like the best pottery. It walked with the assurance of a confident adult and all the grace of a deer. It wore trews of animal skin and a rough tunic of the same stuff. Its hair was dark as the night, heavy and straight, and fell to waist length, though it was tied back, away from its face. The figure carried a small bow and a pouch on its hip and walked barefoot.

Jerat held his breath and he knew that Rin did the same. He tried to imagine that he was one with the trees and the bushes, part of the forest, invisible as the foliage. The creature looked around suspiciously and sniffed the air like a wild dog. With long fingers it cautiously snatched at the cloak, smelled it, shook it out and wrapped it around its slight shoulders. The cloak was far too long, of course, but the creature folded it and tied it in such a way that it fell with a certain elegance to the ground.

Jerat should have pounced then, while the creature was distracted, but he could not move. He watched, fascinated, as the creature stooped; its movements were swift but precise and practised. Suddenly it turned so that its face in profile was silhouetted against the silver of the moon, and Jerat could not breathe: its form was delicate as a bird, but made Jerat think of flint, strong and sharp and black. Its face was so beautiful it made his chest ache with unexpected longing and paralysing fear. There was power in the very lineaments of the Hunter's face, and the Hunter was a woman, a woman such as Jerat had never seen. The moonlight briefly reflected in her eyes so that they shone with animal strangeness. He was sure that was the magic of Zeron, the Dark Daughter. Perhaps this was the famous Moon-eye, though surely she was too young to be the old Teller Priest's friend. She made a slight noise in her throat, deep down, like the resonant growl of animal and yet sweet and clear like the call of the summer bird. It made all the hairs of his neck prickle like thistle spines and he could not control a shiver that set all the leaves of his hiding place rustling. At the first quiver, at the very tip of the smallest leaf, the Hunter was gone. She turned and melted into the undergrowth with a speed of response that took Jerat unawares. He was a fool. He should have caught her while he had a chance.

He did not believe she could have gone far, so he signalled to Rin to pursue her as loudly as possible and then, ears straining for the sound of her inaudible steps, he followed too. He hoped that Rin's noisy pursuit might herd her towards him, might make her careless and easy to track and to trap. In her flight she seemed less powerful, too powerless to be the sorceress he both needed and feared.

Jerat felt like one bewitched, and he was very afraid. His body's noises were so loud in his ears that he had to pause for a moment to force himself to breathe to a regular rhythm and convince himself that his heart's pulse was not footsteps. He would not be distracted from his prey. Strangely his bewitching, if that was truly what it was, seemed to help him track the Hunter with unexpected ease. It was as if, having heard the strange music of her sigh, he could hear her breath. Perhaps it was coincidence, but he followed his instinct, his sense of her. Through the long night he trailed her, and as the dawn began to vanquish the darkness and the time of the Dark Daughter faded, his tenacity was rewarded by a flash of movement ahead. He stalked her softly, conscious that Rin's headlong thundering pursuit a way off was forcing her to move more swiftly than she wished. Rin had done well, keeping up his relentless, noisy tracking for hours. Although Jerat had expected Rin to be cooperative he had not expected him to be so effective or so tireless: Jerat had underestimated him.

The Hunter must have been tiring, for Jerat's own legs, strong and fit though he was, were beginning to feel the strain of the chase, and his side ached from his efforts. When the Hunter vanished from view, he was confident that she had gone to ground and never for a moment doubted that he would find her. She would be tired too, and he doubted that she knew how to disappear – for surely she would have used such power much earlier had it been at her disposal? He would search the whole forest until he had her in his grasp.

He saw her then, cowering and trembling, trying to hide in a thorn bush. He reached to grab her, his spear held ready to strike if need be, but her shoulder under his hand was fragile and he could feel her bones like kindling sticks that could be snapped by a child, and his fear dissolved and he felt only pity for a trapped wild bird and sorrow that it was his duty to capture her. He called to Rin who was hot and panting and deservedly triumphant, but he stopped him from touching her and wrapped her carefully in the red cloak before carrying her back through the forest.

He was afraid to sleep in case she escaped or put

him under some kind of spell, so he stayed awake while Rin slept. He tied up the Hunter, who closed her eyes and refused to look at him. He kept her in the shade of the trees as the sun rose higher in the sky and showed him her flint-sharp features in all their cruel-looking loveliness. He could believe she was evil. Evil could reside in beauty, he knew, in the poison berries and in the deadly flower known as the Daughter's Bloom which could kill the unwary, entranced by its perfect petals. He had heard fireside tales that the Night Hunters could not endure the light of Zerat's day so he was careful to place her in the green shadows of a Great Tree. It was easier to keep her captive when he could not see that face. She was so tiny he felt as if he had trapped a child. Rin was at least a head and shoulders taller than her, and her delicacy made Rin, who was a handsome child, look crudely made and brutish by comparison.

Jerat watched her for a long time – he did not know if she slept, but she lay very still. He checked her several times to be sure she still breathed. Rin was snoring so loudly there was little doubt as to his condition. Jerat was very hungry and after a couple of misfires managed to shoot one of the plump and ridiculously stupid birds that strayed too close to their small camp. He built a small fire and managed to light it with the stick and stone trick Verre had taught him long ago. He was pleased with himself, and cleaning and plucking the bird gave him something to do while he guarded his strange captive. His eyes were gritty with exhaustion and his head did not feel properly connected to his body.

The smell of burning meat woke Rin, and even the Hunter stirred. She would not accept the food he offered and would not look at him. He checked that he had not bound her too tightly. Her scent was strange and oddly alluring. She was more lovely even than Lirian. Her eyes when they opened briefly and met his were dark and compelling; they made him shiver.

After he had eaten he had to sleep and so it was not until late in the day that they started walking again. He carried the Hunter over his shoulder like a sack of grain. She was light as a small child and her heart beating against his back beat to a faster rhythm than his own. The feel of it against him was disturbing, confusing. The Hunter had a beating heart and a beautiful face and somehow that made his intentions seem less honourable.

It was night when they finally stumbled back to the edge of the forest and into sight of the Tier House. Avet in his triumph over Galet had neglected the old Chief's cautious regime. There were no guards at the gate of the first quarter, which was foolish as there had been raids from that direction not so long ago. He was not sure at first that Avet had been so careless, so sent Rin ahead through the gate; if anyone saw him he at least could claim that he had wandered off and become lost in the forest, and not even the most thuggish of the Horde would offer him harm.

Rin took a long time to return and Jerat was beginning to get anxious and to try to work out what that might mean, when he heard Rin's panting breath; it seemed that he'd run all the way from the Tier House.

'There's no one on guard, Jer. The Hall door is open and some of the Horde are sleeping outside, but they are all drunk and snoring.'

'Was Avet there?'

'I don't think so. There is a light in the Heart of the Home so I think he is there with the new wives.'

Jerat made a bundle of his possessions and lashed them to the lowest branch of one of the Great Trees. He could not carry his spear and his burden and he would need to be swift and silent. If he were caught he could not fight the whole Horde. He was more afraid now than he had ever been and he realised that his plan was poorly conceived and only going to succeed if they were blessed with more luck than he had any right to expect.

Jerat had, in truth, not thought much further than capturing his Night Hunter, but he had imagined hiding him – he had always imagined capturing a male – in the carrier coop, as it was the smallest, most awkward space he knew, and if the Teller Priest was right and Night Hunters truly feared small confined places it was his best chance of bringing about the panic that might make him use the Magic of the Last Resort. He did not allow himself to dwell on the likelihood that no such magic existed, or on the other possibility that it existed but could not be brought into being by such a crude and hasty plan as Jerat had been able to devise.

He picked up his captive – her eyes were still shut as if she were refusing to even acknowledge that he and her situation existed – and followed Rin across the Hearthfields to Avet's Hall. There was no clearer sign of the change in ownership than the untidy mess of half-eaten food that lay among the recumbent forms of the Horde. Everything was in disarray as if people had fallen asleep where they were, in mid-drink.

There would be foxes and rats and all manner of undesirable scavengers running wild in the Hall if Avet did not start taking control. Keran must have left, for he would never have countenanced such chaos. Jerat had a moment of regret that Keran had gone and had not said goodbye – there was not time for that now. Jerat sent Rin to find Verre to quietly let her know that they were safe and then he began to mount the outside thatch-ladder. He was exhausted, so that even the Hunter's small weight became difficult to manoeuvre, but he placed her inside the coop as gently as he could and checked her bonds. He did not think she could escape, unless she could fly, and no story had ever claimed that of Zeron's children.

When he had settled her he staggered back down the ladder, where a figure waited for him. He found his belt knife and hoped he would have the strength to defend himself. Was it Avet? The person was more slender than his old enemy and did not appear to be armed. He could not bear to have come so far, to have captured a Night Hunter and to be caught. When he got to the bottom rung of the ladder he sagged with relief and almost stumbled – the figure was Verre. Silently she helped him slide the ladder back to its storage position and followed him as he shambled clumsily back out across the Hearthfields. When they were far enough away from the Tier House to be unheard, she spoke.

'What in Zerat's name do you think you're doing? Avet thinks you ran away with Rin, though I knew you would not leave Ro. I couldn't get any sense out of Rin – he can hardly speak for exhaustion. What have you done to him?' She sounded angry.

Jer shook his head. 'Verre, I can't talk now. I have to sleep.'

'I guessed as much.' Her voice softened. 'The next time you come up with a crazed scheme that involves your brother – let me know. I'm on your side, remember. Well, you can't sleep within the Hearthfields. Avet will kill you, and most of the Horde that remain are so drunk they might try to kill you too. The Chief had lost his wits when he chose Avet, I can tell you. He lacks self-control which, for all his many faults, your father had in abundance. The whole place is going to ruin already, and many no-men deserted last night, so we've lost good hands we can't spare.' She paused to breathe. 'Don't listen to my chattering, Jerat. None of it is important, you're back now. I will keep watch while you sleep, but I will have to leave at dawn. The Teller will wait no longer. You can explain just what you were thinking of later.'

She led him to a good place just outside the Hearthfields, the same place, in fact, where he had stowed his weapons. She spotted them at once.

'You are not an utter fool, then,' she said. 'Sleep Jerat, I will keep you safe.' He was too tired to say anything but 'thank you'. He could not think much beyond the fact that he had trapped his captive, his Night Hunter, and somehow he would bend her to his will. With that thought he fell asleep.

TWENTY-SIX

When Nela relaxed her grip in the stone she found Moss staring at her intently. It was still the dark of the night and it took a moment before the hissing crackle of the fire and the reverberating sound of Millard's snoring reminded her of where she was.

'I can't make any sense of this story,' Nela said. Her mouth was dry and her head ached and it no longer seemed as though the story locked in the stone was as important as she had first thought. She and Moss were in deep trouble.

'This woman is not a settler, that is clear enough. Something happened – a man, the Wandering Man, did something to the stone so that it would be . . .' she shrugged, unable to find the words, '. . . whatever it is.' She buried her head in her hands. 'What does it matter? I'm never going to get a chance to be a Findsman if Millard has his way. If I'm not a non-woman I can't publish this material.' She wanted to cry.

Moss touched her lightly on the shoulder; she shivered and recoiled. He withdrew his hand.

'No, it's all right,' Nela said self-consciously. She would much rather Moss's hand, the hand of a bondsman, on her shoulder than Millard's. She would not marry Millard – that conviction was growing in her hourly.

'I know what we must do,' she said firmly.

'I know what I must do,' Moss replied, 'if you will help me.'

'What are *you* planning to do?' Nela said, surprised: she had not thought that the bondsman might already have a plan.

'I'm going to leave tonight, before Millard can convince the Chief Findsman that I tried to injure him. I have no choice. I'll have to take my chances in the forest.' He removed his tether belt carefully and laid it on the ground; she could see the red weals where it had rubbed away at his skin.

'Thank you for trying to protect me,' he said, meeting her eye fleetingly.

'I promised,' she said, relieved that he would still break all taboo and look at her.

'I hope that you find a way to become a Findsman in spite of them all. I am glad I learned something of the woman in the stone and of you.'

Nela was briefly confused by these remarks.

'Oh, no,' she said, finally grasping his intention, 'you don't understand. I'm coming with you. I will not marry Millard – he could put me in a House of Sanctification if he wished. He could call me a hysteric and have me locked away if I ever upset him – it

211

would be easy enough with my condition. My father would convince himself it was for my good. I do not trust Millard and I have no other protectors. My aunts have long thought me touched by Zeron. If I come with you I could not be married. Millard would not have me if I ran off with a bondsman.'

Moss flinched slightly when she said that, but nodded.

'Let's go, then.'

'Wait, I have some things to get.'

Nela made a pack of her notebook, her sleeping furs, her knife and such tools of her trade as she actually owned, a change of clothes and her bowl and eating utensils. Moss took nothing but a small bag of food. He shrugged when she looked at him questioningly.

'I am a servant. I own nothing. I will not be seen as a thief as well as an abductor and corruptor of well-born Chief Findsman's daughters.' He smiled, and if his smile contained any trace of regret or doubt, Nela did not want to acknowledge it.

Nela followed Moss as he ducked under the perimeter cordon. In the soft light of the fire's flames she saw her father lying deep in sleep, his proud face relaxed and vulnerable. He was all she had and she had to leave him behind – he who was so central to her planned future and to her precious past. Tears came to her eyes in spite of everything at the thought of never seeing him again, but he had given her no choices. He had betrayed her by betrothing her to Millard without her consent; she was on her own now.

They walked for some hours in the darkness, Moss a little ahead of Nela, up the steep incline that formed the foothills of the mountains which surrounded the lake. It seemed to Nela that she walked blind and helpless, away from anything that had meaning to her, into an unknown place with an unknown creature, a bondsman. He held out his hand to her in the dense blackness and she took it; it was warm and capable-seeming – in every way the hand of a person who cared enough about her to offer her help. They did not speak. Maybe he was as unsure as she was, maybe he too was afraid.

Dawn came and brought the heat along with the light. They did not stop and Nela dared not suggest that they should rest because her father could be pursuing them even as they rested. The air became heavy and still, like an unaired room, rank and stifling. Nela was soaked with perspiration and the stubble of her head under its cap was itchy and damp. They walked on. Eventually Nela's trembling legs simply refused to work any more and she started to stumble. Moss let go of her hand, which was slick with sweat, and left her for a moment while he scouted around for somewhere less exposed to rest. She felt bereft and panicky without his hand to cling to. She was turning out to be feebler than she'd thought. When he returned he helped her to a cool place by a small stream in the shadow of some rocks.

'We can stay here until you get your strength back.' Even now that they had run away they were awkward together. He did not meet her eyes, though whether that was in deference to her finer feelings or from dislike she couldn't say. 'Are you all right?' he asked her.

'I don't know,' she answered truthfully. There seemed little point in holding on to any pretence. 'I've left everything behind – I feel . . .' she searched for the word, 'I feel lost.'

Moss didn't answer for a while. 'I think this stream is probably safe to drink from,' he said finally, his expression closed to her. He did not offer to fill her bowl for her. She was on the point of giving him an order when she realised that she could not live by the old rules – she too was an outcast now and that made her little different from the bondsman. She got awkwardly to her feet and filled her bowl. She felt a dull kind of hopelessness as she did it. She was too tired to wonder if she'd done the right thing in leaving – nothing was now the same. She looked at Moss as if he were a person and saw his look of his surprise and relief.

'You are an unusual Findsman's daughter, Nela,' he said.

'If you've only just realised that, you're slower of wit than I gave you credit for, Moss,' she answered tartly.

He smiled a small, hidden smile and produced several slices of cooked hare and some camp bread from his bag. Eating made Nela feel better almost at once. She leant back against the rocks and discovered that she felt not so much lost, as, for the first time, free. It was a good feeling.

'You know this whole place has the kind of smell of magic about it?' Nela said, breaking the silence.

'What do you mean? I thought you didn't believe in magic.' Moss seemed lost in his own thoughts.

'Perhaps it is not magic, but I do not have another name for how I feel things when I touch the stone. It has a kind of a scent or a taste, it's hard to describe. It's a bit like . . . you know how after a fire, even when all the detritus has been cleared away, that charred smoky smell remains?'

He nodded, his expression quizzical.

'When I see things through the stone, the magic leaves behind a similar kind of trace. This whole place has that feel of somewhere that has been burned by magic.'

'Maybe. I haven't seen any sign of life,' he conceded, then he continued, 'We should find somewhere to build a proper shelter and set traps if we are to stay here for some time.' Perhaps the irreversible nature of their decision was beginning to dawn on him too. They were exiled together, perhaps for ever.

Nela washed her mouth and greasy fingers in the stream and then, after a brief hesitation, removed her cap and splashed cool water over her whole face and near-naked scalp. Moss carefully averted his eyes. It was not seemly for a non-woman to expose her bald head in public.

'I'm not wearing that thing in this heat,' she said. 'Besides, running away with you is so very indecent it hardly seems worth making a fuss about this.'

Moss looked uncomfortable. 'I don't think you should be here, Nela.'

'Moss, I am here because I don't want to be there –

not with Millard, not with my father. I don't want the life I'd have with Millard – this one may be worse and, if we don't find food, it will be very short, but at least I've chosen it. I gave you my word that I would protect you from the consequences of all this, and I can't protect you and leave you at the mercy of a man like Millard, can I? I don't know how we'll manage, or how we'll get along, but . . .' Her argument petered out. She was tired, and suddenly her decision to run away seemed hard to defend. Moss nodded but without much conviction.

'I don't know how we can live here,' he said gloomily. 'But if your father is going to follow after us, I would like more distance between his camp and ours before nightfall.'

In spite of her weariness, she could not disagree.

TWENTY-SEVEN

Nela and Moss walked until they came to the edge of a great forest that stretched as far as they could see. By this time it was dusk and neither of them had the stomach for entering the gloom of the densely packed trees.

The forest was not wholly dead, but the Great Trees, which were of a size unparalleled in the rest of the known world, did not look healthy and many of the smaller trees were leafless and rotten. Nela recoiled from them; their broken branches which littered the forest floor looked like huge grey-skinned limbs and even the air of the forest had a miasma of decay.

'Must we go in there?' Nela asked, because Moss seemed to be the more competent in the wild.

'Maybe not now,' he answered, 'but I don't think there's any way round the forest unless you want to climb the crags of the mountain.'

Nela shook her head. 'No, I think that may be

worse. Shall we camp here, then?' She took his silence for assent and began to collect kindling for the fire. 'Are we going to take it in turns to sleep?' They had seen no signs of dangerous animal life or indeed of any animal life at all, but it would be wiser to be cautious. Besides, she was embarrassed about sleeping next to Moss.

Moss managed to start the fire after only a few attempts and the two of them sat on either side of it watching the flames dance and leap between them. The burning wood smelled of corpses and they had nothing left to eat. Nela thought of home, of Scraal and the crooked stone villa of her aunts near the Sacred House of Zerat and her father's vaulted rooms in the scholars' quarter. She thought of the bustle of the many markets at the heart of the life of the city which was the heart of the known world, of the gossip of the sewing salons and the daily ceremonies of devotion and civilised politeness that were expected even of a non-woman in Scraal. She would not know any of that again. She did not know if she felt regret or relief.

'What are you thinking?' she asked. She was ignorant of what Moss was leaving behind, what his life had been before he joined her father. Moss appeared startled by the question.

'I don't know. That I've always wanted to know more about my people, but that I never thought it would cost me everything to find out.' He paused and added quietly, 'That you look nice in the firelight.'

'You don't have to say that,' Nela said awkwardly. 'I know I'm ugly and I don't mind so much – I'm used to it and it's better without the aunts telling me all the time.'

Moss looked genuinely surprised. 'I don't think you're ugly. You look miserable a lot of the time, but not ugly, and now you look . . .' she waited anxiously while he searched for the right word, 'worried,' he said at last. 'Your face looks softer in the firelight and very worried.'

She smiled. She was not sure what a half compliment from a bondsman was worth, but it made her feel better anyway. 'We've got quite a lot to be worried about, haven't we?' she answered.

They sat in silence for a while. It was not a bad silence – they were getting used to each other and she no longer felt ashamed and guilty every time she looked at him. Maybe in time she would forget that he had been a bondsman, but at that moment Nela found it difficult to think of anything but her stomach. They had walked a long way and eaten little.

She sighed. 'If you don't mind I think I'll try and learn more about the stone. At least it may take our minds off our other problems.'

She took it carefully from her belt pouch and slipped it from its fabric sheath.

'How did you do that?'

'What?' I had not seen my brother there, hiding in the shadow of a tree as I tried to control the destructive power of my song. It is difficult to get right and the bush with which I have been practising is charred and blackened and I feel ashamed. I chose carefully – a sick tree which even with the help of my chanting has failed to thrive. I had it in my mind to practise on it if it didn't grow, and perhaps that prevented me from concentrating on healing it as I might have done – but that doesn't matter now because Sky is glaring at me with the kind of concentrated venom that only a brother can manage. He has grown tall, Sky. I see him now as if for the first time. He is lean like all of our people and a better hunter than most. But he is always angry. When we sit and sing songs round the summer camp or in the winter caves he is the one who always wants to sing songs of our deprivation, of how the Bear-men have taken and despoiled our land with their crops and stupid over-bred animals. He is something of a leader of the younger men too and it has become very common for them to moan about our lost hunting grounds on Lakeside and how the smell from the walled traps the Bear-men live in carries far on the Northern breeze and how the air is thick with the scent of their pigs and their milk cows and their horses, their baking bread and their beer and their own powerful odour of sweat and excrement. He is watching me with his ever-angry eyes and I don't know what to say.

I shrug, but he is in front of me in a moment, holding me by my shoulders and shouting in my face.

'What did you do to that bush – tell me!'

'Don't shout, Sky!' I shout back, putting a certain resonance into my voice so that he leaps back as if he himself is burnt, and I am worried, because now that I have found the knack of this power it would be so easy to misuse it.

He rubs his fingertips where they have touched me and I see that they are raw-looking.

'Well, Singer sister, it seems you have found a weapon worthy of the name.'

'I don't know what you mean,' I lie, but his gimlet eyes glitter with eagerness.

'Show me what you did – is it a special note? How is it done?'

'Sky, you have never shown any interest in my craft before. Is it so much less interesting to heal than to hurt?'

'I do not want to heal my enemies, sister, I want to hurt them – not fatally, just enough to drive them and their reeking stock away from here. Every year their lands grow and as they grow we diminish. If we carry on taking their leavings there will not be enough free, wild land to support us, not enough strength in the belly of the earth to nourish the wild things – and the earth will be as tired and worn out as their women after birthing their too-large offspring. That cannot be good. You Singers talk of wholeness and restoration, I want wholeness too and restoration – I want the earth to blossom and grow where it wills, free as it has ever been, and I want the restoration of the lands that were ours to roam in. If I could sing up a firestorm I would not hesitate, and if you were true to your calling neither would you.'

I don't say anything because there is nothing to say. I understand how he feels, or think I do, but I can see no point in fighting the Bear-men. Their brute force imposes their will on the land for now, but the earth herself will rebel in the end – all we need is patience. Sky doesn't have any – he never has.

'Show me how you did that!'

I shake my head and this time he dares not approach me.

'You are a traitor to your people, Singer and sister of mine. Your heart is as cold as the stone you carry everywhere. You are supposed to be the best that ever lived and yet how little do your talents benefit us.'

He spits in my direction but I am not interested in his vitriol. I am more appalled to learn that I have some of his anger in me or how else could I burn the bush and bring death to a living thing in my care? My head aches suddenly with the force of this perverse magic I have wielded and I want to lie down and forget all about this too-successful experiment. Could Sky stumble across the technique for this destruction on his own? I do not think so. He has never shown any talent for singing, but if he had, perhaps his inner fury would have brought about this fire at once. I do not know why I of all Singers should have done this. Have I more anger in me than those others? In my heart am I like Sky?

Nela came to with a start and knew that Moss had removed the stone from her hand.

Her own head ached.

'Did I fit?' she asked. Moss was holding her hand, she noticed belatedly; in fact he was supporting her neck too.

'I think you began to, but you stopped when I took away the stone. Are you all right?'

She nodded and inadvertently touched the stone again.

I am terrified. He has trapped me and the forest that has always been my home is a place of shame, for I, the Chief Singer, allowed a clumsy, foolish Bear-man to trap me. I shut my eyes in fear and shame. I feel his finger trace the outline of my cheek, gently as if I were a child. I almost open my eyes out of curiosity. Moon-eye always says that I'm touched by the Womanface, not just chosen by her, and perhaps that is why I know in my bones and in my guts with absolute certainty that to see this man is dangerous. His touch is not brutal, not bestial, but tender, and I, who have ever thought the Bear-men like the beasts they keep in their unnatural caves, consider for the briefest of moments the possibility that I could have been wrong. I feel him move away from me and I open my eyes and see him. I see him in the twilight with eyes used to looking hard and seeing much and I see that he is young and beautiful and his face is strong and kind, but also fierce. Set against the night his hair is pale and falls like a weeping willow tree in a graceful arc to his shoulders, which are large as boulders, and I know that I have done a bad thing, for in looking on him something in Stone is changed and Stone must not change for she is the unchanging voice of her people and change is dangerous and often fatal.

Moss had removed the stone from her hand. Nela saw that at once when she opened her eyes.

'The woman is called "Stone". Oh, Lord of the Earth! Do you think she could be the faerie woman of the song, Black Stone? The stone visions are confusing, because they skip through different stages of her life, but I think she fell in love with her captor, a Bear-man, the moment she saw him. He was one of the enemies of her people, a huge giant of a man, like the bronze statue of Zerat in the Hearthsquare of Scraal. Stone's brother Sky wanted to fight the Bear-men and use her power to bring fire.'

Moss carefully withdrew his supporting arm. 'There, is that more comfortable? I don't know, Nela. Something bad has happened here, I can feel it. Maybe they used the magical fire? I think you should rest now. We ought to begin to work our way through the forest tomorrow and you will need your strength. I'll wake you when I need to sleep. Don't touch the stone again – there's no need. We'll have plenty of time to discover its secrets when we're further from your father.'

Nela nodded gratefully and sleep came to her like a blow to the head. In an instant she was sleeping – one finger almost touching the unsheathed stone on her lap.

TWENTY-EIGHT

Jerat woke to Verre's voice in his ear.

'Wake up, Jerat!'

He felt as though he climbed back to wakefulness up the steep and slippery sides of a deep well. He fell back into it several times, but Verre would not leave him alone and at length he emerged blinking and heavy-headed into awareness.

'It's time for me to go, Jer. The Teller Priest will be waiting and I need to know where you went yesterday.'

'Oh, just away from here, Verre. You know how it is with Avet.'

'I know that! Listen, you have to confide in me. Ro feared you had abandoned him and has been restless as a moon-mad hare, and Avet mistrusted your absence and is intent on sending me away soon after dawn. It's fortunate that I'd already arranged to meet with the Teller Priest. Hela told me what Avet said – she is to escort me out of the Dependency. If I am to take Rin with me I'll have to go at once to wake him.'

Jerat had ploughed deep furrows in his head trying to unearth some germ of an idea of an excuse for his absence the day before, but he had come up with nothing. He needed to get Verre to help him without telling her about the Hunter. He was not sure she would approve of what he had done – he did not think he approved himself. He kept seeing the beautiful, still face of his petrified victim, hearing her tiny breathless whimper as he abandoned her to the darkness of the carrier coop.

'Avet is very nervous. He thinks you are plotting something,' she added.

Jerat shrugged, hopelessly, and it was not entirely an act. 'I wish I were, Verre. There is nothing I can do. Avet was the Chief's choice, he has the Horde on his side – what could I possibly do? He has all the power and he will make us all exiles.'

'You are still going to stay here to keep an eye on Ro?'

'Yes, of course. I have to.'

'Be very careful. The forest is also full of dangers – real ones, not superstition.'

'I know, Verre, please trust me. I am a man now.'

She touched his face. 'I know,' she said.

'We could live in the forest together.'

'No!' She sounded both horrified and surprised.

'You taught me how to live there.'

'And what of the Night Hunters? And what of the winter? It is possible to survive in the summer, I give you that, but even the Hunters move to the Bear Caves in the winter. I do not see how you could do it, and Ro . . . Ro could not survive that life.'

'You could come too and between us we might find a way.' Having lived in the forest for the last two nights Jerat was by no means certain that it was possible, but if his plan to bring about the Magic of the Last Resort failed it was better than abandoning Ro and losing touch with Verre. His whole scheme seemed ludicrous now, doomed to come to nothing. It seemed at odds with all that practical Verre had taught him – a thing of dreams, the fanciful wish of a young boy. Rin would be safe with the Teller Priest, at least; he had no qualms about that. Verre looked thoughtful.

'Perhaps we could try,' she said at length. 'I am worried about Ro. The old Hearth Guard is dispersing quickly. Soon there will be no one to care for Ro but the new Guard, and I'm not sure Avet is recruiting them for their gifts with children. The other Brood brothers will not risk their displeasure to care for him and if Ro dreams one of his death dreams they are as likely to kill him as not. Perhaps the forest is his only chance.' She stopped for a moment as if thinking through all the implications. 'The Teller is meeting me at the gate of the second quarter soon. I will get Rin to him and, after Hela has done her duty and escorted me out of the Dependency, I will see you back in the forest – at the old hunting spot – you remember? Between the three trees shaped like spindles and the jumping rock. I will see you there tomorrow night. I want to go with Rin for a night at least, to be sure he understands what is expected of him. I think it would be best if you stayed away from the Tier House and take Ro soon. I'll take care of your things. You don't want Avet to know that you've been back.'

'I thought I might hide in the carrier coop.'

He heard her sharp intake of breath.

'That is too risky, Jerat. Avet's men will not stay drunk for ever. He will set up a watch and organise the Hall one of these days.'

'Only tonight, Verre, so I can keep close to Ro. You have my word – tomorrow night I'll take him to the forest.' He felt the pressure of her familiar strong hand on his shoulder.

'All right. I will take your things with me.'

'I would like my spear and the other things with me – I may have need of them.'

Verre nodded and left with her usual silent tread.

Jerat had no idea how long it would take for the trapped Hunter to become desperate enough to use the Magic of the Last Resort, if indeed such a thing existed, but whatever happened or did not happen, he needed to get Ro from the Tier House soon; his situation was more desperate than Jerat had anticipated. And what of the magic? He wished he'd listened more carefully to the Teller's tales. Was it true that Hunters could not bear to be trapped within walls? Some said that even in the coldest winter in their winter camp they stayed at the cave mouth where they could see the sky and the moon, the Dark Daughter, Zeron, who was their goddess and their light, but was one night and a day enough, and how would he know when she was ready?

He was no longer even sure he believed in it any more. If nothing had happened before he met Verre the following night he would take the Hunter back to the forest – where, he thought despairingly, she would probably get her tribe to kill him for what he had done. He could not afford doubts now.

He walked through the Hearthfields and waited hidden behind the Hearthyard well for Verre's return with his spear, his war gear and Rin.

'Rin, Verre has arranged for you to go to the Teller Priest,' said Jerat. 'If all goes well and I can make Ro well again I will find you and we will go together to a new place – until then you will be safest with the Teller. Do as he tells you and we will see each other again very soon.' It was hard for Jerat to get the words past the choking lump of grief that blocked his throat, but Rin was looking at him earnestly but dry-eyed.

'Will we be able to live here then, together, like before?'

'Well, not like before, Rin. Avet is Chief now and he's never liked me much. But we'll find somewhere new that will be just as good.'

'How long will I be gone?'

'Not too long, Rin – but remember not to cause the Teller any trouble.'

Verre was carrying a pack and in the fading darkness there was just enough light for Jerat to see her grim face.

'Don't worry, Verre,' Rin said, 'Jer says we'll be together soon.'

Jerat hugged Rin and Verre gave Jerat the warrior's embrace; he could feel her trembling.

'Be fortunate, blood-marked son,' she said in a

choked voice, and, taking Rin, was swiftly gone.

Could the Magic of the Last Resort make Ro well? It all seemed too bleak to hope for very much and, even if Ro were restored, where would they go? How could they ever meet again? The world was large and Jerat had never felt smaller.

Twenty-nine

I am waking from a sleep where nightmares have chased me through the forest of my dreams and trapped me at last in a place of ever-shrinking walls, but it is not a nightmare and I am trapped. I am still hungry – sleep has not taken that away but then why should it? I feel as though I am suffocating and as my mind grows sharper and the last remnants of dreaming are blinked away I realise that I am not alone in the coop, that another body encircles mine like a wild bitch around her young. His breath is the wind against my face, and his powerful masculine smell, the smell of his hair and his exhaled breath, almost dominates the bird smell of my cage, the dove cote. There is very little room to move and I fear that if he rolls over his Bear-man's weight will crush me, and I start to breathe too rapidly, in that hasty foolish way that has been trained out of me so long ago I am surprised to find myself still capable of it. Will the floor hold his weight? This was not a room built for Bear-men, but then I remember Sky complaining that the Bear-men build with so much felled wood that their houses could withstand the earth's most violent moods and that they build each tier so that Zerat himself in all his clumsy bulk could dance on it.

Thin spears of light protrude, sharp and ruthless, into the tiny room. His face in sleep could be carved from rock – it has the same kind of grandeur as the Great Trees and the monumental mountains. I watch him and all the while the tension is building, a tension that is a kind of a panic, a tension in that part of me, my core from which the magic of my singing comes. Looking up at him makes it worse and I become fearful of more than my captor. I fear the emotion that I cannot control, the feeling when I look at him. There is a Hearthsong I learned when I was a child, before I went to live with Moon-eye. It was called the 'The Song of the Promise of Perfection', it was a favourite with the young girls and was all about the love between one of the children of the Womanface and a child of the Manface; I find the tune and long-forgotten words suddenly on my lips. I would hum to calm myself, but I am afraid to wake him.

'Nela!' Moss's voice came to her from a long way away. She woke to see that the stone had rolled on to the ground. The night was strangely quiet without the snufflings and snorings of her father and his party. Moss was sitting right beside her and it was his hand on her shoulder waking her that had dislodged the stone. Had she dreamed this stone vision? She picked the stone up using the folds of her tunic to prevent her from making contact with its surface.

'Is it my watch?' she asked huskily, as if she had forgotten how to use her voice. The side of her that had been away from the fire was cold, and she shivered. Outside the circle of the firelight, the night beyond looked opaque in its darkness and horribly sinister.

'I need to shut my eyes for a little while – will you be all right? Wake me if you're frightened,' Moss said. His voice too was cracked with fatigue.

Of course she was frightened; she had left her whole life behind and who knew what haunted the blackness beyond the flames? Moss lay down beside her and she stared into the emptiness. It was like the iris of some great beast. She had not realised how much she had depended for her security on the presence of her father and his men. With only Moss beside her she felt more vulnerable than ever before. For a moment, she almost considered waking Moss and heading back to the camp by the Lakeside. The thought once acknowledged was unthinkable – Millard would have Moss killed and her father would have her married off to Millard before she could even talk about the things she had learned from the stone.

It occurred to her then that while her father was unlikely to leave the safety of the camp to pursue her, he would not let the precious memory-stone slip from his grasp. If he noticed that the stone in the strong box was not the ancient black stone he would surely come after her. She strained her ears and thought she heard the distant sounds of voices. She tore a piece of fabric from her cloak, wrapped the stone in it and hid it in her artefact pouch. Moving quickly, she kicked earth over the fire to extinguish it and woke Moss.

'I hear voices, Moss. I think my father is coming.'

Moss was instantly alert, perhaps through his long training as a servant.

'We have to enter the forest,' he whispered. 'They will not follow – not until daylight anyway. It is too dangerous.'

'If it is too dangerous why are we doing it?' she whispered back.

'Because we are desperate and fearful for our lives and because I can see well in the dark,' Moss answered. 'Take my hand, keep your head low and don't be afraid.'

Nela's heart was already beating as if she had run from wild beasts, but she gave Moss her hand. It helped her to feel less alone.

'Are you sure you can see?'

'Of course – can't you?'

She shook her head and he gave a low sound that might have been a swiftly suppressed laugh – as if he had seen her.

It was like being blind – the darkness to her eyes was absolute. After a while, as her eyes became accustomed to the nothingness, she thought she could discern the dark ghostly outlines of Great Trees. Now and again Moss warned her of some low branch or a clump of brambles, but mostly they walked in silence into the heart of the forest. She thought she heard her father calling her name – sound carried a long way in the dead-seeming night. She had never endured anything more terrifying.

They walked until her legs ached and she was ready to sit wherever she was from sheer exhaustion. Moss seemed tireless, although he had scarcely rested. They walked until dawn and still kept on walking until green light illuminated lichen-covered trees, so that it was like being on the bed of the lake.

'This is the home of my ancestors,' Moss said at last.

'How can you know?'

'I don't know, but I feel sure that this is the forest of the woman of the stone.'

'In Stone's memory the forest is beautiful and rich and full of life – not like this at all. I don't like this – it is wrong, warped, stunted. I want to get out of here.'

He didn't say anything in response for a good long while and then said, 'If you want, I will take you back to meet your father.'

'It's too dangerous for you. I'll keep going.'

They kept on doggedly as the sun came up over the desolate forest with its dry wood and smell of decay. 'Lord of the Earth, I am a non-woman,' she kept reminding herself, 'I am strong and I can do whatever is needful,' and so she did – she kept putting one tired foot in front of another while the bondsman led the way.

THIRTY

It was difficult to move soundlessly when hampered by spear and bow and all the accoutrements of war, indeed all your earthly possessions. Jerat walked quietly towards the Tier House, fearful of being spotted as every moment the sun rose higher. From inside the newly inhabited Heart of the Home a baby cried and a voice, a young woman's voice, hushed it wearily. Jerat stiffened when he heard Avet's voice, but he seemed to be calling a woman to him, and Jerat carefully climbed up the exterior ladder and into the carrier coop.

His captive lay sleeping, curled in on herself like a creature new born, fresh from the womb. There was only room for his spear if he placed it diagonally across the tiny space, and he had to curl himself round the sleeping Hunter in order to fit his long body into the coop. He did not see how he could avoid waking her, inadvertently hurting her or developing severe cramp.

The place smelled of birds and of her, the sleeping female, earthy, pungent, other. He wished he had been able to speak to Ro, to explain that he had not abandoned him, to assure him that this was all to make him well, but there was not the time. If Jerat's half-cooked plan worked, Ro would know soon enough of his restoration; if it did not, then he would take Ro to the forest and live there as best he could with Verre. It was testament to Jerat's exhaustion that even in the cramped conditions, and with his future so unresolved, he was asleep almost as soon as his head found the feather-strewn straw.

He woke with a start, conscious of being watched. His mouth was dry and he could not move for the stiffness in his neck, his back and legs. It was cold and, through the tiny gaps in the construction of the roof, he could see slivers of darkness, like shards of flint.

Surely he could not have slept the whole day?

'I need to go outside.' It took him a moment to identify the quietly mellifluous voice as belonging to his captive, the dark shadow who lay before him. 'Please – I need privacy.'

Jerat knew what she meant. He himself had need of the soil pit and, as far as he knew, the Hunters had their animal requirements too.

He did not know what to say. He was her captor, he should make her fear him, but he was moved with pity for her perfect beauty and her unjust captivity.

'We can go outside,' he whispered; he could not speak harshly to her. 'I will keep you tethered to me,' he added, so that she would know that he was serious about keeping her trapped.

It was as difficult for him to get out of the tiny opening designed for birds as it had been for him to get in it. He listened hard for any sounds of activity. He did not know what quarter of the night it was nor whether Avet had finally set a watch on his Hall. The thatch ladder was set to the rear of the Hall door for privacy, but was usually well guarded by one of the Hearth Guard. The pitch of the thatched roof prevented him from seeing anyone down below so he had no choice but to partially dismount the ladder. He could hear Avet's laughter from the Heart of the Home along with other female voices. He felt his guts tighten with hatred and jealousy; his Brood brother did not deserve this Hall.

It looked as though Avet had failed to protect the entrance to the Heart of the Home – maybe he thought he was invincible. Jerat helped the Hunter through the small entrance of the carrier coop and carried her down the ladder over his shoulder. She weighed considerably less than Ro, but even that small additional weight made climbing down awkward. The rope he had originally placed around her wrists was too tight and, in the moonlight, he could see that they were chafed and sore. Even so, he could take no chances, and he tied her hands together at one end of the rope and, holding firmly to the other, allowed her to see to her needs. Then, when she reappeared, he tied her to the Hearth tree while he attended to his own business. He saw something glint in her hand and at first tensed for fear it was some kind of hunter's knife, but then he saw that it was only a stone, like the dark eye of an owl, round and black in her hand.

The night was cool, though not yet cold, and a much depleted Horde slept inside the Hall. It was still warm enough to cook outside. The communal cook pot with its heavy lid was left abandoned on the ash of the outdoor hearth. When Keran was in charge the pot was scoured daily, but Avet's new Horde chief was less scrupulous and there was enough cold broth left in the bottom of the pot to provide nourishment for him and for his captive. He scooped out some of the cold glutinous mass with a couple of the clay drinking vessels that had also been left lying around. He moved as quietly as possible and loosened the Hunter woman's bonds so that she could eat. She turned away from him as she ate, as if taking food in front of him was somehow shameful. He ate his own portion swiftly and then felt hungrier than ever.

'We should get back inside,' he said as he stretched out muscles that were stiff and slow to respond to his desires. 'But perhaps it will do no harm to stretch our legs first.' The woman did not respond, but when he untied her rope from the tree and held it so they could walk she did not complain. He ought not to have been so kind, but he found it hard to be cruel.

They walked away from the Tier House so that the small sounds that they made would not arouse suspicion.

'Why are you doing this?' she said at last.

'Because of the magic,' he said.

'What magic?' she said contemptuously. 'I can help a tree to grow strong and ease the pain of a difficult birth but I cannot keep alive that which is ready to die or do any of the fanciful things the stories claim we can.'

'You know our stories?'

'Probably as well as you know ours,' she answered.

'And what of the Magic of the Last Resort?' He tried to keep his voice emotionless, so that she would not guess at his desperation.

She didn't answer for a long time and at last said, 'I do not know if it even exists, for I have never heard of anyone that has used it or seen it used.' She looked at him steadily. 'It is a story for children and I hadn't thought you a child.'

She almost had him convinced there for a moment, convinced that there was no such thing, but then he realised she had no reason to tell him the truth; if he did not believe in that magic there was no reason for him to keep her and he would have to let her free. He smiled.

'We must go back now,' he said. She looked briefly and longingly at the moon as though in silent communication with it – perhaps she was, for Zeron, the Dark Daughter of their religion, was one with the moon.

There was a sudden movement in the bushes and the lumbering figure of a Horde member suddenly lurched into view. He appeared to have been patrolling the Hearthfields because he was both armed and sober. He settled himself close to the thatch ladder to guard the Heart of the Home and albeit unknowingly to bar their return to the carrier coop. Jerat could not afford to keep his captive outdoors for long, fearing that it would reduce the pressure on her to perform the magic. He took his sling and levered up a couple of good round stones from the flattened soil near the Tier House with the end of his belt knife. He weighed them in his hand and then, using his sling, hurled them with all his force and skill, deep into the olive grove that shaded the walkway to the gate of the first quarter. His first shot did not go nearly far enough, though the guard leapt to his feet at the sound. His second shot soared high into the night sky and landed with a rustle of leaves a good distance away. While the guard investigated, Jerat bundled the Hunter on to his shoulder and ran up the thatch ladder. He could not quite believe his good fortune when the guard did not look round to check his abandoned post as he surely ought to have done – he was certainly not of the old Chief's Brood Trove.

Jerat was pleased that he had not needed to tell the woman that the guard and those inside the Tier House were a greater danger to her than he was; she seemed to grasp that instinctively and was silent as a hunter should be. He liked the neat way she moved and her quiet, self-contained pride, even in her fear. He was ashamed to be acting as he was and so tried to compensate with consideration.

He could not prevent the floor from creaking as he lay down – there was insufficient headroom for him to sit. They lay so his body curved around her back, but he was careful to avoid touching her so that she knew he meant her no physical harm; he could not see her face, only sense the feline curve of her spine, rigid with emotion, taut as a stressed bow. Her breathing however was steady, slow and ever the same, and so he reasoned she could not be so afraid. Should he try to frighten her further to bring on the magic? He was not sure he could do it. Though she was quite unlike his brothers in every respect, and lying next to her was different in every way from sleeping close to his brothers in their infancy, he was reminded of them and his heart ached for safer times and he could not help but feel protective of her. She did not seem like a thing of evil, an enemy of his people. He had to remind himself that he was doing this for Ro, to keep them from the forest and an early death. He dared not speak for fear of disturbing the new Chief and his wives below and, though he dozed, he was no longer tired enough to sleep. Time seemed to slow; he slept a little but he was himself oppressed by the close walls of the Tier House and the knowledge that his enemy slept downstairs.

As the night wore sluggishly on, it seemed as if the woman became like a dark flame blazing with silent power, burning coldly like black frost. She branded her image on his eyes so that even when he closed them she was all he could see. When he drifted into a brief, light sleep, she ran towards him in his dreams, her arms open and her face indescribably sad. In the darkness of the carrier coop she even seemed to glow a little as if suffused by moonlight, while all else was dark. Something was building in her, he could feel it. His foot briefly brushed hers and he felt a jolt like lightning, that set all muscles and tendons in his feet tingling. He could see her trembling like the gut string of a bow when the arrow is loosed. The movement was rapid and slight, less like someone shivering than like a fragile pot vibrating on its shelf to the distant rumblings of the earth itself. Jerat checked his own hands. They were steady. Whatever she was responding to was unknown to him. His prisoner curled herself more tightly, as if to control her quivering, her breathing slowed too, and he began to be worried about her.

'What is it? Are you all right?' he whispered, and touched her shoulder. 'Ouch!' He had not intended to make a sound but his hand pained him as if it had been stung by a comb full of bees, and it felt numb for a moment after.

'Let me go.' She said it softly, so softly, as if it were her dying breath, that he had to put a cautious ear closer to her mouth to make out her words.

'I can't do that,' he said, though it pained him, 'I need you to make Ro better.'

'Please, this is so wrong – what you're doing – how can good come of such torture?' She seemed to be finding it difficult to talk – her teeth were chattering as though she was cold and yet she was sweating now, like a man labouring in the heat of the day, and her shaking was becoming convulsive. Her smell, sour with her distress, filled the carrier coop and made him wrinkle his nose. The Teller Priest must have been right; Hunters could not be confined, but he had not appreciated that to trap her thus was to cause her real suffering.

'All you have to do is to wish to be free and I will wish for Ro to be well and everything will be all right,' he said. He knew he sounded desperate himself, he did not want her to suffer like this and yet he could not give up his plan so close to its fulfilment. 'Please, just wish and it will all be all right.'

The rocking of the carrier coop in rhythm with her juddering seemed to give the lie to that. The floor vibrated with her shaking as if heavy invisible men were jumping on it; he could not see how her light weight could make it tremble so. There were sounds down below, shouts and the sounds of running footsteps as if Avet and his wives were running out of the building. He heard screaming and the sound of awkward feet making their clumsy and desperate descent down the thatch ladder. He heard Avet's voice bellowing in panic and the wives all running out of the Heart of the Home without waiting to be lifted down in the barrel. They were shouting and crying out in fear and the new babe was screaming. The whole solid bulk of the Tier House seemed to sway in time to the Hunter's thrashing. Jerat did not understand why she had to destroy the Tier House to be free – it seemed an unnecessarily violent way of making a wish for freedom come true. He hoped that someone would have the wit and the mercy to help Ro out of the Tier House? Surely someone would? Would Ro drag himself from the shuddering, heaving Hall or would Jerat have to drag himself down there to rescue him? Jerat was torn. He almost ran away then to make sure Ro was safe, but he realised that if he did that he might miss the moment of the wish. The moment had not come yet, but it was very close. He would have had to be a fool not to know that. It was agony but he made his decision to stay.

The Hunter no longer seemed to control her limbs and Jerat was fearful about trying to still them – not wanting to be stung by the force that flowed through them. It was frightening to see the way she trembled, as if torn apart by an uncontrollable force, like a kind of violent possession by Zeron, the Dark Daughter.

'Please!' Her voice was so resonant it made Jerat's ears ring, it reverberated like the Teller's drum. He could not answer because before he could open his mouth she started to produce a low note. It did not seem to come from her mouth but from every part of her skin, from every part of her, as if her whole shaking, convulsing being was an instrument of the gods made simply to produce that note. It was like the humming of insects, the crying of the birds in their carrier coops, the groaning of the trees in the wind – it was an extraordinary sound, thrilling and terrifying. Jerat's heart began to pound hard against his chest like the mallet they used to soften meat. The sound grew louder and higher until he could smell it, breathe it, until he became part of it. There was nothing else in the Dependency and in the wide, unknown world beyond it, but that note. It flowed though his blood, pounded in his ears and he shook with its terrible power. The sound became a force of the earth like the wind. The walls of the coop shattered outwards, as a badly made pot sometimes bursts in the kiln. The walls burst like a seed case and Jerat heard the Horde screaming in terror and fear and then the roof blew away, carried on the note that grew broad as a river in flood. He held on to the floor of the coop with straining fingers.

The noise made him feel like he was drowning, as if in breathing only the song he had lost the gift of breathing air. He had to hold on to awareness and to the disintegrating Tier House so that when the moment came he could make his wish; but would the moment come before he died? It came to him then, as the unnatural wind that was really a river of sound threatened to wash him away, that he knew what she was wishing, and it was not what he wanted at all. In the instant before the blackness came, when his own most precious desire, his own wish was ripped from him in the torrent of terrible murderous noise, he had just enough time to regret that he had ever forced the Hunter to this. The Teller was right: this was a warping of the world. He was glad when the blackness came.

AFTER

THIRTY-ONE

Jerat was woken by bright sunlight streaming through the partially unshuttered window of the Heart of the Home. Beside him the small dark beauty who was wife of the first and probably only quarter turned to him and smiled.

'It's a fine day,' she said in her quiet melodious voice that made him think of flowers opening in sunlight and water gurgling in a stream. It was warm and he was sleeping on a raised platform bed of the kind the Chief had favoured. Something about this struck him as strange so he walked to the shutters and opened them. He looked down over virgin fields surrounded by a defensive ditch, and away in the far distance he could make out the familiar fields of home and smoke from the cook fires of his father's Tier House. That was wrong – hadn't his father's Tier House been destroyed, or was that a dream? And where was he? He could not remember there being a Tier House or fields beyond and above his father's house, only forest and mountains. Something was strange.

The woman lay in the bed and looked at him blearily. 'What is it?' she said. The woman was beautiful but strange, with dark hair that had made a kind of fan of darkness around her head. He knew her sharply angled face, but not intimately. He could not remember how he knew her or the details of their courtship. Perhaps he was not properly awake yet. Jerat could not isolate what was bothering him and could not answer the dark woman; there was only an indefinable sense of wrongness.

'I'm just going to check on things,' he answered.

He unfolded and pulled on the fine woollen trews dyed a glorious unfaded purple that lay on the robe chest. They fitted him perfectly as he had expected, and yet in another part of himself he was sure that he had never worn such a colour before. He climbed out of the wide roof window on to the thatch ladder. The sun had warmed the new, golden thatch of the roof. He had overslept; it was long past dawn and the sun was already high. He needed to see Ro, check he was all right. He felt that this was very important, but could not remember why.

He opened the great door of the Hall and was assaulted by the familiar mingled smell of beasts and humans together. Keran, Hela, the Teller Priest and Verre were sleeping peacefully too – well beyond the time of wakening. He was surprised that Keran and the Teller Priest were there because he was sure they had gone away somewhere. Beyond them, behind the unfaded quarter curtain, in the sleeping place of the first quarter, Rin and Ro snored in their furs, abandoned to dreams. Dreams. There was something dreamlike about all this – a strong sense that things were not quite as they should be. The smell of new timber confused him. This was not his father's home, but a new Tier House built of still-green wood. He checked the grainstore on the raised platform that kept it from vermin – it was full, but this land had not borne a crop this year. He could not remember how the grain had got there.

He went back up to the Heart of the Home and his wife, whose name he did not seem to know. She was still in the bed, her face sharp as a fox and dark as the most fertile earth.

'Well, is it all as you wished?' There was a hardness in her voice that surprised and confused him. He had no memory of upsetting her; in fact, as he was beginning to realise, he had very little memory of anything at all – was he ill?

'Everything is fine – I think – but . . .'

'I see you have forgotten what you made me do – forgotten the Magic of the Last Resort.'

'But honey-touch . . .' He wanted to use her forgotten name rather than some crass endearment, but however hard he tried to remember it, it didn't even hover on the tip of his tongue. The words 'Magic of the Last Resort' echoed in his head – he had heard of that, he was sure, but he couldn't remember where. The name made him feel a little uncomfortable, guilty in such a way that he didn't much want to probe his memory to find out why. The woman went on talking. She had a beautiful voice.

'My name is Moon-stone, known always as

"Stone", Chief Singer of the Long Hill Summer People and the Bear Caves Winter People, and I have made the world wrong.' Unexpectedly she began to sob.

'But Stone, beauty, all is well,' he said soothingly, grateful to have a name for her. He touched her shoulder to comfort her and found it was rigid, unyielding. She reached for a smooth round pebble that lay beside her and clutched it in her hand: that almost tripped and snared a memory, but no, it was gone. He carried on reassuringly, 'I've checked, there's grain in the store, and the core of the Hearth Guard and my brothers of the quarter – they're all well,' but even as he spoke he knew that she was right. 'What did you call it again?'

'The Magic of the Last Resort.' He remembered then a fragment of something and a wish from the heart. There was something important he had to dredge up like a corpse from the Lake. He had made this woman do something she had not wanted to do, something that had caused her pain, something that had changed everything. He found the shadow of a memory. 'But you were supposed to wish for your freedom and I was supposed to wish for Ro to be well again. He saw the dead and could not walk and . . . oh, by Zerat! What happened?'

She wiped tears from her eyes with the back of her hand, which was fine-boned and delicate.

'You misunderstood the Last Resort and I did not believe in it. I should have known better. I should have run away, or killed myself. I had the means, but I did not really believe in it. It is a secret of our people that was kept even from me – or at least if I was told of it I took no notice. You were such a fool to meddle with such terrible power.'

Her distress brought to mind the sudden image of her begging him to free her, and he was suddenly ashamed.

'What have I done, Stone? I don't understand. I meant no harm, only good. I did not think it would hurt you.'

'And when you found out that it was hurting me – you didn't stop, did you?'

As the memory returned he hung his head in shame. 'No, I thought it would be all right if it made Ro well.'

He touched her gently on the arm and she flinched.

'I'm sorry,' he said, pained by her response. She must know that he loved her and wouldn't have deliberately harmed her.

'No, *I'm* sorry,' she said wearily. 'I should have known myself better, should have fought against it harder. This is my fault and I fear we will pay for what we've done here.' She looked desperate, desolate, but Jerat still didn't understand what had happened. His thinking was as sticky as cold corn porridge and he couldn't will it to flow faster.

'I still don't understand,' he said. 'Please explain to me what has gone on.' He wrinkled his face and rubbed his hands across it as if he could squeeze his memory out. 'I remember you singing – no, you didn't sing, but you made a note that flowed like the river in flood and everything started falling apart – at least, I think that's what I remember.'

His head ached with the effort to make sense of his hazy recollections. The carrier coop and the wind that blew away the roof of his father's Tier House seemed too unreal to have been true, whereas the solid feel of the oiled wood floor of the Heart of the Home, the smell of new wood and the feel of his soft wool trews, all that seemed inarguably real, and if the one was true – surely the other had to be false?

'We, the Night Hunters, still live to the rhythm of the earth, sing to the music that made all things – by singing it was all made and by singing it can all be unmade and remade.' She moistened her lips which looked dry. Jerat was struck again by her extraordinary beauty and the way his heart felt full and joyful when he looked at her. 'Stone', a strange enough name, but not unfitting – her skin had something of the look of a polished pebble, and her will, her certainty, was hard and unyielding as stone.

'The gift of unmaking and remaking is hidden within us all; we carry the secret knowledge of its sound in our blood, in the pattern of our bone, it is buried in the shape of our sinews and is there even in the beat of our heart; it is the music of creation itself. For my people that secret is made known by longing.'

She glanced quickly at Jerat and then looked down and smoothed the thick fur of the bed cover with a gentle touch which made Jerat feel strange.

'The stories talk of it as the Last Resort because the longing for freedom or the longing for life are powerful enough to release that note of power, but there are other desires.' She stopped and looked at Jerat, who was blind to anything but her beauty and her distress.

'Go on,' he said.

'Jerat, when you trapped me in the carrier coop I wanted freedom, but as you waited with me for the magic to take hold it was not freedom I desired beyond all else, but you. That is the longing that released the power. I'm so sorry because now I have you and it is because of the magic. I have twisted the world out of shape so that you might love me.' Tears rolled gently down her perfect face like rain off the surface of a glossy winter berry; Jerat wiped them away with his finger. He stared thoughtfully at her before speaking.

'You are saying that the way I feel about you is because you remade me to feel this way?'

She nodded.

'I don't believe you. I felt this way when I saw you first in the forest.'

'No, you didn't,' she said firmly. 'If you loved me you would not have made me suffer the throes of the power – when I fought against it and begged you to let me go. You let me suffer – you did not love me then.'

Jerat was silent because he knew that what she said was true. After a long and uncomfortable pause he asked, 'But what of all this, the Tier House, the land . . .' He waved his arm to encompass the whole room.

'The stories have a kernel of truth – you can make a wish at the moment of change, at that instant when the world is remade, but it is a wish of your heart, not of your thinking. It is your most precious desire that warps the world, not what you ought to want. In your heart what you most wanted was not to make Ro well, but to have a Tier House of your own, to be Chief.'

As she spoke, the memory of what had happened and why it happened grew clearer, as if her words were the cold and unforgiving winter sunlight that dissipated the obscuring mist. The mist had been kinder. He had persuaded himself that anything he did for Ro's good had itself to be good, or at least justified, but no good had come of it for Ro.

'Then Ro is not cured?' he said bleakly.

'No, Ro is as he was.'

'But that was the whole point! So, no good has come of this magic?' He felt rising horror. 'I trapped you against your will for this! I have been enchanted to love you and the world has been enchanted to give me a Tier House of my own.'

'Yes,' said Stone, in a voice as cold as her namesake. 'And I don't see what good can come of any of it, and I'm sorry.'

She lay back down on the bed and sobbed. Jerat wanted to comfort her, make the sorrow go away, but he did not. She was a Night Hunter, one of Zeron, the Dark Daughter's own, and she had enchanted him. Ro was still as he had been and all the world was made wrong and it was all Stone's fault – except that it wasn't; it was all his fault and he knew that too, knew that in the pattern of his bone and the shape of his sinews, and he would always know it.

THIRTY-TWO

Moss and Nela walked without talking; Nela was beginning to wonder if marrying Millard could be worse than starving to death. The forest was as dead and yet still green as a weed-choked pond. It was eerily quiet and she was by no means sure there was enough left living in it to sustain life – or more particularly her life and that of Moss. She watched him trudging ahead of her with a kind of casual strength. She still felt shame at watching him, for even free of his bonds he was still a bondsman. In the end she spoke to break the silence, to reassure herself that she was still there and could still be heard. Moss did not ignore her exactly, but he was so self-contained, so assured in the way he just trudged on that she had begun to feel invisible.

'He'll want the stone back, you know,' Nela said at last, and Moss stopped to answer her.

'You mean your father? Yes, I'm sure he will – we can't let him catch us. Will he check the stone in the strong box, do you think?'

She nodded. 'Millard will surely have told him his suspicions.'

She didn't like to suggest a rest, though she was struggling for breath and was very grateful when Moss himself suggested one. The air seemed stultifying under the canopy of yellowing leaves that trapped them like flies in liquid amber and made every step an effort.

'Moss, do you think we can survive here?'

'The trees are not quite dead or they wouldn't have any leaves, and there are some berries around. I don't know, Nela. We don't know what's beyond the next ridge – somewhere there may be a place that is better.'

'You look at what you've got, not what you haven't, don't you?' She was aware that as a bondsman that might be an essential quality.

'Yes, don't you?'

Nela still found it strange that he spoke to her as if they were equals; she was going to have to get used to it.

'I don't know. I suppose so, but I'm hungry and I find it hard to be cheerful when I'm hungry.'

'Keep alert for nuts and berries – anything edible, and animal droppings.' At her look of horror he added, 'Not to eat, Nela, as a sign of life.'

She smiled. 'Let's go, then. Perhaps if I imagine meat around the corner it'll be easy to get through this place.' It wasn't – only the thought of her father taking away the stone and dragging her back home to Millard kept her going.

Further on they found some berries. They were

vibrant and orange and looked a little like the candied festival berries sold in the morning markets of Scraal. Of course the resemblance to those delicacies might have been coincidental and the wild berries could be poisonous, but Nela found that she didn't much care. She ate a handful of them against Moss's advice and had such terrible stomach pains that she had to lie down.

'Are you going to be sick?' he asked, but she did not answer because she could not; she was sick.

'I'm sorry,' she said at last, 'but I don't think I can walk just yet.'

Something flitted across his face – was it contempt? Was it impatience?

They sat in an even more awkward silence than usual and then Nela said, 'Moss, you know what there is to be known about me – I know nothing of you. How did you come to be bonded?'

He shrugged, 'My family farmed the hill land in the north. We can trace our line way back to the old people, the hunters, though no one hunts for a living any more. Most of us bondsmen are descended from the ancient hunters, as I'm sure you know. I was my mother's first born and the Singer Teller at my birth named me "Moss", which is a name given to those of whom much is expected. I was raised to be a leader of my people, a Singer Teller. But the land is not good and we had many years of poor yields and sickness in our herds so that I was sold before I could complete my training. It's not what you think,' he said, as she exclaimed out loud. 'Someone had to be sold and I volunteered because I am young and strong and fetched a good price. It is an honour to save the family, and besides I was promised by a man of influence that I would be brought here, to Lakeside. Many of our tales are about the lake and the forest, so I think it was once our home, not yours, "the cradle of *our* civilisation".' He gave a wry grin. 'I have been trained to remember, so it is only fitting that I should be the one to come here to find out what can be uncovered about our past.'

Perhaps that explained Moss's lack of proper servility.

'I don't see how either of us can tell anyone about what we've found while we're stuck here in the middle of this place.' She was embarrassed to recognise that she sounded petulant.

Moss got to his feet. 'We need to keep moving – there may be better land further in. Are you well enough to walk?' She felt dreadful but she did not want to appear weak in front of Moss, so struggled to her feet. 'You can take my arm if it helps,' he said.

She did take it and it did help, though she had to stop more than once to be sick. Moss accepted that she could not go on without a longer rest. He left her while he set off to find something they could eat and some clean water. She built a small fire from dead leaves, because the sickness had left her cold and shivery – and it gave her something to do. She did not want to think too much. Her bout of violent sickness left her feeling exhausted so she shut her eyes for a moment and fell into a restless kind of doze. She checked the stone and touched it briefly and found herself standing in almost the same spot as her and

Moss, staring at the same stretch of blighted forest but through the eyes of Stone.

So they are going. I cannot blame them. The land is no longer fruitful and I cannot sing it back to health. They take their horses, and their pigs, their oxen and their cattle, and soon there will be nothing here but decay. Is this all my fault?

When she woke her father was standing over her. She blinked.

His face was paler than usual and the dye of his hair had all but washed away, leaving it an unremarkable brown, streaked with grey. He looked old and worried.

'What has that bondsman done to you?' His voice contrived to sound both angry and frightened.

'I'm all right, Father.' Her words sounded guttural and strange. She could smell the acrid stench of vomit, and saw that her cloak was encrusted with the stuff.

'Has he hurt you?'

'Who? What do you mean?' It took her a moment to work out where she was, longer still to realise that her worst fears had been realised: they had been found.

'The half-breed servant, of course,' he said, impatiently: her father had not changed.

'No, Moss has helped me.' Her father jerked her into a sitting position and a wave of nausea overwhelmed her – she retched drily.

'This is not his fault. I ate some berries.'

'Which ones?' Millard's round face emerged from behind her father's shoulder. She showed him one that she still held clutched in her hand.

'Eyes of the Forest,' Millard identified them. 'They can be eaten if cooked, but are poisonous raw – no need to ask how your daughter consumed them.'

Nela held her aching head in her hands. Then the thought struck her: where was Moss?

'What have you done to him, with Moss?' she asked the men – her father and her putative husband-to-be.

'Not yet what he deserves.' Millard sounded savage. 'Where is he?'

Nela found herself relaxing slightly – they had not found him yet, then.

'Father, you don't understand. I left the camp under my own free will. I will not marry Millard.'

'I doubt that Millard will have you – you have brought shame on all of us by consorting with this bondsman. What were you thinking of? Here, cover yourself.' Her father handed her one of her own scarves with which to cover her stubbled head. She saw that Millard averted his eyes from the ugly nakedness of her skull and she found herself obediently tying the scarf around her head.

'He took the black stone from my strong box too – that Zerat-cursed-bondsman-thief, but we'll get him – you need not worry yourself about that.'

'Father . . .'

'What, girl? You have shamed me, Nela. I don't want to hear any foolish justifications. It is as well your mother is not alive to see you thus.'

That was a low blow. Who knew what her mother

would have thought if she'd lived?

'Where is the bondsman?' Nela's father had her hand in his strong grip and was squeezing her wrist.

Nela shrugged. 'He went and took the stone with him,' she lied, hoping Moss was close enough to hear her and to run away. It was over. Her father was going to take her back. She had not wanted to die in the forest, but now she found no joy in the thought of leaving it. It was hard to bargain when she was disorientated and afraid, but she forced herself to sound strong and reasonable.

'I'll come back with you, Father, if you don't try to follow him.'

'He is a thief and he tried to harm a Findsman.'

'That isn't true, Father. I tried to harm Findsman Millard; it had nothing to do with Moss.'

'And you expect me to believe that? You forget, Nela, I've known you all your life and you've always been sweet and amenable. You have never harmed anyone. I will kill this bondsman – he has corrupted you and shown a degree of arrogance that cannot be tolerated in his kind!'

Nela was momentarily nonplussed. 'Sweet and amenable' – did her father not know her at all? Or had he simply ignored all her many arguments with him and forgotten they had ever existed? It took her a moment to think past his extraordinary statement and recognise the threat to Moss.

'Father, please. He has done nothing wrong.'

'Don't be ridiculous, child. Is your head so thoroughly turned by a handsome face that you can no longer use your wits? You are alone here in the forest. Why, he has obviously abandoned you.'

Nela was startled to note that her father had actually noticed and evaluated the bondsman's appearance. She allowed him to help her as she got shakily to her feet. She thought she glimpsed Moss watching her from behind a tree. She mouthed 'Run!' at him, but not before her father saw her and, following her direction of view, also saw Moss. Lord of the Earth! That was a stupid thing for her to have done.

'Millard, he's there!' Millard had a heavy knife in his hand and Nela noticed that her father had something similar around his waist. They were Moss's butchering knives and had been sharpened to a razor's-edge sharpness.

'Run!' Nela screamed at Moss, as both her father and Millard lumbered after him. She started to run herself, though not towards Moss, but a little to his left out of view of her father. She felt light-headed and shaky but would not allow that to affect her. The dead wood snapped under her feet like bones cracking and splintering. It didn't matter, her father and Millard were making so much noise – shouting and cursing words she'd never heard her father use. She could see Moss just ahead and to her right.

'Moss!' she shouted with her remaining breath. He slowed down to wait for her and grabbed her hand, dragging her after him, running heedlessly, careless of obstacles. Nela's face was scratched and her clothes caught in brambles and tore; she had a pain in her lower belly that felt like her stomach might burst open and spill what little remained in it, but still Moss pulled her after him. She did not dare slow for that would put them both at risk. She had never run so fast for so long in her life. She could hear the roar of water and they ran towards that.

'Father?' she panted.

'I tripped them up with the rope tied between the trees,' Moss said tersely.

'Hurt?'

'No! They're following.' Moss was right. She could hear her father shouting her name.

The river when they reached it was fast-flowing, a wild roaring beast of white water gushing through a narrow channel. There were rocks on either side that looked slick with weed and bright green moss. They stopped panting at the bank.

'Can you jump that?'

Nela shook her head. 'I don't know.'

Then she heard Millard's voice calling to her father not far behind and changed her mind.

'Yes!'

'We'll jump together.'

She wanted to argue, because it was surely safer to jump in turn, but the water made such a noise and she was so desperate that argument was beyond her.

Moss had her hand firmly and shouted, 'We'll take a run up and when I say "jump" leap with everything you've got.'

The sound of the river was deafening. The spray was soaking her scarf and cooling her clammy face. She did not have time to be frightened. They ran and jumped and stumbled and Moss half pulled her up the slippery surface of the rock. She'd lost a shoe and it had gone straight down under the water, sucked under by the treacherous currents that roiled and bubbled under the surface. She clung on to him, shivering with the sudden damp freshness in the air and the shock of what they had just done.

'Did you see what happened to my shoe?'

He nodded. 'Let's get away from here,' he said. Nela really couldn't move fast now. She took off her other shoe, but her feet were soft from her city life and the rough ground made her walk too cautiously.

'Do you think they'll cross the river?' Nela asked.

'Your father's old and Millard is rather portly, and we only just made it. They might try further upstream or downstream. I don't know. I don't think we can afford to rest for long.'

Nela nodded and wiped her face with her soaking head scarf. The cool water helped a bit.

'Thank you,' Moss said, looking at her directly. 'I heard what you said to your father, and thank you.'

'I –' she began.

'No time for talking, let's get going,' he said, cutting her short. Perhaps he knew how she felt.

Moss gave her his boots. They were not as good as her own and were too big, even though he had quite small feet, but they saved her from the worst of the terrain. Moss's own feet were calloused and tough-looking – as a farmer of the hills he was used to going barefoot. He led the way and she followed, but in truth neither of them knew where they were going.

THIRTY-THREE

Everyone in Jerat's Tier House overslept. Jerat went back downstairs to see how they fared.

'Jerat?' Verre said sleepily, when she saw him. 'No – go away, you're in danger. Avet will see you.' When she sat up and saw the Hall familiar and yet subtly different, she was quiet for a moment. 'What –?' she began.

'It is the magic,' the Teller Priest said, rubbing his temples as though he had a headache. 'The magic has wrenched the world out of shape. Hasn't it, Jerat?' He sounded calm but angry.

'What do you mean? I don't understand.' Verre was not at her sharpest when she first woke and she was looking at Jerat blankly and rubbing the sleep from her eyes.

'Tell her, Jerat.' The Teller Priest's voice was low and cold: there was no avoiding the explanation.

'The Teller told me about the tales.'

'I did not tell you to act on them, boy. You don't

put the blame for this at my Hall door,' the Teller interrupted.

'I take the blame, Teller, don't you worry about that,' Jerat answered. 'I thought that the only thing that could save Ro and make him well was the particular magic of a trapped Night Hunter. When we went missing Rin and I were tracking one and I hid her in the carrier coop. I forced her to use the Magic of the Last Resort. It did not work as I'd planned, it is not what I understood it to be. Everything went wrong. Ro is unchanged, but I now have a Tier House and a wife.'

Verre's face was both shocked and confused. She put her hand on his arm. 'A wife? And what of Ro?'

'I'm here, Mother.' Ro limped into the room, leaning heavily on Rin. 'Jerat, do you hate me so much as I am that you would break the world to change me?' He spoke with a stifled sob, his eyes huge dark pits in his pale face. He, like the Teller, seemed to have understood exactly what had gone on.

'No, Ro, it wasn't that!' Jerat almost shouted in horror. 'I wanted you to be free of the dead, that's all.'

'And not be such a burden on everyone,' Ro finished. Verre hugged Ro to her.

'Your brother, whatever he was trying to do, was doing it with the best intentions, Ro,' she said softly. 'I'm sure we'll see that when we understand better what is going on.' She stroked Ro's hair and looked at Jerat quizzically, as though she was not sure it was true. Jerat was at a loss to know what to say next.

'He has done a very wicked, foolish thing,' the Teller said gravely, 'and I want no part in it.'

Keran and Hela exchanged a look.

'You say you have a Tier House, Jer, and that at least seems to be true. Fine new wood, good-looking stock and plenty of space for a full Hearth Guard and Brood Trove, but where is it? Do you also have a Dependency?' Keran, ever practical, showed a remarkable and swift grasp of the changed situation.

'I don't know – I'm very close to our old Dependency . . . I saw my father's place through the window upstairs. I don't know anything else.'

Keran and Hela looked grave, but asked none of the questions he'd expected.

'And who, by Zerat's hand, is your wife?' Verre asked then, as though discovering that her son had changed the world through magic was of no account. At that moment the large Hall door creaked open further and the slim figure of Stone appeared in a beam of bright sunlight. She looked taller than Jerat remembered – she was certainly bigger than when he'd carried her through the forest; she was suddenly not much smaller than Verre.

'This is my wife – she is called Stone,' he said. He could not help smiling when he saw her, because there had never been a more beautiful creature, and he felt such love for her that even though he knew that love was a kind of enchantment, he was overwhelmed by it.

'She is a Night Hunter?' Verre sounded incredulous. Hela grabbed her spear.

'Yes,' Jerat said.

'You are the one who has done this?' The Teller Priest gazed at Stone with a fury Jerat had not

269

expected. Stone flinched.

'Old man, are you not the Teller Priest that Moon-eye told me about?' she said with controlled calm. 'I know you by her description. She had much to say of you that you would be pleased to hear.'

'I thought well of her too, but her acolyte is perhaps not so laudable.' He spat on the ground in front of her and Jerat found his hand around his fine, new belt-knife in a moment.

'I am not her acolyte. I am Moon-stone, Chief Singer of the Long Hill Summer People and the Bear Caves Winter People, and I had no choice in the use of this magic. If you had not passed on our tales in mangled form and told your people lies about the Last Resort perhaps we would all be better off.' She spoke fiercely and Jerat glowed with pride in her. She was right not to let the Teller Priest bully her, and she was right that perhaps he should take some of the blame.

'She's right,' Jerat said.

'No, she's not,' the Priest answered, furious. 'I have never said that this magic was other than evil. I wanted the Lakesiders to understand and tolerate the Night Hunters, not use their magic for selfish ends and not marry them either – the very idea is ridiculous.' His face was red.

'Don't worry about that, Teller Priest, we can have children together if that is your concern,' said Stone. 'We *will* have children together; it was part of the wish, and they will be neither Bear-men nor Night Hunters, but something else. Perhaps this is the will of the Womanface that the night people and the day people be reunited. Do you know a tale about that?

270

We have a song, an ancient hearthsong, but we sing it still. It is called "The Song of the Promise of Perfection". There is no getting away from it. This will happen; it is the way the magic works.' She turned away, dignified and inscrutable. Did she regret what they had done? Jerat didn't know.

Verre stared after her. 'She is beautiful, Jer, but she is not one of us. She is one of Zeron, the Dark Daughter's own. How could you do this?'

'I was trying to keep us together, Verre, keep everyone safe, but the magic has not worked as I expected. Am I to blame for that?' He was not going to tell Verre that Stone had bewitched him into loving her. Now that he did love her, to say such a thing seemed disloyal, and their attitude towards her already seemed unnecessarily harsh.

Keran and Hela, with the resourcefulness typical of them, made breakfast. Jerat's wish, while it included plenty of food and beasts, including his favourite hearth dog, and a well appointed Tier House, did not include the large numbers of no-men it took to keep such a place going. It was a child's picture of a Tier House, lacking all that made it workable. Still, it gave Jerat pleasure to eat again with those he loved in his own Hall. He tried to ignore the fact that Stone had disappeared and that the Teller glowered at him over his meal and would not speak.

THIRTY-FOUR

'What happens now?' Keran asked as they ate.

'What do you mean – what happens now?' Jerat said. He was still struggling to work out what had already happened.

'Well, do you think Avet will tolerate a new Tier House so close to his Dependency? I've looked around and we're just a quarter of a morning's walk from the northern gate – the gate of the third quarter. Are the farmholders to give their tithe portion to both of you? There can be nothing but trouble for us in this, Jer.'

It was a problem Jerat had not considered, but then he had so little time to consider anything. He tried to behave as a Chief might. He chewed slowly on his corn porridge to buy himself some time.

'If I have carrier birds could you send messages to those of our old Horde who may wish to join us, Keran? I can see that we will need to gather a fighting force – perhaps we can tempt those of the Brood Trove who have not yet sworn fealty? And maybe some of the no-men – Heron and Frinkip were with us in the old place so long, would they come?' Keran shrugged and Hela simply looked overwhelmed. Lacking the support he needed there, Jerat turned to his mother. 'Verre, could you go and see if any might be persuaded to join us? Your reputation is enough to tempt some to our side.'

Keran was looking at him in surprise. 'You are serious?'

'Of course. Now I have this place, however I came by it, I will defend it. I will not let Avet take it.'

Verre seemed torn between admiration and disgust. 'You want war again so soon after the last?'

'Do you want Avet to send us from our homelands – to separate us?' Jerat countered. 'Or do you want us to keep what Zerat has brought us?'

Verre paused. Ro and Rin were both sitting as close to her as they could and, Jerat noted, as far away from him as it was possible to go. Verre was holding their hands. 'I do not know if it is Zerat or Zeron that has brought this about, Jerat.' She sighed with something that might have been despair, but Jerat couldn't see what she was looking so miserable for – they were still together, weren't they? 'I'm not sure any good can come of it,' Verre finished. Ro and Rin were looking at him as if they did not know him, as if he hadn't raised them himself, as if he'd not done all this for them, or as if he had not thought he was doing it all for them.

'I am Chief of this Tier House and I will be a good leader – I promise you that,' Jerat said earnestly, in an effort to cheer them.

'Very well,' Verre said, reluctantly. 'I will go with Keran and Hela to speak to some of your Brood brothers whom I know are less enamoured of Avet than loyalty demands. If I go at once they will no doubt be as confused by the appearance of this Tier House as we are – perhaps Avet will not realise the danger and will refrain from killing me on sight.' Perversely, the thought of such risk seemed to make her more cheerful.

'Be careful, Verre. Take no risks.' At Jerat's concerned tone she looked at him. She nodded and he knew that whatever happened she was, however reluctantly, still on his side.

Keran, Verre and Hela left Jerat alone with the Teller. Jer lowered his eyes under the Teller's piercing gaze.

'I never expected this, Jer. The Hunter is right – I should not have told you the legends, but I never thought . . .' He sounded bitter, raw.

'I am grateful, Teller Priest. I am pleased to have this place. If Ro is not well, at least I can keep him safe.' Jerat would not confess his doubts to his mentor. He was a man now and would be true to his own judgement, even his mistakes.

'Can you keep Ro safe? Moon-stone's tribe will be gathering. What will they do when they know you have taken their Singer to wife? She has betrayed her people as surely as you have betrayed yours.'

'I don't understand. How have I betrayed you?' Jerat could not quite keep the pleading note from his voice. He had hoped to make the Teller proud of him. He had not expected this fury, these accusations.

The Teller turned to him angrily and spat, 'If the blood of the Bear-men and of the Night Hunters mingles, what will become of the Bear-men? What will become of the Night Hunters? We will each belong neither to the night nor the day, neither to Zerat nor to Zeron. We will lose our place in the world and all will become chaos.'

'Teller, Stone and I are only two people – there are thousands of Bear-men and thousands of Night Hunters – we are no threat to anyone,' Jerat answered quietly.

'You have turned the world upside down, used magic to distort the natural order of things, and you can say that?'

'Yes, I *can* say that. I want only the best for our people, for my brothers and for you. I want us to be together and happy as we were before. How can that be evil?'

'I'm sure *they* will tell you,' the Teller Priest said sharply, and indicated the arrival of fifty or so young men dressed in the animal skins of the Night Hunters. All but one had an arrow notched on their bowstring and all regarded Jerat with suspicion. Jerat glanced briefly at the Teller – surely he would know what to say? He had dealt with Stone's people before.

'What are you doing razing the forest and building a new Tier House on our precious hunting grounds? We will not tolerate this any longer. You think we are fearful because we hunt in the dark. We are afraid neither of you nor of the daylight.' The speaker was a small but stocky man, young to be a spokesman for the Night Hunters with him. He looked barely older than Avet. His face had the same flint-hard quality as Stone's and, loving her as Jerat did, it was harder to hate the man in front of him or to be as afraid as he would have been just a few long nights ago. The Teller Priest had clamped his mouth shut and so it was Jerat who had to answer.

'I am Chief here. My name is Jerat. Perhaps I can offer you hospitality and we can talk about your complaint against me.' He kept his voice level and calm and it was easy to do so because in the strangeness of this day nothing seemed quite real or really threatening. The day was clear and hard-edged but Jerat felt that if he were to look away it would all disappear like mist in the forest. Stone must have re-emerged from the Heart of the Home because Jerat heard her speak.

'Sky?'

'Stone?' The stocky Night Hunter turned to face Stone, who walked slowly to stand beside Jerat. Jerat could see quite clearly that she was now more than twice the size of the Hunter who stood before her, though still small and slight compared to Jerat himself.

'What have you done, sister? You are changed.'

'It was the Magic of the Last Resort, Sky – I am Jerat's wife now.'

She looked ill at ease, though her face was not particularly expressive and Jerat might have been imagining such a response. Her hand sought his and he took it; it was damp and trembled a little in his.

'No!' Sky shouted. 'This is not your work?'

Stone nodded. 'This is the new world, there is no

going back. Through me, the souls of the Bear-men and Night Hunters will be joined in our children. There is no fighting it – this will be so.'

'Then you have betrayed us, Stone, and you are no longer my sister or our Singer.'

The man Stone had called Sky was about to turn away when she stopped him.

'Sky, don't go yet. I may be able to help you and you may be able to help me.'

He turned and gave her a look of searing dislike.

'And what have we ever done for each other since you were grown? You have no love for me or for any who see the world through questioning eyes.'

'I have not always been right, Sky, but I have always been your sister, and changed though I might be, I am your sister still. We have a problem – we lack a . . .' she seemed to search for the word she wanted for a moment, before saying carefully, 'a battle chorus, a Horde. I think the people further down the valley will attack us and try to take this place from us and then they will use up more of the forest as new people come here. They are the kind who fear the forest and have to destroy it as we would not. If you help us fight them we will make a solemn promise not to encroach any further upon the forest but to protect it. Won't we, Jerat?'

Jerat nodded firmly. Stone must have overheard his discussions with Keran and Verre and was admirably quick to understand their predicament and to respond. Sky looked at her for a while, unmoving and apparently unmoved. Perhaps something passed between them that Jerat did not see, but Sky seemed calmer suddenly.

'We will go and talk with the rest of the Night Hunters,' he said at last. 'This is too big a decision to make alone. I do not make decisions for all of us without discussion. Perhaps it would have been better for us all, Stone, if you had not.'

'It was the the Last Resort, Sky – what choice was there?' She sounded desperate and Jerat understood completely; it was not pleasant to be rejected by those you thought you served.

'The choice is made of what you are, Stone, a traitor at heart.'

He left without looking back and the men he brought turned wordlessly and followed him.

When Jerat looked round to discuss with the Teller Priest what he had witnessed, the old man was gone. Jerat was more troubled by that than by anything else that had happened on this strange morning.

THIRTY-FIVE

Rin recovered quickly from the shock of the change that the magic had brought about and was delighted with the new Tier House and with everything that went with it – his beloved brother was Chief even if, beside the Tier House and immediate land, he was not Chief of very much. Ro was still far from happy.

'Big death coming,' he said cryptically.

'Ro, don't you see, you have a home here with me for ever?' Jerat said, placatingly, but Ro merely looked at him with blank, unfathomable eyes.

'You don't want me. I know that, Jer. You want the old Ro of long ago.'

'That's not true –' Jerat began.

'It doesn't matter,' Ro interrupted, 'Verre and Ro will go to the water together soon.' He turned away then and ice seemed to freeze Jerat's heart – did Ro mean the water of the dead?

Jerat did not dare to dwell on Ro's response. He might have meant no more than that the two of them would fetch water from Jerat's well that day – for the Tier House had a fine well and even a Hearth tree and olive grove as ancient-seeming and as fruitful as that on the old Chief's land. There was enough grain for the winter and enough land to grow more. There were beasts enough in the byre to provide milk and meat, but without the 'gifts' of dependent farmholders the Tier House could not support a sufficiently large Hearth Guard to defend itself, let alone a large Brood Trove, if they were to be so blessed. Jerat was torn between irritation at the incompleteness of his heart's wish and untrammelled joy for all that was there. Keran, fine Horde leader that he was, had understood all that perfectly from the first.

Verre returned in time for the noon breakfast, bringing twenty of the Brood brothers and fifteen no-men, including Heron.

'If war was not inevitable before, it is now,' she said gloomily, as the new Hearth Guard offered fealty and Dependency. 'Avet is trying to recall everyone who left the Dependency after the victory celebrations. He's trying to gather them all back to his Hall, and that was a lot of people. He was a cruel leader and the way he slaughtered Lirian was shameful, but the men will follow him because his toughness is proven and because he won. I imagine he will try to attack within days. I would in his shoes. He will try to take advantage of our confusion.'

'Did you see him? Is he not confused?'

'He was clear-headed enough to threaten to tear my head from my shoulders with his bare hands if he ever saw me again. Yes, he was confused. He has had nightmares that his Tier House was destroyed by a great storm and he has no recollection of your Hall being built – though he pretended he remembered. He told me he told you that the move was ill-judged from the moment you first asked his permission! So he is pretending he knows what has gone on – he was furious at my recruiting from his Horde, once he worked out what I was doing. I tell you I was lucky to get away, thanks in no small part to Heron who let the horses out to distract him. My thanks to you, Heron,' she said in the direction of the largely silent no-man who had been a steady presence through most of Jerat's childhood. 'He will have upwards of two hundred men in a matter of days, and we have twenty-four – thirty-nine if you count the no-men.' She looked at them questioningly and Heron nodded. 'I presume your "wife" does not fight?'

Stone looked up from the cook pot, her flint-face keen and alert. Her voice carried the sharpened edge of a weapon made by a craftsman at the height of his powers. Jerat shivered when she spoke.

'You may call me "Stone" – should I call you "Mother"? It is our custom.'

Verre's face darkened and she looked like someone drinking sour milk. 'You may call me Guardsman Verre – that is ours.'

'Guardsman Verre, you might wish to remember that it is Jerat who trapped me and imprisoned me and put me through great anguish and pain to rip from me the magic which has torn and twisted our world. When you look around for someone to blame do not look blindly. I chose this only when I had no choice.'

Verre looked as though she might attack the smaller

woman for an instant, but then, unexpectedly, she smiled.

'You are a stranger and strange enough, but I recognise pride when I see it and a warrior's will. I will not set myself against you, Stone, but don't expect too much from me. I respect your people – without Moon-eye's help I would be dead in childbirth like most of my Brood sisters – but you are not one of us, not one of the Bear-men. What you have done here for good or ill has given me more cause to fear you than to love you.'

Stone smiled herself, a rare expression and one swiftly gone. Her voice, as Jerat was rapidly learning, was the best indicator of her mood, as well as a tool she used with great precision. It was less lethally sharp when she answered, 'I am a Singer – we are always more feared than loved. I have Jerat's love, I don't need yours.'

'Now that we understand each other so well, do you wish me to show you how to administer a Tier House?' asked Verre.

Jerat was more relieved than he could have predicted when Stone answered with something like genuine warmth, 'That would be most helpful.'

When the new Hearth Guard had been fed and introduced to their quarters, when the no-men had been assigned their jobs and when Keran had talked about defending the pristine Hall at length with anyone who would listen, Tanit, formerly of the first quarter, arrived carrying the old Chief's ancient carved talking stick which denoted that he had been granted the power to act as Avet's spokesman. His message was clear and predictable.

Jerat had usurped the authority of the Chief of the

Dependency by building his Tier House so close to Dependency ground. Either he gave appropriate tithe goods and disbanded his Hearth Guard or Avet would attack and give no mercy. Trove and Horde were equally forfeit: that meant, in effect, Ro and Rin and the thirty men and no-men whom Verre had persuaded to join them.

'Tanit, Brood brother; I am sorry that it has come to this. If you want to join us and be free of Avet's yoke – be welcome. I remember how he used to put salt in our milk when we were children. Do you want to be ruled by such a man?'

Tanit laid the talking stick down carefully on the floor to show that he was no longer speaking for Avet.

'You can't win, Jer, and there is a rumour that you have used the vile Dark Daughter's moon magic to get this place. Please, Jer, give it up. It may be that Avet would take you back as part of the greater Battle Horde, if not the Hearth Guard.'

'You know that's a lie, Tanit. Avet would have me killed now whatever happens.'

'I'm sorry Jer, I wish this hadn't happened, but battle is coming whatever I want. Avet is out of control – you know how he's always hated you.'

'But you don't have to fight for him.'

Tanit shrugged. 'He would not have been my choice for Chief, but he is our father's legitimate heir. He has proved himself an adequate war leader. I must fight for my Hall, even against you, Brood brother.'

Jerat could not argue with that. Tanit was an honourable man, and had never been more than normally vicious to the brothers of the other quarters.

'Thank you, Tanit, for your honesty. Can I offer you

food or some ale?'

Tanit shook his head. 'I should only have spoken the words Avet gave me. I hope you can stay out of his spear's way, but expect no mercy from Avet. He is ruthless and cruel in battle. Maybe you could send Ro and Rin away. I would not like them to fall into his hands.'

'Perhaps I'll do that, Tanit. Go and give the message to our Brood brother that I desire no mercy, for we are not powerless. We harm no one by our presence here in land that was never his.'

Tanit picked up the talking stick and nodded. 'Oh,' he laid the stick down again so that the carved head rolled into the dirt – a bad omen, 'Kellatt said it would dishonour the second quarter were you to give up now and he wishes you luck, though he fights for the old Hall. Does that make any sense to you?'

Jerat smiled at that. Kellatt, one of the oldest of his own quarter, was known for drinking too much, but for once Jerat understood what he was saying; he knew what Kellatt meant – he had no choice but to fight Avet.

'Perhaps. Goodbye, Tanit. Keep safe.'

This time Tanit picked up the stick and wiped the dust off the extravagantly decorated carved head. He bowed a quick goodbye and walked away back to Avet.

'Death coming,' Ro said gloomily.

'Thanks, Ro,' Jerat said, and hurried off to try to find the Teller Priest.

Jerat found the Priest talking earnestly to Hela, who looked as upset as he had ever seen her. She turned away when she saw Jerat coming and waved a cursory farewell in the Teller's direction. The Teller had readied himself for a journey.

'Are you going?' Jerat asked, though he feared he already knew the answer.

'I can't stay.'

'Please.'

'Jerat, it grieves me that you have done this. I had thought better of you – I never would have told you that tale if I'd thought that you would have tried to bend the world to your purpose this way: it seems as if you truly are blood-marked.'

Jerat hung his head, but shame was only part of it. He had always thought so well of the Teller that to find the respect was not reciprocated was not an easy thing to bear.

'I suppose you have to do what you choose,' Jerat said as steadily as he could. 'I am grateful for all that you taught me and for saving Ro.' He would have liked to clasp the smaller man in a warrior's farewell, but it did not seem right so instead he just said, 'May Zerat bless your steps,' and turned away.

He was surprised to see a woman standing behind him, because he had not heard her arrive. She was of Stone's people and was small and lean as a deer. She was looking past Jerat to the Teller.

'Teller Priest!' Her voice was as commanding and chilling as Stone's own.

'Moon-eye?'

'What have you to do with this abomination?'

The Teller shrugged. 'As little as possible, old friend. It seems our friendship has brought disaster, not understanding.'

'You are leaving this son-of-your-heart to manage without your guidance?'

'I am going. This is not what I wanted for any of us.'

The woman was small, childlike beside the Teller who was the smallest Bear-man Jerat knew, but when she touched him he shrank away from her as if she had struck him.

'Must you run?'

'I cannot stay in a world made wrong.' The Teller pulled away from her. 'I'm sorry,' he said, and hurried away so swiftly he almost stumbled. It was not what Jerat had expected of him. Jerat and Moon-eye watched the Teller leave until he was out of sight.

'Are you going to blame me too?' Jerat said.

'Don't get above yourself, young Bear-man,' she answered tartly. 'Perhaps it was the will of the Womanface, whom you know as Zeron, the Dark Daughter, that our peoples be united. I thought so once and so did your Teller Priest. I am sad that he changed his mind.'

'You don't think I was cruel to Stone and that I've pulled and pushed the world out of shape?'

'I'm sure you were cruel to Stone, but it seems she has had her revenge. You are doomed to be despised by both your own kind and ours. You are doomed never to know if you love her for what she is or because of the magic. You were blood-marked at birth, Jerat – I saw it then, and as for Stone, she is touched by the Womanface – there has never been a Singer like her. She far surpasses me in strength, if not in wisdom. I ask myself why two such people should meet if it were not the will of the Womanface. If the world is turned upside down, perhaps it was due for turning.'

Jerat looked at her in surprise. She smiled a broad

gap-toothed smile. She lacked Stone's unearthly beauty but her face was strong and kind, like Hela's face or Verre's – smaller and darker but not so different, not when she smiled.

'The Teller has admired my people as creatures of mystery and power. He has sought to understand us, but he has always fought the understanding that we are so much the same. Even in your stories Zerat and Zeron are born of the same earth. We of the Night Hunters have many stories to explain ourselves – did the Teller not tell you? My favourite is that Zerat and Zeron are the two faces of the Unmade One, the male sun and the female moon, who watch over the night and the day. Their song made the earth and their song drew all that lives from the womb of the earth except for the Bear-men and the Night Hunters. The people of the day, the Bear-men, were begun by Zeron and finished by Zerat, and the people of the night, the Night Hunters, were begun by Zerat and finished by Zeron. You see, Jer, we are both of the day and of the night. We were always meant to be together, sharing the night and the day as the Unmade One is one with two faces, the Womanface and the Manface.'

'Is it true?'

'It tells us something that is true – that is all I know. Such is the way with stories. I have spoken to Stone. She is waiting for you in the Heart of the Home.'

He felt himself flush. 'I'll go and find her, then,' he said awkwardly, but Moon-eye had walked away from him, having said all she needed to. She stood some distance away lost in her own thoughts, looking out across the Hearthfields, watching the Teller's way.

THIRTY-SIX

Stone was sitting hunched by the cook fire of the first quarter. The room smelled of new wood and resin, of spices and of Stone herself.

'Moon-eye at least does not think we have done wrong,' Jerat said softly.

'She sees us as fulfilling a dream of her own, that is why. She has been in love with the Teller Priest these forty winters, Jerat. It is never spoken of, but I have always known it.'

'Well, the Teller Priest has gone. He thinks I let him down.'

'Perhaps he is angry that he never had the courage to take Moon-eye to wife all those winters ago.'

'Or perhaps he is merely angry with me,' Jerat said.

'We have gathered bracken for our own sleeping place, Jerat. We alone lie on it.'

'I would like that,' he replied. She laid her small cool hand on his arm.

'Then let us enjoy what the Womanface has given

us, for however long we have.' She spoke persuasively and earnestly, her voice beguiling and sweet, and while Stone touched him he found it hard to disagree with anything that she said or to deny her anything she wanted.

'Stone,' he said much later while they shared sweet-leaf tea in front of one of the pottery cook fires. 'Why did you change yourself? You are taller than you were, aren't you?'

'I am what I need to be so that the wish can be fulfilled and we can be together and have young together. If the others of my people find partners among your people the same thing will happen to them. It is the way the world is now. The Magic of the Last Resort lives on in the very fabric of the world until the wish is fulfilled.'

'My wish wasn't such a good wish though, was it? A Tier House without a Dependency.'

'Perhaps part of your wish was for your own Dependency, the one you have always known. True wishes, that come from the deepest places, aren't easily put into words. They are as complex and as simple as a seed and sometimes you won't know the full import of the wish until the seed is grown. That might take generations.' Her voice was soft as lamb's wool, warm and seductive. Try as he might he could not look upon her as an evil enchantress; she seemed so honest, so truthful when she was with him.

'I cannot regret the wish, even though I hurt you,' he said quietly.

'I will never forget the anguish of it, Jerat.'

'But do you think this is worth it?'

She smiled, and looked young and happy for a moment. 'You think that I think you're so wonderful that I'll say yes?'

Jerat laughed.

'Well, I thought that you might be glad that we are together – yes.'

The smile disappeared and she looked serious again, and Jerat could see that she was still under much strain. 'I don't know if we both might have been happier if what you did had not been done – but now, well, it cannot be undone.'

'Even by another wish of the Last Resort?'

'I tell you truthfully there is no one anywhere who sings as I do. My voice has more power than any other – I have always been told that this is so and now I finally believe it. This singing, this wishing, is like the colours that run through your weaving. It will be there until the fabric is finished, however long that takes. No one alive has the power to undo it.'

'Are you afraid now to be in a Tier House like this – closed in?'

She shook her head. 'No, that too is a thread in the weaving. I will be what I am needed to be to make our wishes come true.'

Jerat was chilled by that, by the thought that the magic had twisted their emotions, their true nature, in that moment of change. He could not look at himself and find the person who did not adore Stone; she could not look at herself and see someone who needed to be in the forest. It made him uncomfortable to think of it, and regretful – if the magic had done that, then perhaps if he'd been able to wish otherwise, Ro could have been saved. Magic that could change his nature could surely have restored Ro's. He pushed his thinking back towards more practical matters.

'And your brother, Sky, will he join us and fight Avet?'

Stone shrugged. 'I think he will, but there will be a price, and I know what that will be.'

'Will you pay it?'

Stone's voice grew harder edged, like the flint she so often resembled. 'We will both do what we need to do, won't we? To keep what we now have.'

Jerat could not disagree.

THIRTY-SEVEN

If Nela's father had followed them they did not hear him. They walked on into the forest, as the light faded and darkness fell softly as snow in the silence of the almost-dead place.

'What can have happened here? Nela whispered. Her voice sounded curiously flat and featureless, almost as if the forest had swallowed up the sound.

'I can't imagine – bad magic. I don't know,' Moss said, his voice lost too in the silence of the forest which seemed to swallow everything.

'Maybe. Perhaps if it is Stone's forest the stone will tell me.'

They built a fire and shared some berries and some eggs that Moss had found while Nela was recovering from her sickness. They settled themselves quite comfortably before Nela took out the stone again. It was probably not wise while her father was in pursuit, but it had become a kind of compulsion. There was too much she did not understand that she wanted to know.

She looked at Moss to see if he approved. He nodded and she slipped the stone from its covering.

Lilith is playing in the meadow beyond the Tier House Hearthfields. I can hear her laughing and the sound makes me less fearful. Her brother Moss is chasing her and I would like to go and check that he is not being too rough, but the baby is crying and I feel that prickling sensation and go to fetch her and feed her. I am tired, I cannot deny it. I ought not to have borne so many babes so close together, but they are beautiful and strong and I love them. The blight is not so far advanced that we cannot live here. The land is good and we yet have enough loyal Dependents to farm it, though so much grain makes my belly bloat and sometimes I long to run across the long hills in the moonlight like I did when I was free. So many have gone, I should be glad that there are enough left to keep the Tier House going.

'Come, sweet one, honey-touch, moon-washed child of my heart, come to Mama.' I love it when her small hands grab and she looks at me so gravely with the wisdom of infancy. Her skin is red-brown as Jerat's and her eyes are black as mine, my changeling child, neither Night Hunter nor Bear-man, but simply herself. I wonder if it was maybe the will of the Womanface, this uncanny union that brought my sweet ones into life. The fireside of the Bear Caves seems too long ago. In the upper room of the Tier House I cannot feel the earth beneath my feet or see the Womanface rippling in the water,

I no longer vibrate like the plucked string of a Hunter's harp with power that resonates with the world. I am a broken string, a cracked shell. I am no longer Chief Singer of the Long Hill Summer People and the Bear Caves Winter People, and my voice is an instrument of destruction. But I will not think of that.

I named this baby Skylark after the brother I lost and the joyous, free-flying songbird that I once wanted to be. Her warmth against me is what I have now, her soft skin and fragrant head, her eager pink little mouth suckling and her dark hair curling damply where she lies, flushed with my heat against me. Her perfect tiny fingers curl around my breast. I love what I have and what I have lost is gone.

Nela woke to see Moss's face, the beacon by which she now navigated.

'You were crying.'

'Stone did something. I don't know what, Moss. Perhaps it had something to do with the fire. She is sad about something she has done. She has children, and one of them has your name – how strange. I think they are the children of the Bear-man who trapped her, Jerat, and she is living in a Tier House, but the land is blighted and many people have left. I can't work it out. Do you think it's safe to rest here a bit longer? I could try to find out more, or should we go on?'

'Nela, I think you have to rest. Here, you can lean against me if you like. I will keep watch for a while. Your father may yet find us.'

She leant against him gratefully, and he surprised her again by starting to sing. She could hear his chest vibrate as he softly began the Evening Song in the ancient tongue.

THIRTY-EIGHT

It was late evening when Sky and his men returned to the Tier House. Jerat met them by the outdoor cook fire. Contrary to the long-established custom of his father's Hall, Jerat and the wife of the first and only quarter ate with the Hearth Guard and the Brood Trove – Ro and Rin – at the outdoor cook fire.

The new recruits looked curiously at the unmasked wife, who, though tall and dressed in conventional clothes, was clearly one of the Dark Daughter's own. Jerat admired the way she ignored their scrutiny. Much as he liked the comfort and luxury of the Heart of the Home, it seemed foolish to Jerat to eat alone there with Stone when all the people he had fought for were below. Keran and Verre and some of the no-men had expertly caught and cooked a meal from what was at hand. Sky and his men accepted Jerat's hospitality and there was enough for everybody. There was ale too, like the full corn store, a blessing of the Magic of the Last Resort.

It would not have been seemly for Jerat to ask Sky about his decision until he'd eaten his fill, and in that the two peoples seemed to share a common understanding. Only when all was finished and cleared away did the two leaders move a little away from the rest.

'We have spoken amongst ourselves and are agreed that we will sing in your hunting chorus, your Battle Horde, if Stone will teach us the secret of the song of fire.'

There was a silence, which indicated that Jerat and Sky had not been as discreet as they thought – everyone was listening to their low-voiced talk and everyone was now focusing, with rapt attention, on Stone. She continued eating for a while, apparently oblivious to the tens of pairs of eyes staring at her. She wiped her mouth fastidiously and took a sip of ale.

'It is not easy to sing, brother. As we have discussed before, you have never shown much interest in it. The healing songs take years to master – I don't know if you can learn the song of fire in the time I have to teach you.' She spoke with a kind of arrogance, which Jerat found surprising, and yet Moon-eye had spoken to him in much the same way – as if she did not expect to be questioned. Perhaps her tone was normal for the Chief Singer, but Sky looked angry nonetheless and there was a murmuring from his men. Stone's night-black hair was unbound round her shoulders and she had abandoned the hunting trews of her people for a red woollen robe. She looked like she belonged neither to the Night Hunters nor the Bear-men – she looked completely and uniquely herself, and Jerat felt ridiculously proud of the level way she spoke to Sky, though the air around was charged with violence and it would only take one spark, one incendiary note, to ignite it.

'If you give an oath of fealty and Dependency to my husband, Jerat, I will teach those able to learn the secret of the song of fire.' She put up one hand to forestall his response. 'I do not know if anyone else can do it. As far as I know I am the only Singer to have developed the art, and I will not have your support withdrawn if none of you have the skill or the determination. I will have that known and witnessed now. But . . .' With the same intensity as the Teller Priest she swung round and seemed to look at each of the assembled men eye-to-eye so that more than one shifted uncomfortably on the packed earth floor. 'You swear fealty tonight.' She held Sky's eye for a long time until he nodded and the moment of danger passed.

Jerat spotted the slight trembling of her hand when she swept her hair away from her face, and took this to mean that she had been more concerned than she had appeared. She sensed him looking at her and smiled and he understood that this was the price she'd known she'd be obliged to pay for her brother's cooperation.

The elaborate oath-singing took much of the night and then all Stone's people sang the Evening Song together, which Jerat had never heard before; it made his soul shiver with the beauty and the joy in it. If he were never to hear music again he counted himself lucky to have heard that song. Each of the singers seemed to sing a different part so that the melody and harmony rose and fell like the waves on the lake, changing like the patterns of the sun on the water.

The weather was still mild and Sky's hunters arranged to guard the fortified Hearthfields between them. Although they hunted at night by preference, they did not, as Jerat had always believed, sleep during the day and live their lives in darkness, but simply seemed to need less sleep than the Bear-men. He did not feel entirely safe being guarded by those he had been taught to fear.

'They are honourable,' Stone said in her softest, most reassuring voice; she seemed to read him as easily as he read her. Jerat changed the subject.

'This song of fire, what is it – more magic?'

Her expression darkened and she looked uncomfortable. 'It is something I happened upon – a gift for destruction which I did not know I had and which I did not want. But maybe nothing comes without a reason and we will need it now.' She sounded resigned to its use, but Jerat knew she was less certain than she appeared and a moment later she added, 'I don't know what Moon-eye will say when she discovers what I can do. It is not something she will care for.'

'Will she stop you?'

'I am Chief Singer, so she cannot stop me, but . . .' She pulled a face and her meaning was clear enough.

Jerat found her hand and squeezed it. 'We have to do whatever is necessary to hold what we have taken, Stone. It is as you said.'

Jerat was not happy depending upon a weapon he had never seen or heard of before, any more than he was happy depending on the Hunters he had long regarded as his natural enemy, but with his small force he could not afford to refuse anything that might help; for better or worse they were allies now.

Jerat slept badly, his rest punctuated by dreams of battle and of loss. The Teller Priest shook his finger at him and called him 'blood-marked'. He woke with a start at dawn to find that Stone's place beside him was empty. The Tier House was vibrating as if the earth trembled, so that he felt it in his bones. He heard something, something strange that made him feel sick and cold in his stomach, that made him viscerally afraid. He dressed quickly and made his way outside.

The Night Hunters stood together in a cluster around Stone. All had their eyes closed and seemed to be concentrating hard on something, a note so low and strange that he almost did not recognise it as the product of a human voice. It was a cool, misty morning and the Hunters looked almost like figures of stone emerging from the roiling mist. Was this his defence against Avet's spears and arrows and stone-shot that would shatter shoulders and skulls and tear the meat off a man and bleed away his life?

The note began to rise and intensify and Jerat shivered so that the fine hairs that covered his arms and legs all rose at once. The noise grew to a pitch that hurt his ears, it resonated in the base of his skull and made his head feel painfully tight and, as he covered his ears to protect them, a bush just at the edge of the Hearthfield burst into flame. As one body, the Night Hunters in the mist exhaled. The bush blazed and crackled with flame of unusual intensity.

'You see,' Stone said. 'If you are going to practise, stay well clear of the Tier House.'

With her words Stone seemed to release Sky and his men from their peculiar stillness and they began to talk amongst themselves. Sky seemed very excited but Stone appeared weary, drained and unhappy; a small trickle of blood emerged from her nose and ran down her face.

'I don't like it,' she said, and shuddered. 'It feels wrong – against the spirit of the Womanface.'

'Does the power of singing come from her?' Sky asked.

'Yes.'

'Then how can this be not of her too?'

'I don't know, Sky, but because I do not know the answer it does not mean that I am wrong.'

She walked towards Jerat, wiping the blood from her face with her fingers. Jerat could see that she was crying.

'This is not right, Jerat, but when you have so many enemies what are we to do?'

'It is a powerful thing, Stone, but it makes me feel . . .' he thought for a moment, 'it feels as if my bones and the ligaments of my body have all been loosened and tightened in new ways – as if my skin is too tight for my skull.' He took her hand.

'Have you seen Moon-eye?' Stone asked Jerat, who shook his head. Stone's voice quivered as a Singer's voice never did. 'Moon-eye came to see what I was doing. She said that she could believe that in the Magic of the Last Resort I might have been following the true will of the Womanface, but that this song of fire opposed it. She told me that we would pay a high price for this, and like the Teller she has gone. I am no longer a child of her heart. She has been my mother of my heart for so long and as dear as the woman who bore me. I do not know how I will manage without her.' Her words broke into sobs, quickly swallowed. Jerat comforted her while she cried, but she only allowed her grief to show for a moment before she recovered herself and was again proud, unyielding stone. 'We can't indulge ourselves in might have beens, Jerat. We have remade the world this way between us and we have to get on with it. Don't we?'

She was tense and taut like the bow-backed woman she had been in the carrier coop, fighting to remain in control. He understood how she felt. Things were rushing away from them like a snowball rolling down a hill, gaining pace and size, escaping from their control. They had scarcely had time to work out what had gone on before they were having to prepare for battle and the loss of all they had so recently gained.

'I'm sure we can win,' Jerat said, 'but I am going to send Rin and Ro into the forest until it is over. Is there somewhere they should go or somewhere they should not go?'

She knew what he was asking. 'If Sky has agreed to serve as part of your Horde others of the Night Hunters will have agreed it, though not perhaps all. I will take them to the place my sister usually camps at this time of year. It is likely that she will take them in.'

'Thank you. It would be good for them to know your people better. I don't want them to grow up thinking . . .' He tailed off.

'That we are different?' she finished. 'But we are, Jerat. We are different, though not as different as your Teller Priest thinks, but we are not evil and we are not your enemy – your enemy is your brother, Avet.' Then she added in a softer voice, 'All my life I have tried to do the will of the Womanface, but now I'm not sure what I'm doing any more – I don't know what her will is any more. I found you and lost everything else.'

'I know that you are not evil, Stone. I knew that before the magic . . .' For some reason he had developed an aversion to calling it by its common name. 'Perhaps I am the evil one, because I wanted what I wanted too much. I wanted it so much that I was willing to change the world to get it and trap an innocent in the process.' Jerat shook his head; now that battle was coming, he wondered at the wisdom of what he'd done. Stone seemed to understand.

'We will survive, Jerat, we have to – it's how it works.'

'How can you be so sure?'

'I feel it. I know it, like I knew how to use the magic.'

'Yes, but even if we're to be safe, what of the rest? Some of Avet's Horde are of my Brood Trove, my brothers, and what of Verre?'

'She's strong, Jerat, and she must have been lucky to have lived so long.'

'You know Moon-eye helped her, don't you?'

Stone nodded and squeezed his hand. 'What has happened has happened. If the deer is lost we hunt another.'

He was not entirely sure that he knew what she meant, but he walked back to the Tier House to prepare Ro and Rin for a journey into the forest and the Horde for battle.

·

THIRTY-NINE

Nela woke first to discover Moss snoring lightly at her side. Had she slept through her watch? All was quiet and still – there was no sound to indicate that her father might be nearby or that they might at any moment be ravaged by wild beasts. She reached instinctively for the stone, moving carefully to avoid disturbing Moss, who slept so close to her that his legs almost brushed her own.

Nela's dreams had been strangely vivid and clear and they remained in her memory when she awoke. She had dreamed of Scraal; she was locked out of her childhood home and had mislaid the key somewhere about her person. Then she had been trying to translate an old song but could find no one who could help her with one all-important word. An old woman she'd passed on the way to the fish market had said to her 'Pebbles weight the eyes of the dead' and she'd been afraid and run all the way back to the House of Zerat, which was barred by a huge boulder. Lord of the Earth, but it seemed clear enough even to her, who knew little of the philosophy of dreams, that there was something important that she needed to understand. She hoped that the stone might have the answer; she could not leave it alone.

'You have made things bad.' Ro looks at me, his face fierce.

Rin, who is helping him stagger awkwardly over the dense undergrowth, tries to hush him, his tone anxious as if he too is afraid of me. 'Don't say that, Ro, don't you remember what I told you earlier? This is Jerat's wife of the first quarter. You can't be rude to her. She's taking us somewhere safe.'

'Nowhere is safe. Not when songs destroy.'

I feel sick, not the sickness of uncooked berries, but the sickness of the heart. I want to slap the boy, the one who Jerat says is no longer right in the head. I want to slap him to erase the pain of his words or rather to turn it into his pain as well as mine, but he is right and I know it. He has been chosen by the Womanface to tell me what no one else would. I stand taller in all the glory of my greater stature that magic has brought me. It is a truth and I will bear it as a Singer should. The truth of form and sound and resonance is at the heart of healing and also of destruction.

Rin looks mortified. He is a good boy, loyal to Jerat and loving and patient with Ro, who does not seem to be grateful. I know when I look on Ro that he has been plucked from the path of death too late, though Jerat has not been anxious to tell me the whole of that story. I guess that the Teller Priest who saved him from drowning used the Song of Return when he should have sung the Song of Parting, but, as I know all too well, we all make mistakes. It is not unknown for the Womanface to use such people as her voice, and so I am very worried by what he may say next. I want to hear the voice of the Womanface. I have grown distant from her in these latter years when I have been so busy with the needs of my people rather than the needs of the Womanface. I do not think she will be pleased with what I have done with her moon gifts – sweetness has soured to bitterness and my voice is not the instrument of pure truth it once was. The fingernail-moon-shaped scar on my palm itches slightly; I do not take that as a good omen and I grow still more afraid so that I almost lose my place in the forest that has been my home all my life.

I take over the task of carrying Ro. He is heavy and awkward, an uncooperative weight, like some deer carcass. I chat to Rin about nothing much, about the path through the forest and the names of the trees and birds. He is an obliging boy and he talks back of the fine splendour of the Tier House and of the animal stock. He knows the names of all the animals and tells me and behind all that chatter I know that he is afraid too, for Jerat and for Verre and for his new home.

306

'Don't worry, I won't let anything happen to Jer,' I say, certain of myself where the magic is on my side, 'and my sister, Hearth, has boys of her own and she will have something good to eat and may let you do some hunting.' But Rin is not so young that he can be fobbed off with vague promises and the hope of something good to eat, though I remember it worked with Hearth herself until she was quite old.

'You can't keep Verre and Hela and the rest safe though, can you?' His face, handsome in its Bear-man way, is taut with his concern and his brave attempt to hide it.

'I promise you by my status as Chief Singer of the Long Hill Summer People and the Bear Caves Winter People of the Night Hunters that I will do the best that I can,' I say in my best Singer's saying-voice, and I shiver because in my stomach I fear that will not be enough and because the memory of the bush aflame with that curiously white-hot flame makes me afraid. Is that how I will defend Verre and Hela, with that song of destruction?

'The song that destroys cannot heal,' Ro says to the forest floor as if he has stolen the thought from my own head, or seen through my outer case of flesh into what lies within. When he turns to look at me I see in his eyes an expression that tells me that no child looks out on me, but something altogether more knowing and more strange. I feel suddenly cold and Ro says in an oddly singsong voice, 'After Verre and

Ro have crossed the water there will be no healing and no end until moss buries stone in this forest and the song magic flows again in your children.'

'What do you mean?' I ask, my heart fluttering in my throat with fear. I sense that this is somehow the true word of the Womanface, and it fills me with foreboding.

Rin lays his hand on my arm. 'I don't know what's got into Ro today – he doesn't say that much usually, and more of it makes sense.' I ignore his kindness and look to his brother.

'What do you mean?' I ask Ro again and I know that my hard-won control of breath and voice falters and my voice trembles and he answers, with that strange un-childlike look, 'You know what I mean, Singer.'

The stone slipped from Nela's hands as Moss rolled over and jostled her arm. It took a moment for her to recover herself, still longer for her to recover the stone and pick it up carefully in the scrap of cloth. The fire had burned down almost to nothing but she did nothing about it. She thought instead of what she knew of Stone – she had been taught to be a Singer, she had learnt the secret of the song of fire, and somehow she had destroyed rather than healed. It fitted the ancient song of Black Stone, who 'unmade the dark lands'. The woman in the stone had been hunted and trapped by Jerat and then somehow she had ended her days in a Tier House with Jerat, a Tier House full of babies and guilt, no longer able to use her singing magic while the blight on the land spread round her. The blight that still plagued the land. This last memory – was it a missing piece, a clue as to the nature of the blight? Was it because she had misused magic? She remembered Ro's words spoken in that odd singsong voice: 'There will be no healing and no end until moss buries stone in this forest and the song magic flows again in your children'. She started to shake Moss.

'Moss, Moss, I've just worked it out – wake up! Wake up! I think I know what it all means – what we have to do!'

FORTY

Avet's men came that afternoon – there were three hundred at least. Hela climbed to the top of the Tier House to scout for them. Jerat had decided that there was not enough of a Horde to defend the Hearthfields so they had grouped in a circle round the Tier House itself – the source of Jerat's new status and Avet's envy.

They had dug a circular trench, four good steps around the perimeter of the Tier House. Jerat would have liked to place sharpened timbers in the bottom, but the Hunters would not permit the destruction of any more trees and Jerat had promised through Stone not to encroach further on the forest. Instead, Sky and his men brought armfuls of thorn bushes with thorns as thick as a man's wrist and their branches and roots still intact and laid them in front of the ditch. Stone sang the roots into the ground, which was an extraordinary sight. She stood a little way away and sang a succession of notes and at each note the roots of the bush burrowed into the ground like a colony of worms, wriggling purposeful into softened soil. She smiled when she had finished, as though much happier with this task than with the song of fire. Jerat also constructed a raised platform of earth, baled hay and timber from the interior of the Hall to provide a base from which the Hunter archers could attack. He placed a few of the Bear-men, whose accuracy with the slingshot was better than their skill with a spear, alongside them. Jerat's tactics were wholly defensive: stand and fight until the enemy ran away. He had little hope of success – they were so badly outnumbered.

Sky was remarkably cheerful, his enthusiasm for the task ahead contrasting strongly with the grimness of the veterans Verre and Hela and Keran. They had honed the flints of their spears to a finer edge than ever and had made extra arrows for their bows, though not as many as they would have liked. They were not well provisioned; they had only a limited number of arrows, spears and stones for the slings, and the veterans were worried by the lack.

There was no need for Jerat to rouse his troops with inspirational words, and he knew it. Those formerly of Avet's Horde who had fought with him against Galet already knew that they were better off dying in battle than throwing themselves on Avet's mercy, for he knew none. It made their decision to fight the more courageous. Instead, Jerat spoke with each man individually as he heard the approach of their enemies, yelling their war cries and shrieking their bloody intentions. Jerat's men were subdued.

'I'm sorry to have brought you to war again, Verre. I'm sorry if I let you down.'

Verre shook her head. 'I'm sorry too, Jer. This will be a massacre, it can be nothing else. Don't be sorry for me, though, for I have seen at least one of my sons grow to be a man and a Chief. For myself I'm more than happy with what I've had.' She hugged him fiercely. 'Be a good father to your sons, Jerat, a good brother to Ro and Rin, and do not be too anxious to sell your daughters into marriage.'

'Verre, you will survive this as you have survived so much else.'

She shook her head. 'I am old and this new world of magic is not for me, Jerat. Where I grew up – far from here – it is said a warrior knows when she will fall. This is your Hearthfield, not mine. Make it a good one – you are blood-marked for greatness, I always knew it.'

Jer nodded, too full of emotion to speak, hoping that they would have time to laugh at the gravity of this exchange later when they feasted in victory in his Tier House, but he did not think it likely. He moved on to Keran. What could he say to the rock of his childhood?

'Keran.'

Keran hugged him in a warrior's embrace. 'Victory be ours,' he said with a smile like broken pottery, jagged and sharp.

Unusually, Hela smelled of ale, and her bright eyes were mournful. 'I hate goodbyes,' she said, 'so don't you worry, I'm not saying goodbye to this world yet – and if I am, I'm taking Avet with me.'

As the sound of the approaching Horde grew louder Jerat took his place next to Stone on the Tier House ladder and Sky began to sing the Song of the Fallen Stag.

Jerat scowled in confusion at Stone, who smiled at his discontent. 'Jer, it's what the hunters sing before they go to kill the stag – it is not a lament, it is a promise – the stag will die! Listen!' And when he did listen he could feel that the song had a magic of its own – the sound of the massed male voices singing in unison had a powerful and compelling rhythm. As the song built, the singers emphasised the beginning of each phrase and stamped their feet together so that the earth shook with their song, and the war cries of the enemy, which had seemed so fearsome a moment earlier, seemed less threatening, and for the space of several of Jerat's loud and rapid heartbeats, petered out altogether. Jerat allowed himself to hope that this was a good omen and for a moment hope flared.

'They will not kill us,' Stone said calmly. 'And they march to their deaths.'

When Avet's Horde finally appeared they were a breathtaking sight, a sight to set Jerat's already battering heart beating even faster. They wore their finest cloaks in the colours of their own quarters, in blue and purple and yellow and red. Some had painted their faces as Verre had done and combed their corn-coloured hair so that each man's head was surrounded by a corona of light, catching brightness like the light of the sun.

'They are truly children of the Manface with their hair like the halo round the sun,' Stone said in awe as the Horde rushed towards them, screaming wildly and shaking their spears, their faces set in a grimace of fury. There was a small volley of arrows from Sky's men, but the wind was against them and few found their mark – one man went down with a cry but one man made no difference to the tide of warriors approaching the ditch. Sky's men still sang the Song of the Fallen Stag, though more raggedly as each stopped as they took aim and let loose their shot. Jerat could see Avet throwing his spear into the midst of Sky's singers. As he threw it with a strong true aim, so that one of the Night Hunters fell, he screamed, 'By this spear I claim the Tier House of Jerat, his wives, his Horde and his Brood Trove to do with as I wish.'

His own Horde ululated wildly in response and began firing their arrows. The encircling thorn bushes made a formidable barrier and those of Avet's men who tried to cross it were pinned there, making them easy victims for the stones and arrows of Jerat's Horde. Then Jerat saw the flame-carriers at the rear of Avet's party who set about firing the bushes. They were living bushes, thanks to Stone's magic, so that the living sap-filled green wood smoked badly, and the wind which favoured Avet blew the smoke right into the faces of Jerat's Horde. After they brought fire Avet brought water to put out the flames and to allow his men to leap easily over the charred and crumbling barrier of the thorns and engage directly with Jerat's men.

It was hard to make out what was going on under the fog of black smoke. There was no singing now, just screaming and the sounds of exertion and pain as men, no-men and men-women fought hand to hand using knives, stones, spears and fists.

'When you are ready and you think we cannot win any other way – do it,' Jerat shouted to Stone over the noise, and leaped down from his vantage point to join the fray by Verre's side.

His impressions became immediately more confused. He dodged a spear and thrust his belt knife in the direction from whence it came – someone groaned as Jerat's knife sliced through green woven cloth and turned it red. The smoke was choking and Verre's face was blotched with it, her eyes two red-rimmed holes peering through soot. She was hard-pressed by two men. Jerat had an impression of ale-soaked breath, the whiteness of teeth bared in an animal growl and a grunt of surprise as his knife, still slick with the blood of his first victim, struck home.

'Watch!' Verre's warning only just came in time. A flung spear grazed his shoulder and landed a little way behind him on the ground. He picked it up and plunged it with all his force towards the line of bodies still pouring over the burned barrier and into the desperate defence of his Horde, his Brood brothers, his friends and Verre. Verre was strong and vicious in attack. Jerat saw her take out one man with a spear through his eye before ripping the knife from his other hand and thrusting it into his own guts. The man fell at her feet and she stood on his back, the better to fight the next one. Beside her Keran was no less effective, if the grunts and cries of pain from his direction were anything to go by.

There were too many of Avet's men too eager for first blood. They came too tightly packed to properly use their spears, and the growing mass of injured or

315

dead was making it difficult for them to keep their footing. Jerat struggled himself to stay upright as a fallen man of Avet's Horde grabbed for his leg and tried to pull him down. He stamped hard on the man's face but almost overbalanced and lost his bloodied knife. He would have been in trouble, but that he was able to grab a fallen arrow as he dropped to his knees and plunged it into the man's flesh. There was not enough force behind the blow to kill him and the shaft of the arrow splintered in his hand, as often happened, but the man rolled away in agony and Jerat staggered to his feet and kicked him away.

'Knife?' he said, and Hela thrust one into his hand. At least he thought it was Hela, though she looked like a creature from his darkest nightmares, blackened and bloodstained and laughing maniacally as she spitted a young man with his own spear. Jerat feared it was one of his own young Brood brothers but tried not to look. It was hard to breathe and Jerat's eyes streamed so that he saw the whole through distorting, blurring tears. He did not see what took Verre. She was there one moment fighting like a wild beast and then suddenly gone. He tried to look for her on the ground but two men came at him at once and he struggled not to fall under their charge.

'Stone!' he cried. 'Now!'

How she heard him he did not know. Perhaps she saw him from her higher vantage point and knew he was in trouble, but suddenly Stone sang out that note that made his innards shrink inside himself and his skin crawl. All other sounds seemed to cease, as if the only thing that existed was Stone's voice and that note, that terrible destructive note. It was very hot where he was standing and there was a terrible smell of cooked flesh, and then someone screamed a sound loud enough and dreadful enough to be heard above Stone's singing and the man in front of Jerat was suddenly on fire – shrieking and burning. Stone's voice was joined by others, by Sky and his men, so that the air buzzed with the terrifying wrongness, the ugly dissonance, and men all over the Hearthfields burst spontaneously into flame. Jerat froze in horror and the same paralysing shock seemed to afflict everyone in the fields. It took moments before Avet's men realised what was going on and then Avet, who for all his faults was not slow of wit, yelled above the mayhem of the killing music and the dying screams, 'Withdraw!' just as he too burst, like a torch of pitch-soaked wood, into flame.

Jerat moved at last and ran to his Brood brother. He snatched his own spear which he had not had a chance to use in the tight throng of close combat. He could not stand Avet's screams. This was not the way he wanted to win the battle, nor the way his brother should die. He threw the spear of his manhood, carved by the Teller Priest with his own hands, at the figure of his brother aflame and in agony, and he threw it true. Perhaps the runes of the Teller had some potency because it found its mark in spite of the distance and pierced his brother's heart: Avet fell dead to the ground. Jerat stood back for a moment as the flames engulfed the body of his brother and rival, but then ran towards him, trying to extinguish the blaze with his cloak. The body was burned and charred beyond recognition and Jerat did not escape the scorching of the flames. Somewhere he hurt but he did not know whether the pain was outside his body or inside it.

The sight of his Hearthfields was so terrible. The unearthly music stopped and there was silence. The blackened earth was littered with burning corpses. The wind blew the scent of charcoal and scorched flesh and the ripe smell of ordure and death into the Tier House; into the Hall and the Heart of the Home and into the carrier coop and the thatch and the fabric of the building. Jerat saw the way the wind blew and wondered if he would ever be free of that smell or if his Hall would always be sullied by it. Stone ran towards him, stumbling a little over the fallen, her ash-marked face stained with blood from another nose-bleed. She looked shocked and bleak; her eyes were haunted, red-rimmed and streaming.

'Are you all right? I can heal your burns,' she said, her eyes scanning him for signs of injury. She tenderly held his blistering hands where he had tried to beat out the flames that engulfed Avet. She opened her mouth to sing, but no note came out, no music emerged, only sobs.

'What have we done, Stone?' Jerat asked. 'What have we done?'

He staggered back to the ground he had fought to hold, the small square of land between Verre and Hela. It was heaped with bodies that were stinking and charred and heavy to move, but he moved them all anyway in a kind of frenzy of desperation, tearing his nails and skinning his burnt fingers, until he had found the fallen body of the former wife of the second quarter, the comforter of his infancy, the companion and teacher of his youth, his mother, Verre, who had died defending his warping of the world. He knelt beside her battered body and wept.

The worst was not over. Keran lived, though he had lost an eye, and Jerat found Hela somehow still breathing under a heap of foe. Although wounded she was likely to live, and the news of Avet's defeat brought her heart. Stone stood beside Jerat silently, her eyes unseeing.

'I don't know that the Womanface will ever smile on me again,' she whispered in a voice dry as fallen leaves. Jerat tried to hug her, but she was as unyielding as her name.

'Can you take me to Rin and Ro?' he asked.

She nodded without speaking, and then managed to croak, 'I'm sorry about Verre. She was someone I would have been proud to know better.' It was Jerat's turn to nod; he had no words to add and no tears left to shed.

She led him through the forest, and every Night Hunter they saw on their way turned from them as if they were not there. Stone's expression grew ever grimmer. When they came to a clearing Jerat saw Rin standing alone a little way from the well-camouflaged tents. Even at a distance something in his stance filled Jerat with dread. When Rin saw Jerat, he gave a little strangled cry and ran towards him.

'You're alive!' Rin said, gulping down his distress, 'you survived the battle! But Jerat, something terrible has happened. Ro drowned – he's really dead this time. We were playing and he slipped in a slimy rock at the narrow place they call the "giant's stride", and the water pulled him under and I ran and screamed but he did not come back up and then Hearth found him way downstream all white and dead, and Jerat, he was smiling.'

Rin broke down then in Jerat's arms. Jerat himself could think of nothing to say. Poor Rin – he had lost mother and brother in one short day.

'It was all for nothing, then – I didn't save him,' he said to Stone.

'I don't know, Jerat. I don't know anything, but I have to go to my sister Hearth, Jer, to explain that it was not her fault. I fear that Ro's death is the will of the Womanface, Jerat. He should have died before, that other time – this had to be.'

She touched him lightly on his cheek. 'I'm sorry, Jer,' she said.

'Is this part of the price that Moon-eye spoke of?' he asked.

'I think there's more to pay, Jer,' she said in that stranger's voice from which all the beauty and resonance had been leached away. He watched her walk towards the tents, wrapped in a grief of her own. Jerat hugged Rin tightly and wished he'd never heard of the Magic of the Last Resort.

FORTY-ONE

'Moss!'

Moss opened his eyes at Nela's voice and was instantly awake.

'What is it? What is the matter?' He leaped to his feet.

'I touched the stone again. I think we are meant to do something to finish Stone's story. I don't think it can be over until we do. I think she is trapped because of what she did.'

Moss rubbed his eyes and blinked as if to clear his vision.

'I'm sorry, Nela, I don't know what you're talking about.'

She did not have time to explain because suddenly another cry broke the silence of the forest.

'Millard! Nela, she has the black stone!' It was her father's voice – she did not know where he had come from, but as soon as she turned at his voice she saw him running towards her. It was not very light under the trees – dawn had barely broken and it was dim anyway under the canopy. Nonetheless she had a clear view of her father's face contorted by fury as he lunged towards her and the precious artefact that still lay in her lap. It was instinct that made her grapple for the stone and then of course as her hand tightened on it she felt the clear presence of Stone and the song of fire was almost on her lips. Before she could open her mouth, Moss managed to drag her father off her, his youthful strength more than a match for the older man's greater bulk.

'Help me, you fool!' the Chief Findsman hissed at his companion, Millard. But Nela's father was struggling to speak, as Moss had his arm twisted behind his back and was forcing him to his knees. Moss removed the butcher's knife from the makeshift sheath the Chief Findsman had made with his belt. Millard, hovering in the background, looked most unlikely to run to the Chief Findsman's rescue. Millard was limping and dishevelled; his dyed red hair had come unbraided and was hanging in a tangle of twigs and leaves around his waist. His beard was similarly unkempt and he looked far from happy. His knife appeared to have been lost.

'This is ludicrous,' he said. 'Bondsman, release the Chief Findsman. We're not going to harm the slut to whom I'm supposed to be betrothed and I certainly have no plans to return her with me to civilisation.'

Moss did not move.

'Do as he says, bondsman,' Nela's father echoed, but Moss still did not move.

Nela got slowly to her feet. She had slipped the

stone back into its sheath of fabric but knew that the power of Stone's song of fire was only a heartbeat away. That she had almost used it again frightened her.

'Father, I'm not coming back with you. I'm not marrying Findsman Millard, and I'm afraid I can't let you hurt Moss either.'

'Moss, who is Moss?' her father said.

Millard laughed. 'Moss is the bondsman's name. They are obviously intimates.'

'Don't be ridiculous, child. I have indulged you sufficiently. You are coming home with me.' Her father did not seem too quick to understand where the power lay.

'I'd like you to go now, please,' Nela said calmly, 'Moss will let you go when you promise to leave without attempting to harm either of us or steal the black stone.'

'You can stop your game now, Nela. Your father wants you to return with him, even without the promise of marriage. We can leave the bondsman here – he will die soon enough in this blighted land, without us having to soil our hands – but we must have the black stone. It is the only thing of worth to justify the expedition.' Millard spoke in his exaggerated city drawl and Nela began to feel her temper rising. The stone was hot in her hand.

'Millard, Father, you don't seem to understand. You have no power over us here. Go, please, and leave us.'

'I want that stone,' her father snarled.

'You can't have it!'

At that moment two things happened at once.

Millard finally lurched into action and with surprising speed attempted to snatch the stone from Nela's hand and, as he approached, flame blossomed all around Nela, driving Millard back.

'You see – in my hands the stone can also be a weapon. Don't make me use it, because it somehow holds the power that blighted this land. To use it would be wrong. Lord of the Earth, but it would be so easy! Allowing you to take it from this place would also be wrong, and if you try to take it from me I know which wrong I will choose. Please, Father, once the fire is unleashed there will be no escape.'

Nela did not want the fire to spread, but the ground was littered with dry leaves and branches which, they had already discovered, made excellent kindling. Moss had obviously had the same thought because he had let go of the Chief Findsman and had begun beating out the flames with his cape.

The Chief Findsman got awkwardly to his feet.

'I'm sorry, Father. Please let me be. It is for the best – I was always going to let you down.'

'Please, Chief Findsman, go. I will care for her and see no harm comes to her. You can trust my honesty in this.' Moss made the Chief Findsman look at him by force of personality.

The Chief Findsman looked old suddenly, and less than impressive.

'You were right, Father. I am certain from what I have learned from the stone that Lakeside was a centre for civilisation long ago, and I will find the artefacts to prove it. Your reputation will be safe. I want to be a Findsman, Father. I want to be a

Findsman like you, still.' Nela could not keep the pleading, placatory tone from her voice; even after all that had happened she still wanted her father to understand and approve.

'You are not like me, Nela,' he said quietly. 'You are nothing like me, with your fits and wanton waywardness.' He looked at her with a stern, cold look. 'I do not expect to ever hear from you or of you again.'

'Come,' he said, turning to Millard. 'I have no daughter, and there never was a black stone.' He gestured imperiously and Millard reluctantly helped the older man to return the way that they'd come.

Nela could not prevent her tears from falling. Moss left her alone for a while and quietly tracked the Findsmen to see that they really had left. It was hard for Nela to accept the incontrovertible proof that her father did not love her. Nela was grateful that Moss had given her some time alone.

The sun was high when Moss returned.

'I think they have gone now,' he said. 'I think the fire really frightened them.'

'It frightened me too,' Nela answered. She had wept a little and felt better, though her earlier enthusiasm for what she had discovered about Stone had all but disappeared.

'I found some food that your father had dropped – it is wholesome. I saw it fall from his bag.'

They shared what there was – cold meat that Moss had cooked himself days earlier and stale flat bread, but it helped to revive both of them.

'I understand now, I think,' Nela said, wiping her

hands on her headscarf. 'I think the blight in the forest is something to do with the fire song – I think everyone left because the perversion of magic turned everything bad, and I think Stone and her people lost the power to make things grow properly – so nothing did grow well any more, and that is why it is all not quite dead, but not properly alive either.'

'Are you sure?'

'No – not certain, but it makes sense. And there's more – I saw Ro, a strange boy Stone believed spoke for the Womanface. He told Stone that nothing would be all right again until moss buried stone.'

'And that means?'

'That I think you should.'

'What?' Moss looked at her in confusion.

'What Ro said was: "There will be no healing and no end until moss buries stone in this forest and the song magic flows again in your children." And Stone believed it was a true prophecy of the Womanface. And I think we are her children.'

Moss scowled his puzzlement. 'We are not the same, you and I – we can't both be her children.'

'Moss, we are both human. Stone wasn't and Jerat certainly wasn't – he was a giant, truly a giant. I think we are their children – a mixture of faerie and giant. What else can we be? I think my father was almost right, and that this is truly where the human race was born.'

Moss shook his head. 'I don't believe it. Listen to yourself. The shock of your father's abandonment has unbalanced you.'

'Moss, please, think about what Ro said.'

'But the stones here are covered in all kinds of moss and lichen.'

'No, Moss – *you*. You have to bury this stone.'

'No!' Moss shook his head violently.

'What do you mean, "No"?'

'I mean that this is a precious artefact that can tell us more about the origin of my people. Not your people, my people. You said it yourself – Stone was a Night Hunter, and if I am to be a Singer Teller it is my duty to find out all you can tell me, at least when you are not overwrought. I'm not burying our only fount of truth. I'm not burying the thing I risked everything for!'

'Moss, what else can what I saw mean?'

'I don't know. It might mean nothing at all – just a coincidence of names. I don't see how the black stone could know about me.'

'Ro knew about you, not the stone, and the stone remembered. She took a deep breath. 'Please, Moss, if it doesn't work I'll never mention it again.'

Moss held out his hand with a long-suffering air – an expression she had never seen on his face before – and she dropped the stone into his hand.

'Thank you,' she said, and watched as Moss dug a small hole with his bare hands in the soft earth beneath one of the dying Great Trees. He unwrapped the stone reverently and laid it in the earth.

'I think you have to cover it with earth,' Nela said, and reluctantly Moss piled the earth on top of the unremarkable-looking stone and marked the place with a stick.

'I don't think there should be a marker.'

'Are you trying to make me lose it?'

'Trust me, Moss – just bury it.'

'And then what?'

'Breathe,' said a soft voice, and a dark figure emerged from behind the tree.

She walked soundlessly across the forest floor on bare feet. She was not young but not old either, with a dark complexion and black hair that fell like a waterfall of silk to her waist.

'You have to breathe, child, as you have known me breathe, from the heart of the earth up through your womb. You remember what Moon-eye taught me in the glade?'

'Black Stone?'

The woman smiled. 'Yes, I am Stone, once known as "Moon-stone", though later they called me "Black Stone" when they thought I did not hear. I have not known your name but I have known you and it is good to know that *you* are of my line.' She looked for the first time at Moss. 'Moss, I did not know who you would be, but I named my son Moss, and told my children to name one child of each father "Moss" so that one day a child would be born with that name who might save us. I am pleased to have met with such a one.'

Moss, bemused, bowed his head.

'You need to know the rest of my story, my faraway descendants. You need to understand why I need you to help me.

'After our victory in battle against Avet, my brother Sky and those who fought with him went away. We had used the song of fire to destroy life against the will of the Womanface. They felt the blight creeping upon the land, an echo of the blight upon creation we had performed with our act of destruction. No one knew what became of them, my brother and the young men who were his friends, but they were never seen again and I think they faded from memory. Likewise Jerat's people, the Great Bear-men, went away, seeking more fertile land, land not made barren by Black Stone's singing and Zeron the Dark Daughter's songs. They were not to know how little the Dark Daughter approved. A few only remained – Rin and others we loved most. There were other marriages of Night Hunters with Bear-men, but each year the land grew worse and my children left for fertile lands across the Lake. Jerat grew old and when he died I knew that my own death could not come until I had atoned for what I had done and found a way to reverse the evil I had brought on the land.

'The stone you buried was made as a receptacle for my soul, for my memory and for all that I am, when the Wandering Man washed it when I was a child. I wonder if he washed it in water from the waters of death because I let it take me to a kind of death and it has held me safe ever since. It was dropped somewhere on the shores of the great Lake when one of my descendants fled the dying land. It had to stay here, close to the forest, and I have been waiting ever since, waiting for the mercy of the Womanface to bring me someone with the magic of a Singer of the Night Hunters still in her blood, someone who could hear my voice and release me. It is hard to be a singer and to be dumb, and I am grateful that you have let me sing again, if only in memory.'

Moss's mouth had fallen open in amazement, and only the fact that he too was seeing what she saw convinced Nela that it was not another vision.

'Girl, you have to use the songs again as you remember I was shown. My voice has lost the power to heal: it has been polluted by the deeds I've done. Please sing the healing of the land so I can die at last.' The woman smiled and she touched Nela's face with a ghostly hand. 'You remind me of my Lilith, our first born – she was beautiful just like you, and strong. I know that you have used the fire song; I felt it. Promise me that you will never use it again.'

'I promise.' Nela was so astonished by Stone's sudden appearance that she could barely speak and the sound came out as a kind of a grunt.

Stone touched her hair and smiled. 'Jerat has waited for me too long, my many-times-great granddaughter. Sing now and restore the forest.'

Conscious of Moss's astonished eyes upon her, Nela scrambled to her feet. It was true, she did remember everything. Stone had shown her everything she needed to know. She breathed as Moon-eye had taught her, or rather as she had taught Stone long ago. It was as if she had been doing it all her life. She let the notes flow through her, strong and sweet, tuned to the rhythm of the earth and to her own steadily beating heart. She concentrated on the notes, on the sounds and the song – the songs for the enriching of the ground, for the gestation of seeds, for the growing of shoots, for the safe hatching of eggs and safe birthing of rabbits, for all that Stone's memory had told her was missing from the blighted forest. She lost herself in the music of the land.

She felt rather than saw the sudden swelling of buds on the bare branches of skeletal trees: the tender shoots unfurled a moment later into leaf as she sang; the sickly yellow leaves of the Great Trees shaded to green as the sap rose and health was restored to the giants of the forest. Flowers bloomed in the dappled sunlight and birds joined their own song to Nela's and the silent forest was suddenly alive with the whispering of leaves rustling in the wind, the music of the birds and the multitude of creatures of the earth scuttling in the undergrowth, prowling in the dense shade and burrowing in the newly rich soil.

It was dark by the time the singing was done and Moss had built a fire.

Nela crumpled exhausted to the ground.

'Where is Black Stone?'

'She's gone, Nela.'

'She didn't say goodbye!'

'I don't think she could stay – once the stone was buried she seemed to fade.' Moss spoke matter of factly but Nela thought he seemed as shocked as she was herself by all that had happened. 'Stone told me to thank you for your courage and your voice. She said to say that she is proud of you. You are all she could have hoped for in a descendant.'

Moss offered her a bowl of something hot to eat. Somehow he had found the time to trap and cook something while she sang. She did not know how long that had been.

'There is plenty to eat now and plenty to eat us,'

Moss said in his most practical tone. 'We should probably head for the site of Jerat's Tier House tomorrow – we need to find a proper shelter and I would like to see some solid evidence for what we know to be true. Otherwise I will wonder if it was all some dream brought on by poison berries and bad ale.'

'Surely Jerat's Tier House will be ruined.'

'It was built of Great Trees. Stone thought that some of it might remain.'

'She spoke to you?'

'Yes. While she could.'

'What did she say to you?' Only Nela's undying curiosity kept her talking; she was almost too tired to form the words of the question.

'She said that in us the hope of the Womanface was fulfilled, that we her children were born of Zerat and Zeron and all of us are true heirs of the day, the night and all that is good on the earth. I didn't tell her about being a bondsman, but she knew something was wrong and she just said, "Put it right – if you don't try, who will?" I'm sorry I didn't believe you – about us being her children. It didn't seem likely.'

Nela was too tired to answer but merely shrugged. She nibbled at her supper and struggled to understand what Moss was saying.

'Shall we look for proof, then – that we are the descendants of a faerie woman and a giant man? Who would believe us?'

Moss put his arm round her. He was warm and solid and his being there relieved some of her tiredness. She kept very still and straight, unwilling to move in case he took his arm away.

'If you do all that report-writing and evidence-collecting as your father would have done, you can propose a theory and argue it with the scholars of Scraal. Then maybe you will be credited with Findsman status and all those things that mean so much to you.'

Nela shook her head and yawned. 'I don't think the scholars and merchants of Scraal would believe me, however many reports I wrote. What we've discovered is not believable. Anyway, I know what happened now – I understand. I think that matters more than being a Findsman.'

'Even the first non-woman Findsman?'

'I'm not so sure now about being a non-woman,' she began uncomfortably, not yet ready to say all the things she wanted to say and fearful of saying something wrong. Moss silenced her.

'Shh. Stone said to look into the flames of the fire – she said you'd know what that meant.'

Nela nodded. 'Yes, there is a way of looking into them that enables you to see those that cross the water of death. Look!'

The two of them peered into the flames together. For a long time Nela could see nothing.

'After the battle where Stone killed Avet's Horde, Stone showed Jerat that his mother and brother were together in death,' she said, scrutinising the fire carefully. Suddenly the flames seemed to burn with a strange intensity and Nela's stomach lurched in recognition of the presence of magic. For one brief fraction of moment the flames formed a picture of two figures. Their shapes were indistinct, but they embraced each other in evident joy and then they melted away.

'Is that Stone and Jerat, do you think?' Nela asked from the depths of her exhaustion.

'I think it is,' Moss said, 'but she suggested that perhaps it ought to be you and me.' He looked awkward, and started tidying up the debris of their meal with one hand; he did not relinquish his hold on her waist. 'I don't mean that it should be us going to the waters of death – only that . . .'

'I didn't think –' She let her sentence hang unfinished as he interrupted her.

'This is hard to say, Nela. I'm not ashamed about being a bondsman, I never have been, but if you don't feel as I do – I will understand. I thought that in a way we are like them – not Night Hunter and Bear-man but bondsman and non-woman – and if they could be together, why can't we?'

Nela had no words to answer him. Her mind did not seem able to grasp the events of the day. 'I didn't know that you cared about me,' she said confusedly. Everything had an air of unreality. She had not thought Moss even liked her much.

'Come closer, many-times-granddaughter-of-Stone-and-Jerat,' Moss said softly. 'You have just fought off an unwanted marriage, conjured the ghost of an ancient ancestor and restored blighted land to health. Maybe you should rest a while before changing the world again.' He did not mention her father, and she was grateful.

She smiled. 'Tomorrow, maybe,' she said, and it

seemed to her that her voice still carried the echo of Stone's voice, or rather the voice Stone had given her. 'I didn't think it was possible to feel this tired.' She moved closer to him a little shyly, still not sure that she had understood him properly.

'It will be all right, Nela,' Moss said.

'I wonder if we are what the magic was working towards – you know, uniting the divisions of Stone and Jerat's children.' The thought seemed to take a long time to surface. She was finding it difficult to think at all.

'I think it is – that's more or less what Stone said.'

'I'll miss seeing her, being her – whatever it was.'

Moss shook his head. 'I did not like you going away like that. I was afraid for you. It was as if you were possessed. I was afraid for me too. It was so strange to watch.'

'I didn't know,' she whispered.

He shrugged. 'It's over now – and something else has begun.'

'Has it?'

'I think so – don't you?'

Nela was surprised to discover that she did think so. Her father had gone, but the earth beneath her was alive again and she was rooted into it, a part of it, the man beside her cared for her as she had hoped but never expected, and above all she had found her voice: she was Nela, Chief Singer of Stone's world.